EBURY PRESS

THE GIRL IN THE GLASS CASE

Devashish Sardana is the author of the bestselling *The Apple*, which won the second prize at the Amazon India Pen to Publish Literary Contest in 2019. He also writes 100-word thrillers on 10x10 Thrills, a blog on both Facebook and Instagram, with 1.6 lakh followers. The blog reached over 1.2 crore readers in 2020.

Devashish is a small-town boy from India who grew up with big dreams and an even bigger imagination. After graduating from IIM Ahmedabad, he sharpened his storytelling skills as a brand-builder in a Fortune 100 company for over ten years. Devashish lives in Singapore with his wife and college sweetheart, Megha. Before the pandemic, he flitted across the globe selling hope in a jar (beauty creams).

To know more about Devashish, please visit devashishsardana.com. To read his 100-word thrillers, please visit:

Instagram: instagram.com/10x10thrills
Facebook: facebook.com/10x10thrills

THE
GIRL
IN THE
GLASS
CASE

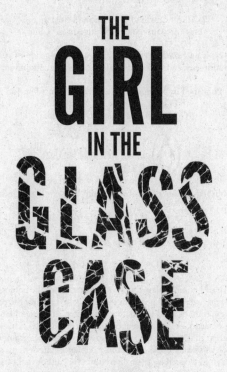

KEEP YOUR GIRLS SAFE.
BOYS SAFER.

DEVASHISH SARDANA

EBURY
PRESS

An imprint of Penguin Random House

EBURY PRESS

USA | Canada | UK | Ireland | Australia
New Zealand | India | South Africa | China

Ebury Press is part of the Penguin Random House group of companies
whose addresses can be found at global.penguinrandomhouse.com

Published by Penguin Random House India Pvt. Ltd
4th Floor, Capital Tower 1, MG Road,
Gurugram 122 002, Haryana, India

Penguin
Random House
India

First published in Ebury Press by Penguin Random House India 2021

ISBN 9780143454373

Typeset in Minion Pro by Manipal Technologies Limited, Manipal
Printed at Thomson Press India Ltd, New Delhi

www.penguin.co.in

MIX
Paper
FSC FSC® C010615

To Suman, the brave woman who raised me.

*To Megha, the fearless woman who raises
me up to more than I can be.*

Prologue

The Night of 2 December 2019

'Shit, it's cold!' cursed constable Daya Pandey, as he stepped out of the police van.

Gusts of chilly, unforgiving wind bit into his nostrils and rushed into his lungs, where they slashed his insides like jagged stones. His eyes watered due to the icy air. He rubbed his arms and stamped his feet as he moved around the vehicle in a bid to shake off the winter chill.

He sniffled and pulled the muffler over his nose. The worn-out rag smelled of mothballs, the pungent odour of naphthalene prickling his frosty, sensitive nose. He gagged on the smell. Every year in February, the family stored all their winter clothing in a sea of mothballs only to retrieve them the following winter—free from moths but smelling like a goddamned embalmed corpse.

Daya knocked on the van's passenger window. His partner Ajay, half asleep, rolled down the window, but only enough to hear Daya's voice. They couldn't risk burdening the geriatric van's overworked heater against the arctic blasts of the night air.

'I'll take a quick look round and be back. Don't doze off again,' said Daya.

'Yeah, yeah . . .' Ajay flicked his hand as if shooing away a pesky fly, rolled up the window and closed his eyes.

Daya sighed and turned away from the van. He knew Ajay would already be asleep. It wasn't surprising. It was 3.40 a.m. The city of Bhopal was fast asleep in its cocoon, enveloped in a heavy fog that made it impossible to see beyond ten metres but they still had hours before their night shift ended.

Experience had taught him that if he took a little stroll, he'd feel more awake. So, Daya hunched, put his hands into his trouser pockets and sauntered into the side street—the 'cursed' street as the locals called it. The road ran along the high brick wall surrounding the deserted Union Carbide factory, the epicentre of one of the biggest industrial disasters in the world: the Bhopal Gas Tragedy of 1984. The air around the factory always felt heavy with the weight of its historical significance, but tonight Daya felt it more strongly than any other night of the year. It was 2 December, the anniversary of the tragedy of that terrible, terrible night. Sixteen thousand deaths. Fifty lakh disabled. The government had made promises—from responsible disposal of the factory's toxic waste and healthcare compensation for the survivors to provision of potable drinking water now that the groundwater was contaminated. The promises were never kept.

The victims, their families and activist groups had staged dharnas earlier in the day, as they did every year. Lifeless placards lay strewn in the street, not to mention empty plastic bottles and crumpled foil containers stained with dried curry.

The event attracted fewer and fewer participants each year. It was like trying to keep a fire burning while the winds of time threatened to destroy it. Now, at this ungodly hour, not a single protester was in sight. Only Daya and his partner remained: the unlucky ones on a night patrol.

Daya heard hurried footsteps ahead. Someone was rushing towards him. He stopped, straining to peer through the smoky fog. He held his breath.

A silhouette came into view.

Daya gripped his baton, ready to strike if required. He waited.

The silhouette came closer. A lone street lamp struggled to bathe in light the lopsided figure that seemed to be carrying a large suitcase in one hand. A woman, possibly in her late twenties emerged. Daya relaxed slightly. The woman was clad entirely in black. A chiffon sari draped over her slender frame beneath a cardigan. In contrast to her dark clothing, her lips were painted gaudy pink, the lipstick shimmering despite the dim light. The only other colour that stood out was the reflective logo—the white swoosh—on her Nike sneakers. Daya had rarely seen a woman wear sneakers with a sari. Maybe it was a new fashion trend. His wife would know about these things. His fashion sense started and ended with the khaki colour of his uniform.

On seeing Daya, the woman averted her gaze and immediately wrapped the pallu of her sari around her face, covering every inch of her face except her eyes. As she emerged further from the fog, Daya realized that the box in her hand was one of those coolers meant to keep beers chilled, a rectangular blue box with a white lid. It was the size of a large suitcase. But noticing the ease with which she carried it, Daya knew the cooler was empty.

Where is she taking an empty cooler at 3.45 a.m.?

The woman met his gaze, slowed down and tightened the pallu that covered her face.

'*Kahan se aa—*'

Suddenly, loud, grating barks erupted behind him. He turned around. The sound echoed in the empty street before Daya saw five dogs charging through the mist towards him. He raised his baton. Good for non-lethal close combat but nothing special. Daya gripped the baton with clammy hands, adrenaline pumping through his veins. He pointed the baton at the charging dogs as if giving them fair warning.

Strike only if needed, he told himself.

Daya stepped off the tar road, retreating into a street lined with mushy shrubs and mulch. His back jammed against the rough brick wall that cordoned off the abandoned Union Carbide facility. His hands gripped the baton, shaking, poised to strike. The dogs were almost upon him.

And just when he thought the pack leader would pounce on him, the dogs ran right past him, completely ignoring his presence.

Daya took a deep breath, relief pouring over him. Beads of sweat ran down his back. He heaved a deep sigh and lowered his baton. He pushed himself off the wall, and looked up and down the street.

The woman had vanished.

'Behenchod!' he cursed aloud.

In the distance, the dogs were barking like the whole city was on fire.

Daya was relieved to have escaped the stray canines' jaws, but he still felt uneasy. Something wasn't right. The woman had been in the wrong place at the wrong time and carrying a cooler that didn't fit. And now she had disappeared.

Daya set off in the direction that the dogs had taken. If his senses were tingling, the heightened senses of the animals would be on fire. He quickened his pace, his beer belly wobbling like squishy jelly, his heavy breathing leaving behind puffs of white mist.

The barking was incessant now. If it was loud before, the noise had risen to a clamour now, intent on waking the dead. As he followed the barks through the blinding fog, he knew from the rising volume that the dogs had stopped running. They had found something.

Daya ran faster.

He reached the Bhopal Gas Memorial site and slowed his pace. A single street lamp lit the famed sculpture by Dutch artist Ruth Waterman-Kupferschmidt: the sculpted figure of a mother crying, one hand covering her face and the other holding her dead child. Daya's heart sank. It always did when he saw the sculpture. A multitude of melted candles stood scattered around the memorial.

A screeching sound, like claws scratching on glass, pulled Daya's attention away from the mournful figure.

A few feet from the memorial sat a three-foot display case. The dogs were scratching, jumping and gnawing at the glass. Built-in lights illuminated flatteringly the contents inside the case, like display cases used to showcase diamonds at jewellery stores, casting an ethereal glow in the darkness of the night.

Rather than priceless jewellery, inside the glass case stood a doll. A Barbie doll. She wore a hot pink tank top, a matching pleated miniskirt and white sneakers. Her blonde hair was pulled back into a neat ponytail, not a single hair out of place.

Her caramel skin glistened as the light bounced off it, only to be reflected back by the glass. Her eyes were open and the edges of her mouth curled up as if amused by the futile efforts of the dogs trying to break through the glass.

The dogs were relentless now, clawing and biting with their sharp teeth.

Why are these mutts so interested in a doll?

He moved closer to the glass case.

And then it struck him.

'Shit!' he gasped.

This wasn't a doll. It was a dead little girl.

Day 1

1

Simone Singh slammed on the accelerator. Her compact four-wheel drive, a Mahindra Thar, responded immediately, lurching forward with a growl. The cold wind rushed in through the half-open window, smacking her in the face. She liked it. She liked winter. She liked the cold. It was her favourite weather and her favourite emotion.

She flicked her head and saw the dashboard clock: *6.10 a.m.*

'Idiots!' she cursed aloud.

The call had come ten minutes ago from the first responder. A brutal crime. A little girl. Encased and displayed. Discovered a couple of hours ago.

Couple of hours? Two hours! Simone had screamed at the officer on the phone.

She should have been called immediately. God alone knew what evidence had been compromised already. Fools! Such tardiness should not be acceptable but had come to be expected in a police force that was burdened with the image of laziness. An image built and strengthened by movies. And the movies were right. Mostly.

Simone had just returned from her 10-kilometre morning run, energized and spirited, sweaty and sticky, when the call had come. She had showered quickly—two minutes. Put on her Indian Police Service (IPS) uniform—two more minutes. Grabbed the car keys. Shouted a quick goodbye to her grandmother, who was just tumbling out of bed, and ignored her pleas of 'Have breakfast!'. One minute later, Simone was tearing through the deserted streets.

Simone estimated it would take her ten minutes to reach the crime scene. She tried to relax but her body remained stiff, more from rage than the morning run. Her hands gripped the steering wheel tightly, her knuckles white. She took a deep breath. Anger would not help. It was her first week back from suspension after 'the incident'—an unwanted blip in her first year of police service.

Simone had graduated at the top of her class at the National Police Academy in Hyderabad. The faculty and officers had high hopes for her; she had high hopes for herself. Her classmates had . . . well, they had wished that she would fall, and fall hard. And who could blame them? She was fearless and feisty but her social skills bordered on deficient—not her words but a former classmate's. Simone hadn't cared. But her classmates got their wish, for fallen she had, and far more spectacularly than they could have hoped for.

She breathed deeply again, blinking away the humiliation of the last forty-five days of suspension and the pain of 'the incident'. She was back at work now, she reminded herself. A fresh start. A new beginning. And anger would not help. Not with her wobbly social skills anyway. She needed friends and well-wishers, at the very least, acquaintances, who'd stand by her, support her or simply not curse her. That's what her grandmother had said. Simone had to change. She had to make an effort. For them. Whoever *they* were.

Simone unzipped her khaki jacket with one hand, while her foot stomped on the accelerator pedal again. She rummaged in the inside pocket, extracted her wireless earphones and plugged one in each ear. She plucked her mobile phone from the passenger seat, without taking her eyes off the road. Simone slowed for a fraction of a second, tapped the Audible app and pressed play. A serene voice immediately filled her ears, picking up where she had left off, reciting her current audiobook: *How to Win Friends and Influence People* by Dale Carnegie, the bible of self-help books.

* * *

Simone slowed the Thar to a crawl as she turned on to Chhola Road.

The serene voice of the audiobook narrator whispered in her ears: '. . . when dealing with people, let us remember we are not dealing with creatures of logic. We are dealing with creatures of emotion . . .'

'Tell me about it,' Simone muttered.

'. . . creatures bristling with prejudice and motivated by pride and vanity. Don't criticize.'

'What crap!' Simone laughed in mock amusement. 'If you don't criticize people, how are they going to learn?'

An outside broadcasting (OB) van of a national TV channel came into view. The channel's crimson logo against the black background screamed for attention. Then, another news channel's OB van came into view. And then another.

Simone caught her breath and sat up in her seat. She removed her earphones. Alert.

How did the media always find out so fast? She sighed.

A police blockade was set up at the only sharp turn on Chhola Road, blocking traffic to the side street. A crowd had gathered around the blockade: a mix of inquisitive residents from the shanties that surrounded the defunct Union Carbide factory, curious passers-by who had stopped their vehicles in the middle of the road, and news reporters and camera persons who were trying to jostle past the traffic police who patrolled the blockade.

What curiosity! thought Simone. The boon and bane of police work. Gets in the way, slows progress but also finds witnesses and leads when there should have been none.

For a fleeting moment, Simone thought of parking her car at the kerb; the police could hardly pull her up for illegal parking—she *was* the police. But rules were rules, and they mattered to her more than most. She looked around for a parking spot. Despite the early hour, it was packed.

'Damn these news channels!' she gritted her teeth.

Finally, when the only other option was turning the car around and going back half a kilometre, an idea hit her.

Simone drove straight into the crowd. She jammed her hand on the horn. The horn shrieked without pause. It caught the crowd's attention. They noticed the oncoming car and scattered, parting the way for the beast intent on running them over. Simone smiled. She parked in the space right next to the temporary police barricade.

The crowd spilled back in, filling every crevice around the Thar, like flies swatted away from food—gone one moment, back the next.

Simone zipped up her jacket. She adjusted the rear-view mirror, which reflected her tonsured head—a self-inflicted reminder of 'the incident'. She was pissed off. Furious. She didn't want to forget the discrimination. So, she shaved her head in defiance of the unfair suspension order. Now she wore it like a badge of honour.

Simone opened the glove compartment and took out a pair of rubber gloves and shoe covers. Maintaining the sanctity of the crime scene was her first priority, even if the foolish first responders failed to understand its importance. She slipped on the gloves and the shoe covers and then her peaked police cap. She slammed the door shut behind her. She was bristling as she surveyed the scene in front of her, her anger threatening to erupt any moment.

'Kuch kaam-dhanda nahi hai?' she shouted at the crowd.

'Ma'am, do you know what happened here?' said someone in the crowd as she jostled past them.

'Move aside,' Simone shouted.

'Is it true, ma'am, that a little girl was murdered?' said another.

'No, I heard they found two dead girls!' someone corrected.

'Any comments for the camera, ma'am?' a TV reporter shoved a wireless microphone in front of her.

'Let me through!' Simone was already regretting her decision to park in the middle of the crowd, even if it was a valid parking spot.

Finally, a traffic constable saw Simone, recognized the assistant superintendent of police (ASP) insignia on her shoulders—three silver-plated metallic stars—and rushed to help. He flailed the baton in his hand, spewing warnings.

'Move aside! Let madam pass or I'll hit you with the baton. I kid you not!'

The crowd parted, letting Simone through. The traffic constable saluted Simone as she stopped in front of him. Simone was too angry for gratitude.

'Do your job and get these people away from here,' she chided the constable.

The constable's shoulders drooped; his jaw tightened. He saluted again and strode past Simone, shouting empty threats at the crowd.

* * *

She crossed the police barricade into the vacant street, leaving behind the din and bustle of the crowd. The street smelled odd—fresh morning dew with the harsh undertones of a pungent chemical. It was also foggier, visibility more reduced than the main Chhola Road. But Simone would know her destination even with her eyes closed. The statue. The memorial of the Bhopal Gas Tragedy.

Simone walked briskly as she approached the monument. A police van came into view. Empty. Two constables stood with a foot each on the front wheel, chatting, joking and lounging with cigarettes in hand.

'You idio—' Simone stopped mid-curse. She was about to scold them for not maintaining decorum at the crime scene and not adhering to protocol. *Don't criticize.* The little voice popped inside her head again. She was determined to improve and give the self-help book a chance. Simone looked away from the constables, even as they quickly dropped their cigarettes and threw her panicked salutes. Simone walked past them. Better to ignore than berate.

The fog cleared slightly and the epicentre of the crime scene came into focus. The first thing that hit her was the sheer number of people fussing about the crime scene— police constables, forensic technicians and the crime scene photographer. All necessary personnel but there were just too many feet compromising trace evidence. For Simone, defacing a crime scene was a crime in itself.

Don't criticize.

Screw it! Simone had had enough.

'What is going on here?' She ignored the little voice in her head, feeling more like herself.

Every head turned. Every hand stopped. Every mouth shut.

'Who is the area inspector who called me?'

A man with a thick, walrus moustache stepped forward and saluted her.

'Good morning, ma'am! I'm inspector Kiri Shukla. I am the one who called you.'

'Inspector Shukla, would you care to enlighten me why you felt it was necessary to invite an army to contaminate my crime scene?'

The inspector opened his mouth, but stopped, as if thinking the better of it. A blush of embarrassment bloomed across his face.

'This entire street, end to end, is a crime scene. I want every person who isn't necessary gone. Now!'

Inspector Shukla didn't even have to command his fellow officers about who was to stay and who was to move out as a swarm of police officers immediately melted away.

This further infuriated Simone. They should all be booked and jailed for intent to destroy a crime scene. Idiots!

'I want every inch of this street photographed.' Simone was speaking directly to the slimmed-down forensics team at the crime scene. 'Every footprint collected; every hair picked up.'

A pin-drop silence followed, except for loud gulps as the technicians swallowed hard. Simone had just increased their work manifold—work that many would have deemed unnecessary but not Simone.

She continued. 'All trace evidence from the body must be collected as per procedure. No compromises.'

She turned back to the inspector. 'Start canvassing for witnesses. Anybody who was in the area after midnight, I want to speak to them. Get me security camera footage going in and out of this street for the last twenty-four hours. There are no public cameras here, so check the shops out front or the Ganesha temple next door. And get me the constable who found the body. I want to talk to him now.'

Inspector Shukla nodded and scurried away.

Suddenly alone, Simone walked the few paces to where the victim was found, her gait measured, her eyes focused, her head churning. The sight was both terrible and mesmerizing, the contrast heightened with the knowledge that the flawless, peaceful doll inside was human. Simone bent down and looked straight into the little girl's open eyes. There was no glint, no warmth, no depth in them, merely a uniform sheen that reflected the dim morning light, like a freshly varnished door.

Simone stifled a gasp. 'Glue . . .' she muttered.

A forensic technician dusting the glass case for fingerprints looked up. He nodded. 'Yes, usually the eyes become cloudy within two–three hours after death. Seems like the killer used a special adhesive to glue open the eyes.'

Simone closed her eyes, bunched her hands into fists, trying to stem the rage that coursed inside her. She only hoped that the eyes had been glued *after* the little girl had died.

'The glass case has been wiped clean of fingerprints.' The technician announced and stood up. 'I'll get somebody to take the body for autopsy,' he said more to himself than to Simone and walked away.

Simone turned her attention back to the corpse. Her top and miniskirt, hot pink and pleated, were in stark contrast to her pale face, arms and thighs. The feet were purplish black, like the little girl was wearing dark purple socks, from livor mortis that had set in hours ago. With the heart no longer pumping, gravity had pulled all the blood to her feet—blood that was now cold, congealed and rotting.

'Constable Daya reporting, ma'am!'

Simone turned. She stood tall, as much as her lean, six-foot one-inch frame allowed while making eye contact with the constable. She was taller than most Indian men and almost all Indian women; a trait that bothered her Grandma. 'Who will marry a girl taller than he is?' Grandma would rue from time to time. Simone didn't lose any sleep over her grandmother's outdated views.

Simone appraised the stocky, pot-bellied constable standing in front of her. Her eyes alighted on the constable's sports shoes rather than the hard police-issued boots he should have been wearing. She scrunched her nose, her face contorted in disappointment. As inept as Simone was at reading people's faces, she was equally bad at hiding her own feelings. Her face mirrored her mind. Always. And right now, her face stretched with scorn at the constable who, to her, represented everything that was wrong with the old guard of the Indian police: unfit and unreliable, undisciplined and incompetent.

The constable lowered his eyes, aware of her scowl.

'Where are your police boots, constable Daya?' Simone simmered.

'At home, ma'am,' Daya answered nonchalantly. It wasn't clear whether he was joking or stating a fact.

Snickering sounds erupted from the side. Simone and Daya turned towards the tittering. It was the technician who had returned with a medical examiner to take away the glass case. Both technicians were giggling, gloved hands over their mouths, like gleeful schoolchildren who laugh when the teacher scolds another kid.

'Something funny?' Simone raised her voice.

The laughter evaporated instantly. The technicians looked away as Simone's glare burnt their exposed skin. They hurriedly got back to work, bending to lift the glass case.

'Be careful with that,' Simone warned them.

Her warning fuelled their panic. They were uncoordinated as they picked up the makeshift casket, one faster than the other. The glass case, slathered in morning dew, was slippery in their gloved hands.

'Hold it!' one technician said to the other.

'Careful!' Simone yelled.

But it was too late.

The case was heavy. The body within was a literal deadweight despite the size of the little girl. The case crashed on the concrete road. The glass splintered into a thousand jagged pieces, each jagged shard representing the jabs of the scolding that was in store for the technicians.

'NO!' everyone shouted, almost in unison.

Simone's eyes flew from the shattered case to what it had housed—the body, the most vital evidence of all. The little girl's body lay on the road, rigid and unmoving.

Simone gasped. The miniskirt had ridden up, revealing the complete nakedness beneath.

A tiny, shrivelled penis nestled in the groin. It wasn't a dead little girl. It was a little boy, dressed as a Barbie doll.

2

The sweet, rhythmic chirping of cuckoos awakened Nalini and she opened her eyes with a smile. She felt light and happy, like she was a balloon tethered to the bed, floating in place.

She had slept like a baby, a dreamless sleep. But good sleep wasn't the source of her happiness. It was the child. The child she had saved last night.

Nalini breathed in and out, a deep breath of satisfaction. She gazed at the clock on the wall. 'Good morning, Snowy!' Nalini blew a kiss at the vivid, albeit slightly worn-out graphic of Disney's Snow White, her best friend, smiling back from her place on the clock's face. The clock hands showed it was 9.55 a.m. Nalini had slept for only a few hours, but she felt refreshed, rejuvenated.

Time to get ready or I'll be late, she thought.

Nalini pushed aside the quilt and felt the first frisson of cold air rushing through the soft fabric of her black chiffon sari. She tittered. She had been too exhausted, too satiated to change her clothes or remove her make-up when she had returned home. She had slipped straight into bed and embraced sleep like an old friend.

Nalini hugged herself tight and scurried across the tiny room, the carpeted floor cushioning her brisk steps. She turned on the heater, immediately smelling dry, burning fumes as the heater cranked up. Her body relaxed a little.

She gazed out of the tiny, square window that struggled to bathe the room in morning sunshine. Nalini stood hunched by the window for a few minutes, peering at the still water of Bhojtal lake glinting in the sunlight, as if the light was infusing the staid water with energy, igniting the ripples on its surface. It was a good sign. The gods were smiling, sending her warm wishes on a cold winter's day. The window was her favourite part of the room, even as a kid, when her father would lock her in the room without food. And water. The window had allowed her mind to escape—not from her own incarceration, but from the heart-rending shrieks and cries of her mother while Dad thrashed her in the adjoining room.

Nalini exhaled and turned away from the window as memories gnawed at her heart.

She glanced at the clock again. 10.15 a.m.

'Oh no, Snowy! You should have warned me about the time!' she said to the clock, suddenly realizing that she had been entranced by the view through the window for far too long.

Timing was of utmost importance that day, more so than the previous day. After all, it was a special day. Today she would save two little boys. Twins.

Nalini switched on the lights. A burst of pink filled the room—the baby-pink wallpaper, the bubblegum-pink kiddie cot that clashed with the yellow-and-navy-blue dress of Snow

White painted on the headboard, a rose-pink kiddie table and a matching kiddie chair, lavender-pink cupboards stacked on one side and a carpet that spanned the entire room, again pink but it had turned dull and musty over the years. Simply put, it was an overdose of pink.

This had been her room as a child when her parents owned the house. It was still her room now that she was renting it from the current owner. The new owner had made only one change to her childhood room since he took possession of the property: he had added a back door next to the window. This suited her perfectly as she could exit the house whenever she liked. But really, the back door meant she didn't need to face her parents' erstwhile room every time she exited her own. Too many memories. Memories best left alone.

There was no time to shower, so Nalini undressed and chose a silk sari, mauve with embroidered corners, from the closet and laid it on the bed. First impressions mattered; a silk sari commanded respect and courtesy. She would need both later today.

Nalini removed yesterday's make-up with wet wipes and reapplied a heavy dose of foundation, black eyeliner, pink lip gloss and a touch of blusher. She was going for a subtle, elegant look that matched her sari. Something a regular secretary in a regular government office would wear. After all, that was the role she was essaying today.

Nalini draped the sari within minutes, fascinated by how it always reminded her of her mother. She put on a mauve cardigan and slipped into comfortable sandals. Once done, she stood before the full-length mirror admiring herself.

'How do I look, Snowy?' she asked her best friend. 'Yes, you are right, Snowy. I need a bindi and sindoor to complete the look.'

Nalini pulled open a drawer in her dresser. She extracted a large, maroon bindi and stuck it in the middle of her forehead. Next, she plucked a liquid wand and applied sindoor, the traditional vermilion colour, on her parting. She wasn't married but she had read a study which claimed that married women appeared more trustworthy than single women; she hoped the study was true for what she was about to do today. As soon as that was done, she twirled a full circle, as if giving Snowy a 360-degree view of her handiwork.

She smiled and nodded. 'I like it too, Snowy!'

Nalini grabbed her purse and car keys, switched off the lights and headed for the door. About to unbolt the door, she stopped, pondering.

She turned and gazed at Snowy. 10.25 a.m.

Nalini chewed her lip, thinking, deciding.

'I know, Snowy! But it'll only take two minutes!' Nalini cried as she swept back into the room.

She dropped her purse and keys on the bed, rushed to the study table and squeezed her slender frame into the kiddie chair.

A single leather folder, thick, large and bulging with papers, lay on the table. She caressed the folder like it was a precious baby. Her fingers traced the length of the folder and then stopped at the letters embossed in the centre:

SEVEN-DAY REDEMPTION

Nalini inhaled deeply, like the embossed letters were touching her, inspiring her. She opened the folder with a slow, measured flick to the first page. The boy she had saved last night was smiling back at her, a toothy grin, an incisor missing. Nalini closed her eyes, bent down and kissed the photo. She was suddenly flooded with emotion. A flutter ran through her heart, her head giddy as goosebumps brushed against the sleeves of the cardigan. Her lips parted in a grin.

'Mama loves you, baby,' cooed Nalini. 'May you find love in heaven. The love you never received in this world.'

She kissed the photo again and turned the page.

The second page had a similar layout as the first one. There was, again, a photo in the centre—twin boys. They were beaming at the camera, their eyes full of mischief. One look and you knew the naughty brats were up to something, conspiring to pull their next prank together. The rest of the page was filled with minute details, bulleted notes, asterisked footnotes—the entire lives of the five-year-old twins laid bare on a page. There were four other pages in the folder. Similar pages. Seven boys in total. Each boy selected, researched, profiled and followed for the last year. A tedious and demanding job, but who said redemption was easy?

Her mother used to say that one should perform seven good deeds to write off the sins one had committed in their lifetime. So, this was Nalini's redemption plan. Seven good deeds in seven days. Seven good deeds before she embraced the light at the end of the tunnel and reunited with her mother. In heaven. Seven deeds to redeem herself for butchering her father.

Nalini closed the folder. She had work to do.

One child saved. Six to go.

3

Simone swerved the Thar into the parking space reserved for police personnel at Bhopal Police headquarters. It was a new, white-tiled building with blue-tinted glass windows. The middle storey jutted out oddly, like a video tape being inserted into one of those old videocassette recorders. The tiles glowed in the afternoon sun in stark contrast to the ancient, videocassette recorder it resembled.

Her mobile phone buzzed in her pocket.

Simone turned off the ignition, tucked the cap beneath her arm and nimbly jumped out of the vehicle. She retrieved the phone from her pocket.

'Hello?' she said.

No answer.

'Hello!' this time she barked into the phone.

'Simo! Heard you were back from suspension. Welcome back!' an excited man blabbered on the other end.

Simone adjusted the phone closer to her ear. 'Who is this?'

'It's me. Karan Kapoor. From the *Times of Bhopal*.'

Simone squeezed her eyes shut and sighed loudly. She should have guessed. Only one person called her *Simo*.

'How did you get my new number, Karan?'

Simone had changed her number after 'the incident'—she neither wanted fake pity nor self-righteous advice.

Karan chuckled at the other end. 'Oh, so you do remember me?'

Simone walked towards the front entrance. Of course, she remembered Karan. The crime reporter in his late twenties and a wannabe YouTuber. When they had first met, Simone had stalked his YouTube channel—'Kal Ki Taaza Khabar'. The page was replete with videos where Karan shared harmless opinions on the news from the previous day in his signature monotone. All his videos combined had less than thirty views. Ever. Simone had taken up the tally to fifty in a single sitting— not because she found the content intriguing but because she found him cute.

Simone scoffed, loud enough to be heard on the other end. 'What do you want, Karan?'

'Simo, all I want is a comment for the concerned citizens of Bhopal.'

'Concerned citizens or your five YouTube subscribers?' Simone hit where she knew it would hurt most.

'Ouch!' Karan put on his best fake laugh. 'How about coffee sometime today? I'll tell you about my subscribers and you can tell me about the kid in the glass case.'

Simone stiffened. Was he asking her out on a date? Simone had never dated. No one had asked her out. Ever.

'I don't drink coffee,' Simone retorted, slapping her forehead. *Idiot! That's probably why you're still single.*

'Look,' Karan sighed, 'I'm writing an editorial on how Bhopal has become the number one crime hub in India. And this new case—the girl in the glass case—represents everything that is wrong with the city.'

So, he doesn't know that it was a little boy and not a girl, Simone thought. *Best to keep it that way.*

Karan continued, 'I want to give the police force a fair chance to comment. And with you leading the case, who better to comment on behalf of the shoddy, irresponsible and inept police department?'

Simone stopped. What did he mean by that? She felt her face twitch, like she had been slapped.

'Get lost, Karan!' Simone snapped and ended the call.

Her face was burning. She flexed and unflexed her fingers. She wanted to punch someone, something, anything.

Simone exhaled loudly and walked to the entrance of the police department.

A constable on sentry duty watched her approach, his gaze riveted to her hairless head.

Simone shook her head. She had been back for a week now but her shiny, bald head seemed to invite attention like she was standing naked in public, every contour, every vein being judged by prying eyes.

She walked up to the constable.

The constable, obviously aware that he had been caught staring, flicked his eyes away to look anywhere else but at Simone. His gaze finally settled on his own feet.

'Have you never seen a bald woman?' Simone's voice was loud enough to attract sidelong glances from people going in or out of the building.

The constable's eyes started sweeping the floor in acute embarrassment. 'Sorry, ma'am,' he mumbled and threw a hurried salute.

Simone made an exaggerated show of putting on her police cap, like the man was a mirror and she wanted to make sure that the cap was on just right. Her eyes never left the quivering constable. His eyes never left the floor.

Then, without a word, Simone walked into the building.

She was letting emotions take over. Emotions she had easily cast aside all her life—roll them, box them and forget them. It took training. It took time. But she had persevered and succeeded. Be it school, sports, officer training—her focused, goal-oriented grit had always seen her through the emotional barbed wire that her peers couldn't escape. Then came 'the incident' which had eaten away at the stone-cold box of her emotions and out spilled every heartbreak, every insult and every betrayal she had striven so hard to hide.

It was 2 October 2019. The date was etched in her brain with indelible ink. Also, it was Gandhi Jayanti, a public holiday—easy to remember if, for some reason in the future, forgiveness found its way into her heart or forgetfulness found her mind. A dry day—alcohol prohibition for a day—was observed to commemorate the birth anniversary of Mahatma Gandhi. Unlike previous years, when people flagrantly violated the law and the police let them, the inspector general of police had decided to set an example this year. *Zero tolerance*, he had pronounced, against sale and consumption of liquor in public places. Additional force had been deployed to support the effort, including detectives from the crime division. Simone had been charged with traffic duty although she thought it was a waste of time for detectives to mind traffic all day, looking for drunk drivers for hours on end, when *real* criminals—murderers, thieves and drug dealers—were running rampant in the city. But she had kept quiet. She wasn't going to fight a direct order.

A few hours in, her team stopped a swanky, canary yellow Lamborghini at the checkpoint. No one in her team, including her, had ever seen a Lamborghini before. It was a rich man's dream, a poor man's fantasy.

The driver, a young adult probably in his late teens, had rolled down his black-tinted window, waggled a half-empty bottle of whisky outside the window as he slurred 'Happpee Ganddi Jawanthee, guys! Cheeeers!'—right in their faces.

Oh, the audacity! Oh, the recklessness! She had brusquely told the delinquent to step out. The boy had laughed, puckered his lips and blown her a kiss. Simone remembered how her face had heated with rage and disgust. She asked him again to get out of the car. The boy had chuckled and said, 'Why don't you come and sit on my lap? I'll give you the ride of your life around town.' Adding insult to injury, the brat had winked, as if the innuendo had been lost on her.

She had taken out her revolver, slammed its butt on the car bonnet and shouted, 'Get out! Now!'

'You, bitch! Do you know who I am?' the boy had mouthed. He pushed open the door, stumbled out and then, for a second, grabbed the car door for support, before twisting around to check the bonnet. The paint had smudged where Simone had slammed the butt of the gun. 'Do you have any idea how much it's going to cost to fix that? More than what you make whoring for a year!'

Enough was enough.

Simone had turned him around, slammed him against the vehicle and tried to handcuff him. That's when things got out of hand. The boy had swivelled, rather lithely for someone this drunk, and punched her. Right in the face and on the nose. Simone was taken aback, her eyes watering and her nose bleeding.

But she had never been one to back down from a fight.

She kicked the boy right in the nuts. The boy had fallen like a tiny bird beaten by the storm. She would have beaten him to a pulp had her colleagues not intervened.

Simone had booked him on three charges, impounded the car and thrown him in jail.

That's when the shit *really* hit the fan.

Within hours, Simone, bleeding nose and all, was summoned to the inspector general's office. The room was bristling with lawyers. It turned out that the boy was the chief minister's son. An official complaint had been filed against her on nineteen charges. Nineteen! She had sat there for an hour listening to the threats and curses of men, old and older, detailing how they would ravage her career and make her pay. She'd gone home thinking—knowing—that her career was over. Best case, she'd be demoted and transferred to another city. Worst case, she'd be transferred to a godforsaken border village where she'd arrive before electricity.

Luckily for her, superintendent Irshad Hussain, her boss, had stepped in and brokered a deal with the inspector general and the law minister. She was one of the best on his team, he had told Simone. He was going to stand up for her. She didn't quite know the details of what had happened behind closed doors. All charges against the boy were dropped and a formal apology was issued by the police in the press. Simone was suspended for two months without pay. Eighteen charges against her were dropped. One remained. She'd heard on the grapevine that the boy wanted to teach her a lesson. He was going to make her pay for damaging the paint job on his Lamborghini. A paint job that would cost a couple of years' worth of salary. She had taken the jab on the chin. She had agreed to the deal, the public humiliation and the raid on her lowly bank balance.

But now, after the agonizing forty-five days, she was back, trying to keep her head held high, raking in the pity and scorn of her fellow officers.

* * *

Simone took the staircase to the right wing on the first floor that housed the Criminal Control Investigation Department—rows and rows of chest-high cubicles. The cubicles were half-empty. Lunch hour. Simone walked the length of the room and knocked on the only office that wasn't a cubicle. A black nameplate was glued to the door. In bold white letters was written:

SUPERINTENDENT OF POLICE (CRIME)
IRSHAD M. HUSSAIN

'Come in,' said a muted voice.

Simone took in a deep breath before opening the door. It didn't help as the stench of alcohol smacked her right in the face. She gagged on the smell.

Simone recovered quickly and saluted. 'Jai Hind, sir! You wanted to see me?'

Superintendent Hussain was busy writing in a ledger. Without looking up, he motioned Simone to take a seat. Simone removed her cap and sat down as directed.

Irshad finished writing, closed the ledger and removed his wire-rimmed reading glasses. He sat back in his chair, clasped his hands and peered at Simone. He seemed to have aged since Simone saw him last week. He was in his early forties but looked much older. Stress spared no one in this line of work, especially if compounded by alcohol abuse. Fine lines had sprouted around his eyes, as had the greys in his sideburns.

'What have we got on the new case?'

Simone cleared her throat. 'A constable found the body of a boy, around five, dressed as a Barbie doll, encased in a glass case and left by the Bhopal tragedy memorial. Most certainly murdered but we're waiting on forensics to confirm the cause of death. Trace evidence was collected and the body sent for autopsy. The constable also saw a woman in a black chiffon sari at the crime scene around 3 a.m. We are trying to identify and locate her. We are canvassing for witnesses. There are no security cameras in the vicinity. A first information report [FIR] was filed at the local police station and we are searching the missing children database to identify the victim. You'll have my report—'

'What about the broken glass?' Hussain interrupted.

Simone pursed her lips. *Who had snitched?* The vein in her forehead started throbbing.

'I want no mistakes on this case, Simone. No mistakes. It has only been a few hours since the kid was found dead, but the media interest—which by extension means future public and political interest—is unparalleled. Do you know how many phone calls I have received since morning? Journalists are outraged because it's a little kid who has been murdered and displayed. I am sure you can imagine the headlines in tomorrow's newspapers. And we know who'll be crucified as always? Us. The police. And it's not just the media. The inspector general of Bhopal called. This case is top priority now,' Hussain paused, letting the gravity of the situation sink in before continuing.

'The reputation of Bhopal Police is on the line. We crack this case and we are forgiven for making Bhopal the crime capital of the country. We don't . . .' he let the last words hang in the air like a hangman's noose.

Hussain's voice softened, 'I understand the last few weeks have been tough on you. Extremely tough . . .'

For a fleeting moment, his gaze went to her bald head. Simone noticed it. She noticed every stare, every ogle at her baldness. She raised her head an inch. She was proud of it. Not for a moment did she miss her soft curls.

'. . . but I want you at the top of your game,' Hussain continued.

'I am back, sir, and just as committed and strong as I was when I first joined the force. There will be no more mistakes . . . you have my word,' Simone retorted.

Superintendent Hussain leaned back, the swivel chair creaking under the sudden shift in weight. He remained silent, assessing, thinking and deciding. Then, he leaned forward and pressed a button on the office phone to speak to his secretary.

'Send Zoya,' he said.

He pressed the button on the telephone once again and then looked straight at Simone, 'While I appreciate the commitment, Simone, I can't take any chances with this case.'

There was a knock on the door.

'Come in!' said the superintendent.

An overweight, voluptuous woman in her mid-thirties walked in. Zoya Bharucha, deputy superintendent of police (DSP). Technically, both Simone and Zoya were the same rank—above inspector but below superintendent. But Simone, a decade younger, was on the IPS fast track—a luxury conferred on a select few officers who had cleared the 'mother of all exams in India'—the Civil Services Exam. Only 0.1 per cent of the lakhs of Indians who sat for the exam each year passed the exam. Simone was one of them but Zoya wasn't. But Zoya had something that Simone did not: popularity. Zoya was revered by junior personnel and respected by senior officers. Almost as much as Simone was shunned.

'Good afternoon, sir!' Zoya saluted with gusto, her leather boots clicking against the hard concrete floor. Simone glanced down at Zoya's weathered boots, more from the weight they endured than the time gone by, Simone supposed snidely.

'Good afternoon, Zoya! You are looking sharp today. Come, take a seat.'

'Thank you, sir!' Zoya smiled, a glint reflecting off her front teeth.

Zoya deposited her bulk into the chair next to Simone with a thump. Her energy was palpable. Her enthusiasm infectious.

'Zoya, did you hear of the dead child in the glass case?' said the superintendent.

Zoya's lips tightened, as if suppressing her sadness. She nodded. 'Yes, sir. A dastardly act. A little child. Not even five.'

Superintendent Hussain paused, struck by the sudden heat of emotions from Zoya. The woman was a mother; she had a son she had lost in the custody battle with her adulterous husband. Nobody could understand how the mother wasn't granted the custody of the four-year-old. But then everybody also understood that the rich got their way in a country where corruption still ran rampant. Zoya's ex-husband owned the city's largest grocery retail chain. All she got in her divorce settlement was a fruit basket.

'May I be of assistance in the case, sir?' Zoya added.

Simone turned sharply, narrowing her eyes, and stared at Zoya. *I don't want your help*, Simone wanted to shout. *I don't want your fake sympathy for* my *case*. Simone wanted to shove Zoya but she restrained herself. She chewed the inside of her cheek instead.

'I like the enthusiasm, Zoya,' said the superintendent, dousing the raging fire in Simone's heart with kerosene.

'I have the case under control, sir,' Simone leaned forward in her chair in protest. 'I *do not* need help.' Simone felt Zoya's eyes pierce her from behind. She didn't look back. She didn't want to get into a glaring match with her.

He continued, 'Even so, Simone. I want my best detectives on this case. It's top priority.' He turned to Zoya. 'I want you to come on board and partner with Simone.' He stopped, clasping his hands. 'I expect a hands-on approach from both of you. Ask your deputy inspectors to take over your current cases so you can focus on this case alone.'

Zoya nodded vigorously, 'Absolutely, sir!'

Simone sat back. She chewed her cheek again. It hurt. She stayed silent.

Hussain peered at both of them. Left to right. Right to left. Then, he bobbed his head in satisfaction. 'Okay then. Get me results, ladies! Off you go.'

Both women stood up, saluted in unison and marched out of the room.

'To be clear, I remain the officer-in-charge,' Simone said bluntly as soon as the door closed behind her. 'I'll let you know when I need help.'

Zoya walked closer, her face inches from Simone's chest, her head raised and eyes glued to Simone's, unblinking, 'Oh, how gracious of you, madam IPS! You are letting me on your team.'

Zoya inched forward and grabbed Simone's left forearm. Simone didn't flinch. 'Let me be absolutely clear,' Zoya continued. 'I am the senior officer here. Ten years your senior. But I understand it's your case first. I would get testy too if the superintendent didn't trust me to solve my own case. So, here's what I am willing to offer. We work as equals. Partners. That's what the boss wants. That's my best offer. Take it or you can go back in and cry foul in front of him.'

Simone's nostrils flared. She shoved Zoya's hand away.

'Fine. Partners it is. But I will not slow down just because your old, fat ass can't keep up with me.'

4

'Hello!'

Nalini cleared her throat.

'Hello!' she said again, her voice squeaky. 'No, doesn't work. Needs more depth,' she said to herself.

Nalini was in the parking lot of Anna Nagar Government Primary School on the outskirts of Bhopal. She sat in her car—a white Maruti Swift. A rental. She had replaced the number plate. A precaution. Swift was probably the most common hatchback in the country. That helped. Easy to blend into the surroundings. No one remembered white. Everyone remembered pink—her usual colour of choice.

'Hello.' This time her voice was deep, bordering on a baritone. She sounded masculine. Nalini smiled. 'Hello,' she said again. It sounded exactly how she had practised for weeks. Like a middle-aged man. Like the father of the twins she was about to rescue.

It was time for step one of the plan: gain the school's trust. Nalini picked up the cheap burner phone she had bought the other day and keyed in the school's telephone number.

'Hello, Anna Nagar Government Primary School,' said a voice on the other end. The receptionist, Nalini had discovered during her recce.

'Hello, Reema!'

'Hello, sir!' Reema seemed pleased to hear her own name. *Always helps to use a person's name. Immediate trust*, thought Nalini.

'This is Vijay Srinivas, father of Ayan and Vyan, class one. I'm calling as I will not be able to pick up the kids from school today due to an urgent client meeting.'

Nalini paused for effect, letting it sink in.

'I'm sending my secretary, Mrs Nirmal Sharma, instead to pick up the kids.'

'Yes, sir. Is your secretary one of the official guardians in our records?'

'No, she isn't, Reema. I have given her an authorization letter signed by me. You can check the letter and then ask the boys to accompany her, please?'

'Sure. No problem at all, sir.'

'Thank you, Reema! Bye.'

Nalini disconnected the call. She shook her head and smiled. One could always trust the lackadaisical attitude of government-school receptionists. Had she tried this act with a top-notch private school, she'd have heard a point-blank no.

Nalini checked the dashboard clock. She decided to wait ten minutes before entering the school gate to collect her prey.

* * *

'Hello! Are you Reema?' Nalini asked the middle-aged receptionist sitting near the entrance to the school's administrative office.

Nalini already knew the answer. She knew more about Reema than the receptionist's own husband, or he would have already discovered her affair with the school's English teacher. But that was not for Nalini to tell. It was none of her business. It was just research, plain and simple.

'Yes, I'm Reema,' said the receptionist. Through her horn-rimmed glasses, she appraised Nalini from head to toe.

'I'm Nirmal Sharma, Mr Srinivas's secretary. I'm here to pick up his sons.'

Nalini handed a letter to Reema.

The receptionist took the letter, unfolded it and read it. 'May I see your ID, please?' she asked.

Nalini was prepared. She took out an Aadhar card in the name of Mrs Nirmal Sharma, a thirty-five-year-old resident of Ashok Vihar, Bhopal. The ID was fake. The photo was real.

Reema examined the card. Satisfied, she stood up. 'I just need to take a photocopy of your ID card and also cross-check Mr Srinivas's signature on the letter with our records. Would you mind waiting a few moments? Why don't you take a seat?'

Nalini felt beads of sweat pop on her forehead. Her pulse quickened. Her mouth dried. Photocopy was fine but she had not expected the receptionist to cross-check the father's signature. Nalini sat down on the chair reserved for guests. Her hand instinctively went to the belt strapped around her right shank. The belt was actually a holster, hidden beneath the sari, carrying a pocket-sized pistol. A lightweight, aluminium-frame, double-action short-barrelled Colt Cobra.

Reema photocopied the ID card and then went to a chest of metal drawers behind her desk to sift through the endless folders it contained.

Nalini started rubbing her right leg as if it was aching. Her eyes were locked on Reema's back. Her stomach churned. Goosebumps ran all over her skin, tension spewing from every pore.

Reema looked back at Nalini and then again at the folder she was scrutinizing.

Does she think the signature is forged? worried Nalini. She told herself to relax; her preparation had been painstakingly detailed. She had spent an entire hour working on the signature. An hour! There was little chance that a sloth like Reema would catch her in the act.

Reema closed the folder, smiled and walked back to her chair. 'Here's your ID card. The signature checks out. I'll ask someone to get the kids.'

* * *

'Is it tight?' Nalini asked Ayan, the twin with a blush-coloured birthmark on his forehead.

'It's too tight, Auntie!' Ayan frowned.

'That's good. Seat belts should be tight. Look at your brother. Is he complaining about the seat belt?' Nalini asked.

'I can't breathe!' Ayan retorted.

'Stop fussing, Ayan. I know you can.'

Irritated and aware that the seat belt wasn't coming off his chest, Ayan crossed his arms and stared sulkily at his feet, frown lines etched on his cute, chubby face.

Nalini stepped back, satisfied that the kids were secure in the car seats she had installed especially for them. They were not going anywhere now.

'Who wants Coca-Cola?' There was genuine excitement in Nalini's voice. She loved pampering kids. She would do anything for the little ones while she could.

'Me! Me!' screamed Vyan, kicking his legs in excitement, with a toothy grin that would have melted most hearts.

Ayan didn't answer. He kept his arms crossed, although the frown was gone.

Nalini laughed. 'Okay, okay.'

She bent down and fished out two Coca-Cola cans and a packet of plastic straws from the back pocket of the front seat. She snapped open a can, stuffed in a straw and gave it to Vyan, who grabbed the can with both hands and started drinking from it.

'Slow down, Vyan or your stomach will hurt,' Nalini mock-scolded the kid, who wasn't paying attention any more.

Nalini turned to his brother. 'How about you, Ayan? Don't you want Coke?'

Ayan shook his head sulkily.

'Are you sure? There are only two cans. If you don't want it, I'll drink this one.'

Nalini twisted the metal ring and popped open the can. She comically exaggerated the process of stuffing the straw like she was pushing the straw through cake rather than Coke.

Ayan's eyes followed her every move. He smacked his lips.

'No, I want it!' Ayan shouted, just as Nalini was about to put the straw in her mouth.

'I thought so,' said Nalini, lovingly squeezing his puffed cheeks. 'Naughty boy, here you go.'

Nalini gave him the can and ruffled his hair. Why was it that the naughty ones were always the cutest?

Nalini shut the rear door of the car before opening the driver's door and slipping into the seat. Her heart was fluttering. She couldn't stop smiling. If there was such a thing as bliss in the world, this was it.

She started the car and pulled out of the school parking lot.

They drove in silence for five minutes before Vyan complained from the back seat. 'Auntie, my stomach hurts.'

'I told you to drink it slowly, Vyan.'

If the kids had looked at Nalini through the rear-view mirror, they'd have seen her lips curl in a cunning smirk.

The plan was working.

5

They had identified him. The Barbie. The boy in the glass case.

The missing persons department had called Simone ten minutes ago. She was both surprised and impressed with their speed. Usually it took them days, sometimes for ever, to get a match but the recently adopted facial recognition software had matched the photo of the dead child with a boy reported missing two days ago. Ankush Dixit, aged five, was a resident of Shanti Nagar, one of the oldest slums in Bhopal.

Simone and Zoya were on their way to break the news to Ankush's father, Ramesh Dixit. A carpenter and a single parent. Simone had called ahead, saying they had more questions about his son's disappearance, and had told him they would meet him at his house. Best to deliver bad news in private rather than asking him to come to the police station. It was the least they could do.

Simone stepped on the accelerator. Her Thar roared on cue and lurched forward.

'Do you always drive so fast?' asked Zoya from the passenger seat, without looking up from an engrossing game of Angry Birds on her smartphone.

'I'm still within the speed limit. And, anyway, it's an emergency,' Simone replied.

'Oh, is that why? Makes sense for someone like you.' Zoya's voice dripped with sarcasm. Out of the corner of her eye, Simone could see Zoya looking at her. After a moment, Zoya shrugged and went back to Angry Birds.

Simone knew Zoya had a doctorate in psychology. *Dr* Zoya Bharucha. She also knew that Zoya had a habit of psychoanalysing everyone she met. She was the unofficial agony aunt of Bhopal Police. She was friendly, the officers trusted her but, most importantly, she listened with an intent to understand and not to retort. Another reason Simone disliked Zoya—a woman of mere words, not action. Simone liked doers, not sit-on-your-fat-ass preachers.

Simone knew what awaited her on the other side of the conversation—the truth, her truth. But restraint wasn't one of her strong suits. 'What do you mean "someone like me"?' She raised one hand from the steering wheel to air quote the last bit.

Zoya glanced at Simone, her head tilted to one side and smiled condescendingly, like mothers do when their toddlers ask cute but dumb questions.

'What do *you* think it means, Simone?'

'Don't use my question against me,' Simone raised her voice.

'Okay,' Zoya sighed. 'I meant a person who is driven, hungry and always wants to prove something and wants to impress.'

Simone snorted. 'You're kidding, right?'

Zoya didn't answer but continued to stare at Simone.

Simone turned a sharp corner without slowing down.

'I am not trying to impress you. Why would I try to impress you? I don't even like you that much!' Simone was shouting now, her pitch rising and her voice shriller, without even realizing it.

Zoya raised her hands in surrender. 'Calm down. I didn't mean it—'

'Yeah, right! That's exactly what—'

Simone's phone buzzed, the ringtone an ode to the bygone rotary phones.

She slowed the car, turned on the indicators and stopped by the kerb. Talking on the phone while driving wasn't a rule she wanted to break, even in an emergency.

She snatched her phone from the dashboard and accepted the call.

'What?' Simone yelled into the phone.

'Simone, this is Marvin.'

Dr Marvin D'Souza was the lead medical examiner on the case. A thorough professional whose love for superhero comics was only exceeded by his love for cadavers.

'Oh, hello, Dr D'Souza. Is the autopsy done?' asked Simone.

Dr D'Souza laughed, as if Simone had cracked a joke. 'My assistant just started the autopsy, Simone. And only because superintendent Hussain pushed the case to the top of the list.'

'Oh,' said Simone, disappointed.

'Anyway, we have finished dusting the clothes and body of the child for prints. And I thought you'd want to know . . .' he paused. There was a rustle of papers, as if he was rummaging through a pile to get to the right sheet of paper.

Simone put the call on speaker so Zoya could hear the conversation as well. Simone had no patience to repeat conversations.

'. . . here it is,' Dr D'Souza said, his voice booming through the speakers, 'no latent prints or trace evidence on the clothing. They were sprayed and wiped with bleach, which, in my opinion, was just precaution. The killer must have been wearing gloves and maybe even personal protective equipment [PPE] because there were no foreign hair follicle or skin cells on the body.'

Simone was becoming anxious, frustrated. *Tell me why you called, doc,* she wanted to shout, *not what you didn't find.*

'But,' there was sudden excitement in his voice, 'get this! There is a thumbprint—neat, crystal clear, intentional—right in the middle of the victim's forehead. The killer put a tika on the forehead using vermilion, just like a pandit puts a tika in a temple on a devotee's forehead. I am sending the print to the National Crime Records Bureau [NCRB] to cross-check. But here's where it gets even more interesting—the tika was definitely applied posthumously because the body's natural perspiration and oils did not interact with it.'

'What are you saying, doc?'

'I am saying the killer put the tika on the boy after he was dead. It has a thumbprint. In all probability, this is the killer's thumbprint. Like an artist signing his or her painting.'

6

Simone had called her aide, an inspector at the NCRB, right after her conversation with Dr D'Souza. She told the inspector she wanted the thumbprint from the victim's forehead cross-checked against the Unique Identification Authority of India (UIDAI) database, which contains biometric information—fingerprints, iris scans and photographs—of 136 crore Indians. Simone knew it was a grey area, an invasion of privacy if the far-Left liberals were to be believed. Privacy laws notwithstanding, this was Simone's best bet at catching the killer. Her fastest bet. No warrant, no red tape, no hassle. She'd have the results within the hour.

'So, our killer's an artist, huh?' Zoya munched her lower lip as Simone disconnected the phone.

'Yes, an artist who likes to mark his sculpted dolls,' said Simone.

She steered the Thar into a narrow lane. A signboard declared: Shanti Nagar—literally meaning Peace Town. *Well, there will be no peace in this town today*, thought Simone.

Simone squeezed the Thar through the alleyways lined with open gutters, the terrible stink, vendors selling sundry goods in tiny shops and brick houses rammed together as if supporting each other from imminent collapse. The Thar bumped over puddles small and big, jolting both passengers and making their ears ring. It was as close to an off-road adventure as one could get in Bhopal. Finally, Simone found the address she was looking for and brought the Thar to a halt.

'Might be better if I do the talking,' said Zoya.

'I'll do the talking.' Simone jumped out of the Thar without waiting for an answer.

'Suit yourself,' Zoya said, more to herself.

An unbearable stench assaulted Simone's nose and crawled down her throat. Gagging, she hastily pulled out a handkerchief from her trouser pocket to cover her mouth and nose.

Simone looked around. All eyes were on Zoya and her. The kids playing cricket in the street had stopped to stare. Neighbours had emerged from their houses, whispering to each other. Simone felt unwelcome here. She was the police after all, the bearer of bad news.

Simone jumped over the choked gutter that lined the street on to the minuscule veranda in front of the house. She knocked on the door. Twice.

A lanky man with cropped hair opened the door. Deep, dark circles surrounded his bloodshot eyes. He had either not slept in days or had been crying. Or both. His unshaven and unruly beard, speckled with grey, suggested the latter.

'Are you Mr Ramesh Dixit?'

'Yes, please, please come in,' his words mixed into each other and he stepped back immediately to make room for

Simone and Zoya to enter the dark, dingy house. He seemed hurried. Like he didn't want to provide fodder for the gossips gathered outside his house.

The neighbourhood aunties will know sooner or later, thought Simone.

Simone was forced to bend her tall frame to avoid banging her head on the lintel of the door. Once inside, she stood tall, the ceiling barely inches from her head. It was a square, one-room studio. There was a sofa—brown, grubby and stained—by the door to seat guests. A mini-LCD TV hung on the wall alongside it. A bed lay in the far corner, the sheets crumpled and the blanket in disarray. It seemed that Ramesh had spent the last few days hibernating in bed. The caustic odour of stale sweat definitely seemed to suggest so.

Two people, a man and a woman, stood in the other corner, supposedly the kitchen. 'My sister and her husband,' said Ramesh. 'They live down the street and have been helping me since . . .' he choked, '. . . since Ankush disappeared. Did you find him, officers?'

'Why don't you sit down, Mr Dixit?' suggested Simone.

'Yes, you too. Please sit,' Ramesh gestured to the sofa. He dragged a wooden stool for himself and sat opposite the sofa. His sister and brother-in-law continued to stand near the kitchen. They hadn't spoken a word since the officers had arrived.

Zoya moved past Simone and sat down on the sofa.

Simone kept standing, her handkerchief on her mouth, her soul cringing at all the germs inhabiting the dirty sofa. Perhaps it even had bedbugs? She shuddered at the thought. There was no way she was sitting in that grime.

'Can I get you something to drink?' Ramesh asked politely.

'Nothing,' Simone blurted.

Zoya eyed Simone, displeased. She turned to the host, 'Water will be fine.'

Ramesh nodded. He was about to stand up to get the water, when his sister said, 'You stay. I'll get it.'

Ramesh sat back down, clasped his trembling hands and forced a smile. His eyes brimmed with deep sadness.

'Sit!' Zoya hissed at Simone.

Simone wrinkled her nose in disgust and shook her head vigorously.

Zoya rolled her eyes. 'Stop being disrespectful! Sit!' she whispered under her breath.

Simone seemed unsure. Then, after much thought, she chose the lesser of the two evils—a wooden stool next to the one Ramesh sat on, praying and hoping it wasn't infested with bedbugs.

'I'm ASP Simone Singh. This is DSP Zoya Bharucha.'

Simone decided to come straight to the point. *Best to rip the Band-Aid off*, she thought. Exactly how she'd like it if she were in Ramesh's position.

'Your son, Ankush, is dead.'

'No!' Ramesh's sister screamed and dropped the tray she was holding.

The three glasses of water and the tray fell with a loud clang and water spilled all over the floor.

Zoya covered her mouth with her hand, embarrassed and completely caught off guard by Simone's words.

Ramesh's brother-in-law rushed towards his wife. He held her as she bawled and wept.

'What? My son is dead?' Ramesh slumped. His face contorted. His lips quivered. He rubbed hands on his thighs, as if trying to calm himself. Suddenly, a flood of tears burst

through, overpowering the wall of self-control he was trying
to build.

'Ankush!' he cried. 'I'm sorry, Ankush!' Putting his head
in his hands, sniffling hard, he tried to push back the tears
intent on running unchecked.

'Why are you sorry, Mr Dixit?' asked Simone, unmoved
and desperate to get the discussion back on track.

Zoya looked at Simone, raising her hands and mouthing
the words without speaking—*what the fuck!*

Zoya took over. 'We are very sorry for your loss, Mr Dixit.
Please take all the time you need.'

Ramesh's sobs turned silent, as if he had just realized that
he had strangers for company. He bent forward and covered
his face, putting back the wall of self-control.

Zoya said, 'I have a boy myself. About Ankush's age. So, I
can understand your pain.'

Ramesh didn't respond. He rubbed his eyes, inhaling and
exhaling heavily.

Zoya went silent.

Simone started tapping her foot, her impatience making
itself known.

'I'm sorry,' Ramesh sniffled.

Simone stopped tapping her foot.

Ramesh turned to Zoya and asked, 'How did Ankush die?'

'The autopsy is—' Simone started to speak, but Zoya
interrupted her.

'We don't know for sure,' said Zoya. 'The autopsy is
underway.'

'Was he . . .' Ramesh hesitated and bit his lower lip. 'Was
he murdered?'

'I'm afraid the circumstances suggest so, Mr Dixit.'

Ramesh pursed his lips. A fresh stream of tears rolled down his cheeks.

'The investigation is on. We will have more information in the coming days.' She paused and then said, 'And that is another reason why we wanted to meet you in person. If it's okay with you, we'd like to ask some questions which will help us in our investigation to find the murderer.'

Ramesh nodded his assent.

'We know from the FIR that Ankush went missing from Government Model School, Shanti Nagar. Where were you at that time?'

Ramesh sniffled, clearing his throat.

'I had a carpentry job at the new pharmacy shop coming up next door. I was supposed to pick up Ankush from school at noon. I was thirty minutes late.' Ramesh looked at his feet, as if ashamed. 'I wanted to finish milling the cupboard planks before picking him up. The shop owner wanted the cupboards done in a day. I had started late and was behind schedule,' he explained.

'What happened when you reached the school?' Simone asked.

Ramesh took a deep breath. 'He wasn't at school. We checked everywhere. Asked all his friends and their parents. Nobody saw him leave school. Nobody found him at school. He . . . he had simply vanished.'

'Did you always pick him up from school or were there days when he walked home alone?' asked Simone.

'No, never. He was just a little kid. Sometimes I asked my sister or brother-in-law to pick him up from school. And sometimes I asked my neighbours. But Ankush was told never to leave school alone or with a stranger. I know my son. He wouldn't have left alone.'

'Okay, we'll need a list of all the neighbours and relatives who have picked him up in the past.'

'Relatives?'

'Yes, Mr Dixit. A close relative is involved in 80 per cent of criminal cases related to children below ten,' Simone narrated the fact with pride.

Ramesh looked stricken, appalled.

'Are you blaming my family for my son's murder?' Ramesh asked, his hands bunched into fists, his face misshapen with rage.

Zoya stood up and cleared her throat, 'Sorry, what my colleague means to say is that it's a possibility we'd like to investigate. We don't know who did it but we will not leave any stone unturned to find your son's killer.'

Ramesh backed off and nodded slowly.

'How was Ankush doing at school?' Zoya asked, as she too sat down.

'What do you mean?'

'Any incidents recently? Any fights? Anything unusual?'

'He was a timid boy. Extremely shy. It was difficult to get even one word out of him.' Suddenly, his expression turned dark, even sinister. 'He used to get bullied because of that. The boy was soft. Easy pickings for any bully, especially older kids.' Ramesh shook his head in disgust. 'He came home one day with a busted lip. On another day, his shirt had been torn, the buttons ripped out. One day his bag got "lost" mysteriously and was found the next day, filled with dog shit.'

Simone ground her teeth; her eyes widened. She might not understand empathy, but bullying she understood. Her childhood nemesis that had somehow never left her in adulthood.

Ramesh continued, 'I complained to the teachers. Shouted at the principal. Nothing happened. No culprits were found. But then, last week, something unusual happened.'

Both Simone and Zoya leaned forward.

'Ankush came home happy. Excited. For a change he was chatty. Completely unlike himself. He said a "cleaning auntie" at school had saved him from bad boys and had given him a chocolate. Of course, I immediately told him never to take sweets from strangers. He said—'

Ramesh stopped all of a sudden. 'Wait a minute! Do you think it could be that cleaning lady at school?'

Simone said, 'We'll look into it. Anything else you can tell us about the victim?'

'Ankush,' said Ramesh.

'Sorry?'

'He has a name. It's not *victim*. It's Ankush!'

Ramesh's voice echoed in the enclosed space, leaving Simone stunned. Silence gripped the room.

Simone opened her mouth to speak. Then, decided against it.

Zoya jumped in, 'Mr Dixit, if you don't mind my asking, where is Ankush's mother?'

Ramesh inhaled deeply before replying, 'She died right after giving birth to Ankush.'

'Oh! I'm so sorry.'

'How did she die?' asked Simone.

Ramesh stared at her.

Simone stared back. It was a valid question. She was within bounds to ask it.

Finally, Ramesh broke the eye contact. 'My wife was born months after the Bhopal Gas Tragedy. She had a congenital birth defect in her heart. Complications arose when she got pregnant with Ankush. They had to operate on her immediately. Ankush survived. She didn't.'

Silence.

The piercing ringtone from Simone's phone caught all of them by surprise. She jumped from her seat and fished out the phone from her pocket.

It was the NCRB inspector.

'What?' said Simone.

'Ma'am, we got a 100 per cent match on the thumbprint.'

Simone's heart raced.

'Tell me,' she said.

'The thumbprint belongs to Ramesh Dixit, the victim's father.'

7

Simone disconnected the call and just stood there for a moment. And then, with a sudden click of the boots, she turned around.

'Mr Dixit, please put your hands behind your back. You are under arrest on suspicion of murdering your son,' said Simone.

'Simone!' Zoya gasped, standing up.

Ramesh was too bewildered to react. He remained seated on the sofa, mouth agape and eyes unblinking. His sister, who had been sobbing in a corner, her head buried in her husband's chest, stopped crying all of a sudden.

'Is this a joke?' demanded Ramesh's brother-in-law, pulling away from his wife.

'What's happening, Simone?' said Zoya.

Simone ignored her.

Zoya felt beads of sweat run down her spine. She walked over to Simone and grabbed her arm. 'We don't have a warrant,' Zoya muttered.

'We don't need one. We found his thumbprint on the body. The thumbprint that was left *after* the kid was murdered and it's a perfect match,' said Simone. 'To me that is reasonable suspicion of a cognizable offence—Section 41 of the Criminal Procedure Code [CrPC].'

Zoya let go of Simone's arm. She knew a 100 per cent fingerprint match, especially one left posthumously, was grounds for arrest without a warrant.

Simone said, 'Stand up, Mr Dixit.'

'But . . . but . . .' Ramesh was at a loss for words. 'I didn't kill my son! Why would I kill him? He was *my* son.'

Simone pulled out the handcuffs.

'Your prints were found on your son's body, Mr Dixit. Now, turn around,' she ordered.

'I don't understand. There must be a mistake,' said Ramesh, hapless and defeated.

Simone turned him around and cuffed him.

Zoya admired Simone's finesse, her focus, her calm, even under stress. Robotic. Clinical. *Only if the woman had a heart*, Zoya thought.

Ramesh started to cry. 'Why are you doing this? I didn't kill Ankush! I swear! I swear!'

'Save this for the court, Mr Dixit,' Simone snarled.

Zoya opened the door.

Simone shoved Ramesh from behind. 'Let's go!'

They stepped out the house. The pesky neighbours were still loitering outside. Give them all a tub of popcorn and it would have looked like an open-air theatre, spectators entertaining themselves on the misfortune of others.

An immediate hush fell among the neighbours when they saw Ramesh in handcuffs. A few gasped. Some covered their mouths in surprise. Others stood still, not knowing how to react to the latest development. It wasn't every day that the police arrested your neighbour in broad daylight, was it?

Zoya followed Simone and Ramesh to the Thar. Ramesh started to sob profusely. It wasn't clear if it was because he had been caught or because he felt humiliated in front of the neighbours.

Simone opened the rear door. 'Get in!' she ordered.

Ramesh hopped inside awkwardly; his movements restricted by the handcuffs.

Simone slammed the door shut.

'Why are you arresting him?' shouted the next-door neighbour, a Sikh man in a purple turban and white kurta-pyjama.

'Mind your own business,' Simone retorted.

This seemed to infuriate the man. He pulled up the sleeves of his kurta, as one does before throwing punches in a fight, stepped off his veranda and marched over to stand in front of the Thar.

'You cannot just come here and arrest innocent people. The poor man's son has been missing. And now you come here and harass him!' He crossed his arms. 'You are not taking Ramesh anywhere!'

It spurred a cacophony of agreement from the other neighbours.

'Yes!'

'You cannot arrest him!'

'Yes!'

Men and women stepped forward and joined the turbaned man. A show of solidarity, a show of mutiny.

Uh-oh! Zoya gulped. Her heart raced. It was no secret that the citizens of Bhopal hated the police. Crime was at an all-time high—actually, the highest in the country. Police brutality was the daily topic of discussion in the local news. In a nutshell, the citizens didn't trust the police and who could blame them? She had heard of many instances, mostly from such small localities, where police personnel were harassed, kicked or beaten, in the line of duty. And here they were, two women against the entire locality. If the locality leaders decided, the two of them would be lynched in broad daylight and in cold blood.

Simone turned to Zoya and said, 'You prepare the memo of arrest. I'll run Ramesh through his rights. We produce him in court today. We don't want a defence lawyer to shred us later and claim the arrest was botched.'

Zoya stared at Simone. It seemed like Simone didn't understand the pickle they were in. They might not leave the locality alive and here she was going on nonchalantly about police routine.

The crowd swelled. A dam waiting to explode.

'Simone,' whispered Zoya, 'what about the neighbours?'

Simone glanced at the crowd, left to right and back, like she was eyeing her opponents in a street fight. 'Get in the Thar,' she muttered.

Simone opened the driver's door and got in.

Zoya sighed, walked around the Thar and got into the passenger seat.

Ramesh cried. 'But madam *ji*, I am telling the truth. I didn't do it,' he said between sniffles.

'Well, we'll know for sure soon, won't we?' said Simone.

Simone faced the steering wheel and the crowd gathered in front. She started the engine.

The crowd started to yell and shout but no one budged.

'What shall we do?' asked Zoya. 'We need to talk to them and calm them down.'

'Won't work with an enraged crowd.'

'Then, what, Simone? We can't simply run them over.'

Simone gave her a ghost of a smile, 'Why not?'

Simone threw the Thar into gear and stamped on the accelerator. The beast lurched forward with intensity, aiming directly for the man in the purple turban, who was standing barely ten metres away.

'Shit!' Zoya shouted.

It was a battle of who would blink first. The outcome would be catastrophic if no one blinked.

The rage in the eyes of the turbaned man instantly turned to fear. He stepped back.

'No!' yelled Zoya.

Suddenly, at the very last second, Simone jammed her foot on the brake, bringing the Thar to a grinding halt. At the same instant, the turbaned man, unaware that Simone would stop the car, jumped aside to save his life. He fell on the ground, his clothes stained brown with dirt.

The others in the crowd saw their leader on the ground and scattered like roaches.

'Fear of death is greater than their love for their neighbour,' said Simone.

She pressed the accelerator again and sped away from the yells and curses of the crowd.

* * *

They produced Ramesh in court within hours of the arrest. A government lawyer was provided after Ramesh declined to hire one. He couldn't afford one and had declared that 'the innocent don't need lawyers'. *A brave, but stupid move*, Zoya thought.

The documents were in order, grounds for arrest strong—the thumbprint match was the clincher. The district magistrate agreed with the arresting officers and remanded Ramesh in judicial custody for a period of ninety days. It was non-bailable custody. Ramesh broke down in court again. The district magistrate brushed him away. Ramesh deserved no sympathy for killing a little kid, more so his own son.

'Well done!' Zoya told Simone, after an inspector had taken custody of Ramesh and taken him to jail.

Simone narrowed her eyes, her forehead creased. 'Do you think I care? Or do you think I need your approval?'

Zoya sighed. It was getting harder and harder to work with this brat. She sympathized with Simone. She'd hold a grudge too if superintendent Hussain thought she wasn't capable of handling a case on her own. So, she, Zoya, was happy to collaborate, happy to let Simone take the lead and let her shine. But Simone wasn't making it easy. Not at all.

'Sorry,' Zoya gave Simone the benefit of the doubt. Again. 'I meant we did well, partner. Bagged our first suspect.'

Simone said nothing. The vein in her forehead throbbed, ready to burst through the skin. It conveyed what Simone couldn't put into words.

'What now?' asked Zoya. She didn't want to ride roughshod over Simone, even though she was the more experienced officer. Collaboration was the best tactic, especially for someone with a short fuse like Simone.

Simone said, 'We have the suspect. Hard evidence that places him at the scene of the crime. All we need is the murder weapon and motive. Case closed.'

Zoya pondered for a moment. 'Do you think he did it?'

'What I think is not important. The evidence speaks for itself.'

'Yes . . . but, what does your gut say?'

Simone sighed. 'I don't trust my gut. And I don't trust people. I trust and follow hard evidence,' she paused, 'which is why I'm not sure if we have the right person in custody.'

'What do you mean?' asked Zoya.

'On the night the body was found, constable Daya saw a woman, not a man,' said Simone.

Zoya's eyes widened, 'Maybe that's the motive?'

Simone inched closer, 'What is?'

Zoya said, 'His wife is dead, right? So, maybe, Ramesh is involved with another woman. A woman who doesn't like the shy little nuisance—the kid. She wants the kid out of the picture. Doesn't want the kid from his ex-wife, a constant reminder of his past. She convinces Ramesh, hatches the plan and together, they murder the kid.'

Simone grinned, revealing her front teeth. It was the first time Zoya had seen her smile.

'It's an interesting theory, Zoya, but we need to ask around, see if there is another woman and check out his alibi. But the way his place was messed up, it looked like he was genuinely heartbroken. Even if he killed his own kid, why display him in a glass case? Why make a big deal out of it? Wouldn't it be better to hide the body? Easier to say the boy was kidnapped and never found. We, the police, would lap it up. Nobody would even suspect him because he lodged the missing person complaint himself.'

Zoya nodded. For all her faults, Simone was right, her logic sound. Zoya agreed, 'You're right. The biggest clue is the display case—an elaborate and painstaking endeavour done at the cost of getting caught. Why dress up the boy as a girl? More importantly, why kill a little boy in the first place. We need to understand the psyche of the murderer. We should—'

'Stop!' Simone turned on her heels. 'I know you are a trained psychoanalyst but let's not make it a bigger deal than it is. We are not dealing with a psychotic serial killer. It's one dead boy. One murder.'

Zoya shuddered at the thought of Simone's cold and frigid heart.

Simone continued, 'We follow the clues, play it logically and we'll find the killer. If current evidence is to be believed, yes, maybe the killer is already in jail. Or maybe not. We need to nip the loose ends in the bud, wrap it up with a red ribbon and throw the closed-case file in the boss's face!'

'So, that's what it's about? Throwing it in superintendent Hussain's face because he asked you to partner with me?'

Simone huffed. She walked towards her Thar.

'Wait! Is that a yes or a no?' Zoya jogged after Simone.

Simone didn't answer or break her stride.

Zoya was sweating by the time she caught up with Simone. 'Look . . . I am . . . sorry,' she said, breathless. 'You're right . . . Let's follow the facts of the case.' She exhaled loudly. 'Let's start—'

Simone's shrill, old-school ringtone started blaring. She pulled out her phone and accepted the call. 'What!' she barked into the phone.

Zoya chuckled. She was beginning to wonder if Simone ever said 'hello' to the caller.

Simone listened to the caller for a few seconds. 'I'm on my way,' she said and disconnected.

'What is it?' Zoya asked.

'The autopsy results are back. I'm heading there.'

'Oh, great! Let's go then.'

Simone didn't move. 'No,' she said, 'I'm going alone.'

'What do you mean?' Zoya was starting to reach her boiling point, both from the short run and Simone's attitude.

'Let's divide and conquer like you suggested earlier. Why don't you go check Ramesh's alibi and talk to his neighbours? See if you can prove your theory of the secret mistress.' Simone unlocked the Thar and hopped in.

Zoya ground her teeth. She had had enough of Simone for a day. 'Fine. Divide and conquer it is,' she muttered. 'Just drop me off at the headquarters. My car is parked there.'

Simone shut the car door and turned on the ignition. The Thar boomed to life. She lowered the window and appraised Zoya from head to toe.

She said, 'I think you'll greatly benefit from a twenty-minute walk, Zoya.'

Simone put the car in gear and drove away.

8

Simone clenched and unclenched her hands on the steering wheel, chewing her lower lip, intent on reducing it to a pulp. Her nostrils flared like a chimney releasing white plumes of smoke. Quite simply, she was mad.

She was mad at superintendent Hussain for not trusting her and forcing a babysitter on her. She wasn't a child. She didn't need a nanny.

Simone scoffed, thinking about Zoya's secret-mistress theory, which was stupid at best. It didn't answer why Ramesh, or his mistress, would dress the boy in drag and display him in a case. *Senior detective, my foot!*

Simone sighed, immediately regretting the thought. Zoya wasn't the culprit here. Hussain was! She was getting blindsided by his behaviour and blaming Zoya unfairly.

And just as suddenly, she got mad at herself for how she had behaved with Zoya, who was only trying to help. She didn't deserve to be left stranded in the parking lot.

Simone slammed a hand on the steering wheel as a gamut of emotions threatened to swamp her.

'Get a grip!' she lashed out at herself.

Simone brought the Thar to a halt at the offices of the Directorate of Forensic Science Services. She shut her eyes and breathed in.

Must stay strong. Stay focused. Be emotionless, she told herself.

She opened her eyes and saw the reflection of her steely gaze in the rear-view mirror. She nodded and jumped out of the Thar.

Simone walked into the reception, registered in the entry docket and took the elevator to the third floor.

She had been here many times. The place always smelled like antiseptic liquid. Always the same routine. Dr D'Souza preferred meeting detectives in his office, rather than sending autopsy results over email or meeting them in his lab.

She walked the length of a corridor and came to a stop outside his door. Simone knocked on the door twice.

'Come in!' said a gruff voice.

Simone entered.

Dr D'Souza looked up and removed his thick, black reading glasses.

'Oh, Simone. Come in, come in!' he softened his voice. It still sounded hoarse and forced, like he had a sore throat. He didn't. It was a birth deformity in the larynx—Dr D'Souza had once told Simone.

The office was small and square, with shelves lining the walls, replete with folders of every conceivable colour. It seemed more like a mini library of dossiers than a medical examiner's office. Dr D'Souza sat hunched with his elbows on the table.

'Take a seat,' he offered.

'Thank you.' Simone sat down.

'How are you doing, Simone?'

'I'm fine,' said Simone. She wanted to get to the point. Small talk made her uncomfortable. Or irate. Or nasty. Sometimes, like today, all of the above.

'How's your grandma?' croaked Dr D'Souza.

'Fine.' Simone forced a smile.

'And Simone . . .' he paused, as if trying to find the right words, '. . . I was sorry to hear about your suspension. It was neither fair nor just. I understand how difficult it must have been for you and—'

'Have you ever been suspended yourself?' Simone interrupted him.

Dr D'Souza fell silent for a moment. 'Umm . . . no . . . I haven't. But I know it takes someone resilient, a fighter like you, to come back strongly.'

Simone gripped the edge of her chair, holding herself in place lest she give in to the urge to run away. She bobbed her head quite a few times. 'You mentioned on the phone that the autopsy is complete?' she said, changing the topic.

Dr D'Souza looked at Simone for a moment. Then, with an understanding shake of the head, said, 'Yes and no.'

Simone was puzzled.

He pushed the folder in front of him towards Simone and turned it around for her to read it.

He said, 'We finished the autopsy, yes. But did we find the *cause* of death? No.'

'What do you mean?'

Dr D'Souza sat back in his chair, massaging his forehead. 'Let me try to explain. The deceased boy had no physical injuries, no internal haemorrhage, no organ failure. Which means no undue force was used. He wasn't strangled—no marks on the throat or pinch marks on the nose. So, we thought the kid was poisoned. But the toxicology report came back negative. Nothing in the stomach, except the remains of a burger and Coca-Cola. We checked twice. Same result.'

'What are you saying, doc?'

'The kid had a heart attack. His heart simply stopped pumping. Poof! Just like that. If not for the way the kid was displayed in the glass case, you'd think he went to sleep and never woke up.'

9

Ranveer skewed his face sideways. He checked himself in the rear-view mirror of his swanky, red Mercedes-Benz SUV. He flicked a stray strand of his shoulder-length hair behind his ear. The charcoal black hair glowed in the dim light of the underground parking lot, thanks to the copious amounts of hair gel he had applied.

It was date night. He felt giddy. The once-a-quarter ritual. Ranveer closed his fists to control the little shivers of excitement. He took a deep breath. It only made him more perceptive of the anxiety that gripped his body, mostly his loins.

'Date night, baby!' he exulted loudly, in an effort to let some of the exhilaration out of his system. It helped. A little.

Ranveer looked outside the car window. The parking lot of DB City Mall was full. The evening traffic still streamed in with a few cars wandering about the parking lot hoping to find a vacant spot.

His date was late. Five minutes and running.

Ranveer took out his iPhone 11. He turned on the VPN set to Cayman Islands, opened the Internet browser and entered an IP address. It took him to a blank, white screen with a cursor blinking in the middle, asking for a password. He was always struck by the stark contrast of the white screen representing his favourite site on the dark web. A timer below the cursor was counting down from thirty seconds. He entered his twenty-character password. No haste. No stress.

The page refreshed and took him to a site called G.B.T. A tagline at the top of the page read: '*The sexy middle if you lose the L and Q*'—a reference to the LGBTQ community. Below were graphic listings of gay, bi and trans men seeking lovers or one-night stands. Ranveer ignored the listings and opened his secure inbox. He entered a different password and all his previous messages showed up. His previous one-night stands with closeted transgender tourists on short trips to Bhopal. He liked to look at the old messages to re-live those nights of passion.

Right on top was a message thread with his date tonight. Cleopatra, 'she/her'—the pronouns she preferred. A fake name, naturally. No way would Indian parents name their boy Cleopatra. There were no new messages from Cleopatra. The last message, sent more than two hours ago, was a selfie of Cleopatra, pouting, her face caked with colourful cosmetics, her lush, red lips almost kissing the camera. A caption under the photo read: *Getting ready! BTW . . . I'm naked right now!* The flirty message aroused him. If he was excited about the date before, the message had ignited raw, uncontrollable passion.

Ranveer had replied: *FYI. I just got out of the shower.* Two could play that game.

Ranveer clenched and unclenched his fingers to calm the little shivers that were trying to gain control.

'Dammit!' he huffed.

'Get a grip!' he told himself. He felt the constant throbbing of the vein in his forehead.

Suddenly, there was a knock on the passenger-side window. Ranveer looked up, surprised, the vein in his forehead pounding.

It was Cleopatra. She was grinning. Her shimmery, silver chiffon gown's V-neck, lined with fake diamonds, glittered despite the dim light. One could always trust a closeted, transgender woman to go all out on a date night in a different city—the few nights of freedom when he could be a woman without a care or judgement. Ranveer preferred it this way. The secrecy. The disguise.

Ranveer smiled at Cleopatra and lowered the window.

'Hi! Are you Ripple?' Her voice was raspy, heavy, fake. Just like her get-up.

For a moment Ranveer was confused but quickly remembered that Ripple was his chosen name for tonight's date.

'Yes, I am. Nice to meet you!'

Ranveer unlocked the car door. Cleopatra gathered her flowing gown with one hand, the grab handle above the car window with the other and got into the SUV. Ranveer couldn't help but notice her matching six-inch silver pumps. His heart fluttered. The tremors in his hand returned. He was already fantasizing about adding those pumps to his collection.

Cleopatra slammed the door shut. Blinked her long, fake eyelashes at Ranveer and said, 'Shall we?'

Ranveer nodded, locking the car, and started the engine.

Cleopatra was his. *Forever.*

10

'How about some music?' Ranveer turned on the car radio without waiting for an answer from Cleopatra. A Punjabi song filled the car with its peppy beats. Ranveer wasn't a fan of Punjabi music. Or Bollywood music. Hard, headbanging rock—that was his jam. But, for now, anything to shut Cleopatra up, he thought. He was getting tired of her constant raspy blabbering. Cleopatra was going out of her way to hide her masculine voice. The more she tried, the more her voice grated on his ears, like a buzz saw cutting through hardwood—jarring, pesky and screechy. He didn't mind the over-the-top dressing. He liked it actually. But the pretentious feminine voice annoyed him. He would have picked up a woman if he had wanted to be with one.

Well, he had been with a woman until she left him. His wife. Ex-wife. The woman he loved. The woman who had crushed him.

Ranveer tightened his grip on the steering wheel.

'Oh my!' Cleopatra squeaked.

Ranveer was jerked out of his reverie, the memory of his ex-wife dissolving into indecipherable fragments—exactly the way she had left him last year.

'That's terrible! Did you hear that?' Cleopatra asked him.

The Punjabi song had stopped. The radio jockey was speaking in a hushed, pained voice.

'Sorry, what?'

'The news. Did you hear the news on the radio? Someone murdered a little girl of five and encased her in a glass case dressed as a Barbie doll, like she was some sort of trophy to be displayed.' Cleopatra patted her chest, as if trying to calm down her heart.

Ranveer shrugged. Thousands died every day in this country. What was one more death?

'Don't worry about it,' said Ranveer.

Cleopatra fanned her face by vigorously flapping her hand. 'Sorry, I get a little paranoid sometimes,' she said. 'You see, I have a daughter of my own in Mumbai. Six years old. I'm just concerned about her. What would happen if a creep like the Doll Maker kidnaps her? I would die, you know. Just die!' Her voice choked on the tears she was struggling to hold back.

Ranveer narrowed his brow. 'The Doll Maker?'

Cleopatra gulped, nodding. Holding back emotions that were clearly ready to flow, she nodded again. 'Yes. That's what they are calling the killer.'

Ranveer shook his head in dismay. *That's what the media does today!* He was screaming in his head. He was annoyed. And, maybe, a little jealous. One murder, just one! And the media gives the killer a nickname. Nine years ago, when he first started, it took him three kills before the media even gave him coverage in a newspaper. Five kills before they christened him. The Clipper. That was what they had called him then. And had been calling him ever since.

Ranveer sighed. 'Relax,' he told Cleopatra. 'Nothing is going to happen to your daughter. The killer is here in Bhopal. Your daughter is safe in Mumbai.'

Cleopatra sighed. 'I guess you're right.' She forced a smile.

Suddenly, Ranveer felt a hand on his shoulder. His arm spasmed instinctively. He flicked away Cleopatra's loving caress.

'What the—' Cleopatra raised her arms in protest. Even her annoyance was exaggerated.

'Sorry. I'm sorry,' said Ranveer. 'I was startled. I don't like anyone touching me without permission.'

Cleopatra smiled with a flirty tilt of the head. 'Okay, Ripple. How about . . .' She shifted in her position.

Ranveer took his eyes off the road for a moment to look at her.

Cleopatra was biting her lower lip. Her eyelashes fluttered at him '. . . how about giving me permission to touch you here?'

Ranveer felt her fingertips on his left knee. Slowly, teasingly, her fingertips started moving up his thigh. He stiffened, slowing the car a wee bit. He tried to calm himself down.

She sidled closer to him. Her fingertips kept riding higher up his thigh before coming to a stop between his legs. She massaged him there with soft, calculated movements, till he knew she could feel his bulge.

Cleopatra scooched over and whispered in his ear, 'That, right there, I think, is permission granted.'

He snorted. Glanced at her, his hands firm on the steering wheel.

Cleopatra winked at him. Gave him a coy smile. And just as suddenly as it had started, she pulled her hand away.

He was left wanting more.

She sat back in her seat and said, 'Just so you know . . . .' She paused, bit her lower lip and gave him the same flirty, sidelong glance, 'You have permission to rip off this dress tonight.'

Ranveer's eyes lit up. Little did she know that he planned to rip off more than the dress tonight.

11

'Hello,' said Zoya, her voice groggy, her annoyance clear in her tone.

'Umm...' Simone had called Zoya, but was now suddenly stumped, unsure of what to say and where to begin. She adjusted the phone in her hand.

'What do you want, Simone?'

Simone decided the apology could wait. 'Anything on Ramesh's alibi?' she blurted.

Simone heard Zoya sigh on the phone.

'For God's sake, Simone. It's midnight! I was sleeping. The case can wait till tomorrow morning.'

'Fine!' Simone raised her voice. 'Go to sleep, *partner*.' Simone drawled, like the last word was a slur. 'I'll be here at my desk the whole night, working the case, while you get your beauty sleep.'

'Look,' Zoya cleared her throat and said in a composed tone, 'there really isn't much to work with. Ramesh's alibi checks out for the day his son was kidnapped. He was indeed doing a carpentry job at the pharmacy next door. The shop owner confirmed his presence.'

'Then, how did his thumbprint get on the dead body?'

'I don't know, Simone. And I think I was wrong about the mistress. None of Ramesh's friends or neighbours ever saw another woman since his wife died. He was a doting husband, apparently. Her death shattered him completely.' Zoya let out an audible yawn. 'Simone, I'm too tired to think right now. If you want to work through the night, be my guest, but I'm going to sleep.'

'Fine. Goodnight.' Simone disconnected the call.

Her heart raced; her head throbbed. She had called to apologize. But she had a feeling that, somehow, she had made it worse.

Day 2

Day 2

12

Superintendent Irshad Hussain entered the crime wing at 6 a.m. A habit. Cultivated and followed for twenty years. It started even before he joined the police force as a brash, young constable.

The office was empty. As expected. Most of the detectives trickled in by 9 a.m. Or later. In the past, he'd have cursed, berated or suspended the lazy bums for their lack of discipline. He was a taskmaster but something had happened a few years ago. He had changed. Not because he had become more understanding. But because a case had broken his conviction, his resolve. The one case he could not solve. The one killer who taunted him. Still.

The Clipper. 'The fucking coward,' Irshad muttered loudly.

He entered his office, closing the door behind him. He didn't want prying eyes to invade his morning ritual. He eased into his swivel chair, opened a drawer and took out a hardbound folder. The original case file on the Clipper, each note, each annotation, each subtext written in Irshad's handwriting. The file had Post-it notes protruding from the side, an indexing system that Irshad had devised. He was the lead detective on the case when the first murder happened nine years ago. He was the superintendent when the last murder happened three months ago. The body was never found. But like clockwork, once every quarter, he'd receive a ripped off . . .

Irshad closed his eyes to burn away those vicious and savage memories. It didn't help.

He opened his eyes and opened the bottom drawer. He knew what would help. It always did. He took out a half-empty bottle of Old Monk rum. His companion, his saviour, his mistress. The brown liquid sparkled in the morning light that dappled through the blinds.

Irshad used to be a God-fearing teetotaller. A loyal husband, a caring father. Never missed a *salat*—five times a day he'd pray to Allah. Gave *sadaqat* or non-obligatory charity from his meagre salary every month. Then, something had snapped in his brain four years ago. He remembered the day most vividly even though he had ended up drunk, doped, beaten and half-naked in the gutter lining Bhopal's red-light district.

It was the five-year anniversary of the Clipper's first kill. The killer had celebrated it in style. Five 'gifts' like five salat had arrived at Irshad's desk during the day. Each gift similar. Each gift gruesome. He had opened them. Stared at them. Touched them. Despite the judgement and scorn in his colleagues' eyes. He was convinced that it would help trigger the anger, the drive and the passion to bring the killer to justice. Instead, it had opened a door in his brain that he didn't know existed. Curious, he had bolted through that door. And never looked back. Now he wasn't sure whether he was trapped or just didn't want to go back.

Irshad unscrewed the bottle cap and took a swig. The liquid set his throat on fire. He swallowed hard. He put the bottle aside and opened the case file.

The first page was a summary of the investigation so far, a page he himself updated after receiving the Clipper's 'gift' every three months or so. Sure, Irshad was the superintendent and could have given the case to a bright, young detective like Zoya or Simone. But this was his case, his killer to find, his case to close. The investigation summary attributed forty kills to the Clipper over nine years—one murder for each of the thirty-six quarters and four extra kills that one quarter to 'celebrate' the five-year anniversary of the Clipper's first kill. The modus operandi (MO) was the same for each kill. A male victim. No body found. A gift sent by the killer, wrapped in the day's newspaper, to the investigating officer—Irshad. As if it was a game. And the killer only wanted to play with Irshad. No prints were found on the newspapers. They were always squeaky clean. As were the gifts inside. It was a dead end.

Then, two years after the killings began, Irshad got his first break in the investigation. He had submitted a request to his bosses for a resource-intensive undertaking—matching DNA evidence from every 'missing person' in the last year to every 'gift' he had received from the Clipper. The request had been denied. He was asking for far too many resources, it was inefficient and a shot in the dark, they told him. But with mounting media coverage, pressure from the local government and his constant nagging, the police brass eventually came around. With no dead bodies, no trace evidence and no suspects, they had to take their chances, no matter the inefficiency. Irshad was given the go-ahead.

The next challenge was getting consent and collecting DNA evidence from the families of the male adults who had gone missing in Bhopal. The NCRB provided a list of more than 4000 missing and unrecovered males over the last two years. It took Irshad and his team several months to contact the families of the missing. Not every family agreed. And even when they consented, it was hard to find objects that still contained the DNA of the missing men.

Then, two years and seven months after the first kill, Irshad got his first DNA match. Then another. After a month, he had four confirmed DNA matches out of the ten murders up until then. Initially, it seemed like none of the four matches had anything in common. A diamond merchant from Surat, a college senior from Pune, an activist from Kolkata and a textile mill owner from Madurai. Then, it struck him—they were all out-of-towners, visitors to Bhopal. Irshad was pumped. He was going to find and bury the Clipper, the bastard.

Irshad shook his head. He never found the Clipper. Never found that positive energy again. Forty kills later, the Clipper was still at large.

Irshad chugged large gulps of Old Monk and turned to a new section of the case file marked 'Hypothesis' on a Post-it. At the top of the page, circled, were two words, 'Sex Trafficking?' These words were scored out. Alongside, also circled, he had written the words, 'Vengeful Woman?'

During the investigation of all DNA-matched victims, it became clear that a woman was involved. This was confirmed by the make-up and, in a few instances, women's clothing left behind with the belongings of the deceased in their hotel rooms. In some of the cases, the hotel staff also confirmed sightings of women going in or coming out of the victim's room. Prostitutes, Irshad inferred. Expected of out-of-town men. Why not dabble in some guilty pleasures, some fun in a strange place, away from their spouses and families? No one would know. But a prostitute in every case was just too much of a coincidence. Irshad didn't believe in coincidence.

Every action by the Clipper screamed serial killer—playing a game, toying with out-of-town men. But a female serial killer? It was hard to fathom since 90 per cent of all serial killers were males. However, it fit the killer's actions. Maybe a woman who had been wronged, now out for revenge? Ripping the very thing off her victims that had traumatized her in the first place. And taunting the police with the 'gift'. Maybe the police fudged her case? Maybe the police didn't come to her rescue when she needed saving or justice? It made sense. The theory fit. So, Irshad had stuck with his theory.

But nothing connected the evidence or the theory to the killer. The Clipper was a ghost. Forty kills and the police still didn't have a suspect. They still didn't know how the killer contacted the victims. No mobile phones were recovered. Even online browsing histories recovered remotely from the victims' phones by the cyber-crime department threw no light. Nothing out of the ordinary. It was like the Clipper had telepathic or psychic ability, communicating directly with the minds of the victims, in secret, untraceable.

He took another swig of the burning, brown liquid.

Suddenly, there was a knock on the door. Irshad gulped down the liquid.

'Wait!' he shouted.

He grabbed the bottle of rum and threw it inside the drawer. He sat as straight as an ironing board. He blinked his ruddy eyes a few times, wide awake.

'Come in!' he said.

The door opened. The peon from the reception downstairs thrust his head through the door.

'Yes?' said Irshad.

'Sir, a package has arrived for you.'

Irshad sat still. His heart thumped. His head pounded from inside.

The peon entered and produced a parcel—a shoebox— wrapped in a newspaper. The wrapping was neat and tidy, like one would wrap a birthday gift.

Irshad gulped. Case number forty-one. He knew the wrapping was this morning's newspaper without looking at the date. He also knew that there would be no fingerprints on the package.

'Just put it on the desk and leave,' Irshad ordered.

The peon did as he was told and left, closing the door behind him.

Irshad removed the wrapping carefully, gently. He knew Dr D'Souza would not like him tampering with evidence. But after forty such instances, he knew the forensics would find no clues to go on. *To hell with Dr D'Souza,* he thought.

It was an all-black shoebox. Irshad placed the box on the table gingerly and inhaled deeply. Every cell in his body wanted to run away, every pore perspired. His heart knocked like it was trapped inside a house on fire. But there was no escape.

'Breathe,' Irshad told himself and exhaled.

He opened the package.

Nestled inside, within a box lined with soft, black sponge, sprinkled with gold glitter, was a pair of cleanly shaved testicles.

13

Simone parked the Thar on the street outside her government-issued quarters at 7 a.m. She was tired, irritable, spent. Her eyelids heavy, her shoulders sore. A small and stubborn part of her wanted to go for a run to shake off the weariness. The rest of her wanted to snuggle up and sleep.

She had spent the night at her desk writing the case report, researching about Ramesh and his dead son, devising theories, scratching out theories. At one point in the night, around 3 a.m., she had gone to the crime scene. *Maybe they missed something, maybe a clue would miraculously appear*, she had thought. But no luck. No clues.

However, she came back with a question. A question that kept her up the rest of the night—why did the killer choose the infamous site of the Bhopal Gas Tragedy to display the dead kid? There was a connection there. Most definitely. But, what? Nothing in Ramesh's history linked him to the tragedy—he had moved to Bhopal from a small village in Bihar nine years ago for work. Sure, his wife was a local and had been born with a birth defect because of the gas tragedy. How did it matter? The answer and sleep had eluded her. Except, now, sleep had come back with a vengeance. Unfortunately, not with the answers she was seeking.

Simone opened the Thar door. She trudged out into the misty morning fog. The cold prickled her face, tried waking her up. Her body rebelled with a fresh dose of irritation. Bed. Sleep. That was what she needed. Not a wake-up shot in the arm.

Simone locked the Thar and walked tiredly across the modest porch to the front door. A deep, intoxicating fragrance of tuberoses and jasmines uplifted her. She smiled. The little joys of life, she exhaled. Her grandma loved gardening, even if all they had was a tiny tract of land—as big as a regular-sized three-seater sofa—adjacent to the front porch, lining the brick wall that surrounded the house.

Simone slipped into the house. She didn't want to knock or ring the bell and disturb Grandma who was usually deep in meditation between 7 a.m. and 8 a.m. daily without fail. Grandma was an ardent follower of and 'teacher' with the Art of Living foundation. Despite her age and escalating diabetes, she was the city coordinator for all Art of Living activities— social service, group meditations, teaching courses, discourses and satsangs. On some days, Simone felt that Grandma had a more active social life than she did. But then, a lifetime spent as the principal of the local army school still served Grandma well.

Simone stepped into her room.

'Simone *bachu,* is that you?' Simone heard her grandma call from the adjacent room. Even though loud, her grandma sounded like a saint giving a sermon—calm and at peace.

'Yes, Grandma!' Simone shouted back; her voice shrill, irritable.

'Come here, *bachu*,' Grandma's voice softened.

Simone dropped her head in dismay. She wasn't in the mood for conversation. Any conversation.

Why? Why? Why can't you keep meditating and let me be? thought Simone. She dragged her feet to the adjoining room.

Grandma was reclining on the bed, dressed in all-white.

'Good morning, *bachu*. Just got back home?'

'Good morning,' said Simone. She didn't answer the question. Wasn't it self-explanatory?

'Shall I prepare breakfast?' Grandma swung her feet off the bed to get up.

'No, no. You meditate, Grandma. I'm too tired to eat. I'm just going to go to bed.' Simone turned away to go to her room, considering the conversation closed.

Grandma wasn't finished. 'Tch, tch!' she clicked her tongue. 'Simone, look at you! It's like you don't eat any more. That tall body needs nourishment. Who'll marry you otherwise?' Grandma got out of the bed. 'Wait, I'll prepare poha. It'll take ten minutes. You eat and then sleep.'

'I said I don't want to eat!' Simone yelled.

Grandma went quiet, her face expressionless, although Simone knew it was her 'I'm disappointed in you' look. It made Simone even more grouchy.

'I don't want to eat. I don't want to get married. And I don't want to have these conversations.' Simone's decibel level increased with each sentence until her voice rang through the house.

Simone stormed out. She went into her room and slammed the door shut behind her. She choked back the lump in her throat. After removing her shoes, she slipped under the snug, cosy duvet.

And, then the emotions she had been fighting for so long came out of nowhere, swamping her, pinning her down and smothering her. She felt overwhelmed with the pressure to perform like her old self before the suspension. She resented her boss for not trusting her. She was cross with Zoya for being the better person. She regretted speaking like a cranky child with Grandma, the woman who had raised her and had provided for her. Probably the only person who *ever* loved her.

Tears poured from the corners of her eyes. Her chest heaved and her lips trembled.

Simone felt alone, broken, hurt. Exactly how she had felt the night her parents left her with Grandma and promised to return. They never did.

14

The shops were shuttered, the kiosks covered and padlocked. DB City Mall was mostly empty at 9.45 a.m. on a Wednesday.

Varsha entered the mall and soaked in the emptiness of the shopping arcade. *As expected*, she thought. 'Come girls,' she said to her two daughters, nine and ten years old. 'Let's take the lift to the movie hall.'

Frozen 2, the movie sequel to the global Disney phenomenon, had finally released over the weekend, after six excruciating years of waiting. It was all her daughters could talk about since the movie trailers first appeared a few months ago. Varsha was excited for her daughters and had promised them tickets for the first day, first show. But then she forgot to book the tickets on time—the bane of a housewife charged with doing *everything* for young kids and a good-for-nothing husband. The tickets had sold out within minutes. Her girls had cried for hours. 'You promised,' they had bawled. It broke Varsha's heart.

But, as luck would have it, she was presented with an opportunity to make it up to her daughters. With record crowds for the movie, Cinepolis at DB City Mall had added a 10 a.m. show. It meant her daughters had to skip school for a day. Varsha booked the tickets without thinking. Her daughters were doubly overjoyed—no school *and* the movie. Varsha was simply relieved.

Mother and daughters took the elevator to the top floor. The quietness of the ground-floor arcade was replaced by the palpable bustle the instant they stepped out of the elevator. Varsha wasn't the only parent who had made her kids skip school.

A thin crowd of restless parents and children on tenterhooks was loitering in the lobby. A queue had formed at the popcorn counter, only one server catering to the morning show crowd. A mall cleaner was mopping the floor, releasing a gag-worthy smell of equal parts antiseptic and must.

The mop cloth needs a change, Varsha thought.

Another mall worker was moving gigantic plastic statues of the Frozen sisters, Elsa and Anna, to the centre of the lobby. Young girls and boys thronged the statues, wanting to take pictures.

'Photo, photo!' cried Varsha's younger daughter, as she ran towards the exhibit, her elder sister in tow.

Varsha wanted to scold her daughters and tell them to behave themselves in public. But she stopped herself and shook her head. Today was about them. She took out her phone to take pictures and walked over to the exhibit.

In the seconds it took Varsha to walk twenty metres, complete mayhem broke out. Kids jostled each other. Parents scolded, not their own but others' kids, asking them to get out of the frame, while they took sweet photos of their own children. A girl pushed another, who started crying and a shouting match erupted between the mothers. Fathers tried to intervene but were soon swept into the burgeoning flood of emotions.

'Mom, there's no space! They're fighting!' cried the younger daughter as Varsha joined her.

'It's okay, baby. We will wait for our turn,' Varsha had to shout to make herself heard over the hubbub of fighting parents and crying kids.

A security guard ran into the fray, requesting parents to step back and stop fighting.

While the shouting match continued in the centre of the lobby, Varsha noticed that the same mall worker—dressed in blue overalls, face covered with a bandana and black sunglasses—brought two more exhibits from the back and placed them in a corner. Two dolls. These were much smaller. Elsa and Anna encased in glass.

Varsha grabbed her daughters' hands. 'Come on, girls,' she whispered, 'let's take pictures with those.' She pointed to the glass exhibits.

Her daughters jumped up in glee.

'Yes!' said one.

'Hurry, hurry!' said the other.

They rushed over. None of them noticed the mall worker who left through the emergency exit.

'Wow! The dolls look so real. Just like the wax museum we visited in London!' said the elder daughter.

'Yeah, yeah,' Varsha ignored her. 'Come on, quick. One of you stand next to Elsa and the other next to Anna,' she said, aware of other parents starting to queue up behind her.

Her daughters complied.

'Smile!' said Varsha seconds before zooming in to get a closer shot.

First, it was only a feeling. She looked up, and then, back at her camera.

'Mom, what are you doing? Take the photo!' said her elder daughter.

Varsha was entranced. She squinted at the camera, zoomed in and focused on the encased figurines. The feeling of dread crept up her legs like a python closing in on its prey. Suddenly, it hit her. The news from yesterday. Then, in a light-bulb moment, her heart squeezed tight. And before she could stop herself, a loud, piercing scream burst from her.

'Mom! What happened?' her daughters screamed in tandem and ran towards her.

A hush fell over the entire lobby. Parents stopped squabbling. The popcorn server looked over. The security guard rushed over.

'What happened?' asked the security guard.

Varsha pointed a finger at the glass exhibits, one hand covering her mouth to force back another scream. 'Those . . . those dolls.' She kept pointing to the encased figurines. Her hand quivered, the finger rocked in place, like a pendulum.

'The Doll Maker!' she screamed.

In the pandemonium that followed, nobody noticed the mall worker walking out of the emergency exit. Except the security cameras.

15

Ranveer was giddy like a kid. There was a spring in his step, a flutter in his heart and a song on his lips. His hand was twitching, more from the anticipation than the anxiety he felt before each conquest, each kill.

He looked up at the cuckoo clock, crafted by the artisans of the Black Forest in Germany, hanging on the living room wall. Twenty minutes until the afternoon news. He had sent a wrapped gift to his old friend, superintendent Hussain, early this morning. By afternoon, the media would have lapped up the story. Even if they hadn't, just to be on the safe side, Ranveer had sent anonymous notes to all major news reporters in the city. *The Clipper has clipped again*—said the notes.

A flutter went up his chest. He loved this feeling—the excitement, the build-up, the suspense—before *the Clipper* was revealed to the world again, his infamy clouding their television sets, his reputation buttered, his ego massaged. He was the Clipper. The fame was his. His alone. It had been so for nine years. He had come to love it all—the adulation, the respect, the praise that the media, representatives of the common people, showered on him. Sometimes, during sleepless nights, he would question whether it was purely the pleasure of killing or the irresistible pull of fame that ignited his passions. Both—he concluded.

Ranveer placed the glass of wine on the side table and sat back in his La-Z-Boy recliner. He pushed a button on the electronic panel hidden beneath the armrest and almost immediately, soft rotors started massaging his back, moving up and down his spine. He closed his eyes, moaning with pleasure. He was reminded of Cleopatra—how she had moaned last night, her fragrance, how she had charmed him with slow, measured moves in the bed, her silky, hairless skin, and how she had begged for more. He had given in to her requests, generously and magnanimously, like a benevolent king. Before he clipped her, of course.

Ranveer's eyes flew open. Blood rushed to his groin. He inhaled deeply to calm down his palpitating heart. He plucked the glass of red wine from the side table. He took a sip, twirled it in his mouth, gargled and swallowed. The smooth, zesty liquid shimmied down his throat. It was a Sangiovese-based, vintage Chianti from Tuscany, aged ten years. His favourite.

A sudden urge gripped Ranveer. He glanced at the clock again. Fifteen minutes to the news. He had time. Just enough to visit his temple. He put the wine glass aside, stopped the massager and jumped off the chair. He walked briskly across the wood-panelled floor to a wide helix staircase that led both to the basement downstairs and to the bedrooms upstairs. He had renovated the house last year, transforming it from the dilapidated farmhouse he had inherited from his father after his mother's death to a minimalist, contemporary country home. Only one room had been untouched since it was first built ten years ago. His temple.

Ranveer peered through the French windows parallel to the staircase—it made it seem like you were walking in the garden outside as you descended, or, as you climbed the stairs, like you were walking on the still water of the lake beyond. A cabin was built in the far corner of the front yard. Ranveer craned his neck, peering at the outhouse. It was dark. Eerily quiet. No sign of the tenant who was renting it from him. Ranveer shrugged his shoulders. He liked people who kept to themselves. He was one of them.

Ranveer walked down the stairs. A soft, melodious hymn—coming from the basement—tickled his ears. The music grew louder with each step. Cold air wafted over Ranveer as he stepped down to the last step, almost as if the air were purifying him before he entered the sanctity of the temple. Ranveer flicked on a switch. The basement was instantly swathed in bright, white light. The basement was as big as the house above—one acre in size, about the size of a football field. And it was empty. Completely empty. There was nothing in it—no furniture, no carpet, no gym equipment. Just square, grey, stone tiles spanning the floor. And mirrors, lots and lots of them, covering the four walls of the basement like wallpaper. It was a room of mirrors, reflecting light in so many directions that it seemed like every inch of space was a spotlight.

Ranveer smiled smugly. This was his favourite part of the house. Made him feel like he was a celebrity musician in the middle of a concert, thousands cheering him on. He liked fame. He liked the spotlight on him. Just him.

Ranveer sauntered to the middle of the large, empty space. A single white tile shone brightly amid the sea of grey around it. Ranveer jumped on the white tile. And then stepped back.

A whizzing sound came from under him. The white tile and the eight grey tiles surrounding it shifted downward and then moved across, together as one large block, to reveal a staircase that led into the dark abyss below. The caustic smell of disinfectant permeated up from the revealed space. The crypt. His temple.

Ranveer undressed. He stood naked and barefoot on the chilly stone tiles. His lithe, athletic body shimmered in the dazzling light that spilled over him.

Ranveer bowed his head in respect and whispered a short prayer, 'For God gave us a spirit not of fear, but of power. Amen.'

Ranveer climbed down the rickety staircase, which creaked with every step he took, the sound echoing in the empty basement above, more ominous, more frightening. The smell of the disinfectant was overpowering at the bottom. Ranveer sniffed and smiled. *The smell of cleanliness.* Exactly how he liked it. Ranveer stood in the dark for a moment, taking in the aroma. Then, he bent down on his knees and flicked a switch. The crypt was illuminated with muted yellow light.

The crypt, like the basement above, spanned the floor area of the house. There were rows and rows of white porcelain bathtubs filled with embalming fluids, each preserving a memory, a conquest, a body. Next to each bathtub stood a mannequin, depicting the female form. Each mannequin was dressed exactly the way it was like in his memory—the clothes and footwear of his conquests. It was a museum of his memories. His temple.

Ranveer walked past several rows. Today, he was interested in the most recent memory. His stomach cartwheeled and his hands shivered. Ranveer arrived at the bathtub that was most recently occupied. Last night. A mannequin shimmered in a silver V-neck evening gown and matching six-inch pumps. Fake diamonds sewn on the dress sparkled in the muted light, exactly as they had hogged attention last night. Ranveer stepped over and gazed at Cleopatra floating inside. Dead. The skin torn where he had slit her throat; a cavity where her testicles had been ripped off. Ranveer inched closer, his naked thighs touching the cold porcelain.

Blood rushed to his groin. He exhaled loudly, letting his breath out in a whoosh. A deluge of memories washed over him.

With slow, steady movements he touched himself. And started to moan.

16

Simone slammed the brakes outside the front entrance of DB City Mall. The crime scene. Simone knew the mall would be locked down; all entry points sealed by the police. Nevertheless, a decent-sized crowd had gathered outside, as expected. Concerned, curious citizens wanted to know: what happened? Media reporters led the crowd, their OB vans parked in the public parking lot across the street.

Simone decided to park in the mall's parking lot. More convenient. Plus, she didn't want a repeat of yesterday.

Simone honked the Thar's horn. The crowd gave way reluctantly, seeing a police officer driving the Thar. A constable checked her credentials at the gate and let her pass. Simone parked in the underground lot and rode the elevator up to the ground floor.

Simone stepped out and was greeted by the sweet aroma of bubblegum and a punch packed with strawberries and bananas. This level was deserted, except for a few police personnel patrolling the area. Simone struck her palm on her forehead.

'Damn it!' Simone swore aloud. Zoya had asked her to come to the movie hall on the top floor.

Simone got back into the elevator and jabbed the button for the top floor. She was still half-asleep, her mind foggy. She swivelled her neck and rotated her shoulders. Wake up, she told herself. Her stomach growled, as if in protest.

The elevator opened to chaos. The cacophony that greeted Simone felt like an assault on her ears. It seemed like every person on the floor was speaking, yelling and snarling, all at the same time. Simone was suddenly very wide awake.

Two security guards stood by the elevator to ensure that there was no unauthorized access. They skittered away like bowling pins upon seeing Simone's police uniform, letting her pass.

'Check the badge!' Simone admonished them. 'Don't let anyone pass just because they are wearing a police uniform.'

They bobbed their heads rapidly like reprimanded kids.

Simone sighed and shook her head. In her experience, common folk carried in their hearts an unspoken fear of the police. The police made them jittery; made them blindly trust the uniform, no matter who wore it—be it the police or imposters.

Simone walked to the centre of the lobby. The entire area from the lobby to the theatre had been cordoned off with police tape. Police constables stood outside the perimeter like human barricades. Inside the cordon, a multitude of technicians hovered and fussed around two glass cases in one corner. The two dolls. Dead twins.

'Look who finally made it!' It was Zoya. She walked over, grinning. 'Good morning, ma'am!' Zoya bowed in mock deference. 'Anything I can get you? Breakfast? Coffee?'

'I was working the entire night,' Simone muttered.

'Well, it doesn't matter, does it?'

Simone knew Zoya was right. There was no point arguing. Swap places, and Simone would have yelled and berated Zoya in public. Simone had zero tolerance for lack of discipline. She didn't like being on the other side of the line.

'I'm . . . I'm sorry,' said Simone, 'about yesterday.'

Zoya stayed silent for a moment. She gazed at Simone, bemused. 'I'm speechless. Never thought I'd hear those words from you.'

Simone rocked back and forth, nodding, saying nothing.

Zoya nodded back.

'So, what have we got?' asked Simone, finally.

'Two victims. Twins.'

Zoya walked towards the glass cases. Simone followed.

Zoya chuckled. 'Gave quite a scare to a woman who had come to see the morning show with her daughters. The woman had to be sedated.'

Simone waved this information away, as if irrelevant. 'Are the deceased boys?' Simone stared at the two dolls dressed as Elsa and Anna.

Zoya nodded. 'First thing I asked the medical examiner to check, after they finished brushing the glass cases for prints. Both boys. Not wearing undergarments. Same as the last kill.'

Simone was silent.

Zoya continued. 'I sent their photos to the missing persons' cell and I've asked them to run facial recognition against kids reported missing in the city, starting from the most recent case. Nothing so far. I also called Dr D'Souza. Asked him to get one of his assistants to check for fingerprints on the victims' foreheads now, rather than at the lab, to save time.'

Zoya pointed to a technician dusting a brush over the pale forehead of dead Elsa. 'The guy confirmed the presence of clear thumbprints on the foreheads. He's collecting them now. I've asked him to send them directly for cross-checking as soon as he's done collecting them.'

Simone said nothing. Her mind was churning. Agony brewed deep inside her. She clenched and unclenched her hands, all the while thinking how it would feel to crush the killer's head with her large, heavy hands.

Zoya glanced at Simone. 'By the way, the boss called.'

Simone stiffened.

'Don't worry,' said Zoya. 'I told him you were somewhere around here. Not at home.'

'Not worried about that,' Simone stared ahead, avoiding Zoya's eyes. Superintendent Hussain had called Zoya. Not her. Despite knowing that it was her case. *Sonofa*— . . . Simone inhaled deeply and tried to calm herself.

'If it helps,' said Zoya, 'I told him that he should be calling you instead. It's your case.'

Simone swung around in surprise. She knew Zoya was nice, friendly, but didn't expect her to be so . . . selfless.

'Thank you,' said Simone.

Zoya shrugged. 'He was flipping out. Not sure if you heard but he received a package from the Clipper today. Another murder. No body. Just ripped off . . .'

Zoya left the words hanging in the air.

Simone bobbed her head in understanding.

'. . . anyway. He went on and on about giving our everything to find the Doll Maker. Results, results, results . . . must have said that word ten times in a five-minute call. Frankly, I tuned out after two.'

Simone could not suppress a loud snort.

'What's funny?' asked Zoya.

'The man hasn't found the Clipper in *nine years*, but he wants us to find this Doll Maker in *two days*? Was he drunk or something?'

There was a long pause and both women looked at each other with a gleam in their eyes, like conspirators who share a secret, and when they couldn't contain it any longer, both burst into giggles. Both knew. The entire office knew. Hussain was a drunk.

They revelled in the office joke for a few seconds, attempting unsuccessfully to stifle giggles that were highly inappropriate at a gloomy crime scene. Their tension released; a bond formed. In front of the recently departed, camaraderie bloomed.

Simone would remember this moment forever, she knew with absolute certainty, for this was the moment when she, for the first time, shared a laugh with someone who wasn't her grandma. Her heart warmed and fluttered like a washed blouse on a clothes line.

Zoya's phone started to ring. The moment passed.

Zoya rummaged in her tight trouser pocket and extricated a phone after a struggle. 'Hello!' she said.

Simone could not hear the conversation. But she sensed the surge of excitement in Zoya's voice. Zoya began pacing around Simone like a lion stalking its prey.

'Thank you!' Zoya hung up and stopped pacing.

'We've got a match!' said Zoya, exuberantly. 'Rather, *two* matches. The victims are Ayan and Vyan Srinivas. Their father, Vijay Srinivas, had lodged a missing persons' report yesterday!'

'Yesterday?'

'Yes, they went missing from school about twenty-four hours ago. I've asked the inspector to email me the FIR.'

Simone shook her head. 'It's escalating. The killer is on a spree. Too fast, too soon.'

'That's how killers make mistakes. Speed. It compromises them, always.'

'Let's hope so,' said Simone. She wasn't so sure. Three kills in two days and it felt like the killer was toying with them, playing a game, tossing them bodies without clues. Simone didn't like to play if she wasn't in control. Her fists clenched at the thought.

'Ma'am!' a loud, shout startled them.

An inspector was rushing towards them from the elevator.

'Ma'am!' he shouted again, as if no one had heard him the first time.

'What is it?' Simone matched the inspector's pitch.

'Slow down, inspector,' said Zoya.

'You both need to come with me. Now!'

'Why?'

'What happened?'

'We spotted the killer on camera.'

17

'This way,' the inspector opened a heavy door marked *Authorized Personnel Only* on the ground floor and led the officers across a congested corridor lined with small, stuffy rooms. The administrative block. The enclosed space was a melting pot of competing scents—the dry wood smell of the furniture clashed with the pungent smell of ammonia from the toilets in the far corner; the artificial fragrance of bubblegum from the mall's air freshener locked horns with the spicy notes of gravy masala. The inspector stopped in front of the security and surveillance room—a posh name for a grey, gloomy alcove that housed two chairs in front of innumerable monitors. Both chairs were occupied by mall security guards. Both seemed upbeat, chirpy, as if the incident was a welcome respite from the boredom that gripped their daily routine.

'Good morning, ma'am!' the security guards said in unison, their grins broad, their teeth yellowed with cigarette stains.

'Good morning,' replied Zoya.

'What did you find?' Simone didn't waste time on unnecessary pleasantries.

The guards stopped grinning.

'Start with the footage from 9.40 a.m.,' the inspector instructed the security guards.

One of the guards clicked the mouse a few times and brought up a grainy, colour footage of a wide, steel door at the end of a spacious corridor, its walls painted green, faded in patches like the skin of a cucumber. A timestamp in the top right corner of the screen read: 9.39. The date underneath was today's date.

'This is the entrance to the building from the loading and unloading bay,' said the security guard and pressed play.

The pixels came to life. Even though the video showed a static scene where nothing moved, the pixels danced like grains on a conveyor belt. It was live. It was happening. They waited with bated breath. Thirty seconds.

Suddenly, the steel door opened outward, revealing the concrete floor of the bay outside. The screen crackled, like a pet dog who hears a sound outside and gets jittery. A trolley entered the corridor, carrying larger-than-life plastic statues of Elsa and Anna from *Frozen 2*, exactly the ones that were propped up in the lobby of the theatre. The door closed. The trolley trundled towards them on the screen. Someone was pushing the trolley with hands secure inside construction gloves. The person's frame was hidden behind the enormous plastic figures. As the trolley came near, they saw that it also carried two rectangular boxes, both identical—blue bases with white lids—ensconced between the giant Elsa and Anna.

'What are those large boxes?' asked Zoya, squinting at the screen.

'Coolers,' said Simone. 'Daya, the constable who discovered the last victim, reported a similar picnic cooler. The suspect was carrying it.'

The trolley came closer, the person pushing it couldn't hide behind the plastic figures any more. The person was short, like Zoya, but slender. Dressed in blue overalls, the person's face, except the eyes, was covered with a bandana. However, the eyes were concealed behind dark sunglasses, the thick-rimmed kind with massive lenses that covered most of the cheeks. The suspect looked up at the camera, her conduct assured, like she expected the camera to be there. The killer pushed the trolley and soon was out of the camera's line of sight.

'The killer is a woman,' said Zoya.

'Don't we already know that from Daya's statement?' retorted Simone.

'Yes, but that was circumstantial evidence. She could have been a passer-by, in the wrong place at the wrong time. Now we have video proof that validates Daya's statement. Two data points.'

Zoya paused. There was a glint in her eye.

'Plus, and this is interesting . . .' Zoya nodded to herself, as if a fog had lifted and her view had suddenly become clearer, '. . . a female killer is usual and common but a *female serial killer* is rare. Less than 10 per cent of all serial killers are women. And . . . now we know our suspect is a woman.'

Simone rolled her eyes. 'Not interested in psychology statistics, Zoya. Can we get back to the tape?'

The glint in Zoya's eyes faded. She crossed her arms and looked away from Simone, whose eyes were locked on the screen. 'Fine,' she said curtly.

'Carry on,' Simone told the security guard.

The screen whirred back to life. They followed the killer across cameras from the loading bay to the service elevator, which was massive. The security guard switched cameras and they saw the woman push the trolley out of the elevator. Signage atop the elevator door told them that she had alighted on the top floor. Another camera switch and the woman halted outside a door marked: *emergency exit*. She swung open the double doors and placed door wedges to hold them open. In the far corner, the footage showed cinemagoers queuing at the popcorn counter, unaware of the crime unfolding under their noses while they jostled for popcorn. Then, with the agility of a fencer, the woman plucked the giant plastic statue of Elsa and trotted inside the lobby. She deposited the figurine in the centre of the lobby and came back for Anna, only to repeat the action. Although the footage was without audio, the clip's current audience sensed an immediate change in energy as a group of kids, their parents in tow, ran to the large plastic dolls and elbowed each other for space, while parents started clicking pictures with their smartphones.

'A distraction,' said Simone.

No one responded, although everyone nodded absentmindedly. The sequence of events was reaching its climax. No one dared to even blink, absorbed as they were in the scene taking place before them.

While the crowd fussed around the large, plastic figures, the woman opened an ice cooler and extracted a glass case. She held it close to her bosom, like it was a newborn and walked gingerly to the corner of the lobby. Here, she deposited the glass case with extreme care. Her movements were slow and calculated. As she stood up, she brought her gloved hand to her lips and blew a kiss to dead Elsa, almost as if she was heartbroken and regretful. The Doll Maker then did the same with Anna. Within minutes of her arrival, she removed the door wedges and ran back the same way she had come.

'Okay,' exhaled Simone.

'Wait. It's not over yet,' said the inspector. He tapped the security guard's shoulder.

The guard clicked a button on screen and the corridor camera came up again, the first camera that had picked up the Doll Maker. But this time, they saw the woman exit the building into the loading bay.

Then, as if she had forgotten something, she stopped and turned around. She walked back to the camera, stood on her toes.

She lifted her bandana, puckered her lips and blew a seductive kiss at the camera.

18

They watched the clip again. Zoya was hooked. The Doll Maker had retraced her steps, her intention crystal clear. It was the alluring kiss that caught Zoya off guard. The killer had shown tremendous restraint till the kiss. Zoya's mind raced. Why did the Doll Maker do that? Did she do it for fame or to flirt or for fun? Zoya shuddered at the thought of the latter. Who this Doll Maker was—not important at this stage—the answer lay deep inside the killer's psyche. All Zoya had to do was find the 'why' and she would be able to lift the lid on the killer. Zoya knew it was much easier with one-time killers; but perplexing and convoluted with *serial* killers.

They played and replayed the entire clip—the Doll Maker's journey in and out of the mall—for more than half an hour. Same scenes. Same outcome. Until boredom set in.

'Do you have cameras in the parking lot?' Simone asked the security guards.

Both men shook their heads.

'How about the security cameras at the entrances?'

Both continued shaking their heads in unison. *It was like talking to clones*, Zoya mused.

Simone huffed; her shoulders drooped. 'Why not?' she snapped in exasperation.

'The purpose is to protect the mall inside, mostly from shoplifters. The basement parking is free and the mall is not responsible for the safety of the vehicle. It's the duty of the car owners but people have to park on their own risk. We have even put up a sign saying so.'

'And your responsibility ends with putting up a sign?' Simone didn't wait for an answer. She turned to the inspector. 'I want you to ask every person who came to watch the morning show if they saw that woman . . .' she pointed to the paused video, the Doll Maker frozen in the act of blowing a kiss at the camera, '. . . driving a vehicle. She brought two large coolers and two plastic figurines. She must have used a vehicle. I want to know which one.'

The inspector nodded.

Simone snatched a Post-it and a pen from the table, scribbled furiously and thrust the paper at the guard controlling the screen. 'Email us the video clips.'

Simone turned to Zoya. 'Let's go break the news to the victims' father.'

Zoya sighed, her mood suddenly sombre. Death notification to the next of kin was the one part of her job that Zoya hated.

'Zoya, are you coming?' Simone was already halfway across the corridor.

Zoya nodded. There was no way out of death notification for this case. Best to accompany a socially inept firebrand like Simone before someone filed a complaint against her.

'Yes . . . yes, coming,' said Zoya.

She walked over to where Simone stood. 'How about a snack on the way?' she asked. 'I'm hungry.'

'When are you not?' Simone rolled her eyes.

'Mind your tone, Simone,' Zoya warned.

'Sorry. I'm just mad at those guards. Why in the world would you *not* put cameras in the parking lot? Why?'

'Not their fault, Simone. And not their call. Mall management decides where the cameras go. The poor guys were just doing their jobs.'

Simone huffed. 'You know what? I'm hungry too. Let's get something to eat before notifying the father of the dead boys.'

Dead boys? To say Simone was 'insensitive', was an understatement.

Zoya's phone belted out the latest Punjabi song, 'Sakhiyan', her ringtone, peppy and uplifting like a mother's hug. She plucked the phone from her pocket.

It was superintendent Hussain.

'Hello, sir!' said Zoya.

'Two more murders! What's happening, Zoya?' Hussain yelled, as if Zoya was behind the murders.

'Sir, it is—'

'The Clipper claimed another victim today and this new serial killer murdered two! It's almost like they are competing with each other and making *my* life miserable.'

Yeah, personal vendetta and competition were *exactly* why they were killing sir, Zoya wanted to retort, but kept her mouth shut.

'I want a report now, Zoya. Right now. In my office. Bring Simone. We are doing a press conference in an hour.'

'We're on our way, sir,' said Zoya.

'I'll be waiting!' superintendent Hussain hung up.

'Phew!' Zoya exhaled loudly.

'What?' asked Simone.

'Forget the twins' father for now. We have our own *mai-baap* to answer to first.'

19

Quack! Quack!

Nalini rubbed her eyes, burying herself deeper under the warm, cosy quilt.

Quack! Quack!

The incessant noise made sleep impossible. She groaned, tossing and turning in her bedclothes, her long tresses spilling over her face. She took a deep breath and hugged herself as if embracing the sweet bliss of sleep itself.

Quack! Quack!

'Oh. My. God.' Her eyes flew open. She threw the quilt aside and jumped out of bed, disoriented and dishevelled, trying to locate the source of the infernal quacking that had woken her up.

Quack! Quack!

The noise was coming from outside her window. Nalini tottered over, half-asleep, partially blind in the darkness. She gripped the chunky polyester curtains, which smelled like industrial disinfectant and parted them a few inches. A brilliant volley of sunbeams stung her eyes.

'Damn it!' Nalini released the curtains, squeezing her eyes shut. The after-image burnt into her retina continued to glow orange though her eyes were closed.

Nalini parted the curtains again and gingerly squinted to get used to the daylight outside. It was late afternoon on a short winter's day and daylight was fading quickly. The grass in the garden outside looked dry and cold, exactly the way Nalini felt upon leaving the warm confines of her bed. The lake beyond the garden sparkled as the sun's rays receded.

Quack! Quack!

The sound drew Nalini's attention to a duck in the garden, pecking at the grassy soil, probably foraging for worms or slugs. A duckling was waddling around the mother duck, quacking with excitement, its bright orange feet almost hidden in the grass.

Nalini smiled. It reminded her of her mom, her confidante, her best friend. Her everything. When she was four or five, Nalini would run in circles around her mom, exactly like the duckling, pretending to clean the house with a toy broom while her mom sipped tea from a toy cup and saucer, feigning delight at how tidy 'Mrs Nalini' kept her house. She loved playing house, for it was in those moments that Nalini could pretend that she didn't have a father. Even though her mom never mentioned it, Nalini knew it was the reason her mom loved the make-believe game too. For a few hours they were Mrs Nalini and Mrs Mom, attending tea parties, splurging Monopoly money, draping saris and slapping on make-up that made them look like clowns rather than the prim and proper aunties they thought they were portraying. There was no room for abuse in their fantasy house. No black eyes. No purple bruises on the buttocks. No cracked ribs that hurt to touch. Mrs Mom had plenty of those in her regular house. It was *the* reason why Mr Dad was not invited to their tea parties. You never knew when his switch would flip.

Nalini sighed. She shook her head slowly. She peered outside the window again. The mother duck and the duckling were waddling away towards the lake, their quacks merry and their gait cheerful. Nalini swallowed hard, holding back tears.

'Miss you, Mom.' Her voice cracked, despite the whisper.

Suddenly, a loud moan from the bed cut through the moment.

Nalini rushed back to the bed and slipped under the covers.

'Shh! Go back to sleep, baby.' She held the little boy close to her bosom.

'Mommy,' mumbled the boy without opening his eyes and grabbed Nalini with his stubby fingers.

'Shh! Mommy is here, baby. Go to sleep. Shh! Go to sleep.'

The boy fussed for a moment and then, almost instantly, started taking long, deep breaths and was sound asleep again.

Nalini drew the boy's head closer and planted a kiss on his forehead. Despite the darkness, Nalini could make out the silhouette of the boy's face while he slept—a tiny chin, slanted eyes, the large forehead and a tiny tongue protruding out of an even tinier mouth—all telltale signs of Down's Syndrome. The very reason she had chosen this boy. He was a special boy who needed special care, a mother's care, even more than the rest of them.

Nalini felt the boy's warm breath against her neck. Deep, unbridled satisfaction swept through her body, like a wave that sweeps through the beach during high tide. Nalini was filled with immense love, maternal love—pure, selfless, enduring. The love she had received from her own mother until she passed away. Taken. Too soon. In cold blood.

Smash! The broken glass.

Crack! The broken skull.

Aieeee! The scream. The broken heart.

Nalini closed her eyes, trying to forget the memories, the nightmares. *Why? Why? Why* did her father always have to spoil such rare moments of love?

She exhaled and opened her eyes, peering at the special boy. Perhaps she would let him sleep some more before she released him from the tyranny of his savage father and reunited him with his dead mother.

20

Simone knocked on the door of the superintendent's office.

'Come in!' a voice growled from inside.

Simone exchanged a glance with Zoya; brace yourself, it said. She took a deep breath, like a zookeeper before entering the lion's cage, and pushed open the door.

Irshad sat in his swivel chair, his hair ruffled, his head buried in his large hands. The office smelled like a tavern. On the table, in front of him, stood a half-empty bottle of rum. Simone couldn't tell the brand. She didn't drink and couldn't care less about the brand unless it interfered with police duty.

Irshad raised his head. His eyes were puffy. Angry. Red.

'Where have you two been?' he jabbed at his watch. 'I called about an hour ago! We have a press conference in ten minutes.'

There was no point in reminding him about Bhopal's traffic problems. Best to shut up and take the heat.

'It has been two days. *Two*,' he held up two fingers, as if words weren't clear enough. 'What results do my two best officers have to show for it?'

Silence.

'An arrest without a warrant!' Irshad raised his voice further, if that was possible, and answered his own question.

Simone sighed. It had been her decision to arrest the victim's father without a warrant. The news had evidently travelled to him.

'We had probable cause, sir,' said Simone.

'Probable cause, my foot! Lazy police work more like it!' he leaned back in his chair. 'Tell me, if it was the father of the first victim, how did he commit two more murders sitting in jail?'

Silence.

'Sit down. Both of you,' said Irshad, his tone seemingly quieter than usual after the rant. He rubbed his eyes. It didn't help. 'We have ten minutes. Tell me what you know so far.'

Simone looked at Zoya, who looked back at her.

'One of you, anyone, start!' he roared.

'Three murders in less than three days,' began Simone in a clinical monotone. 'Same MO in all three murders. Boys, aged five or less, dressed like dolls and encased in glass. Cause of death—heart attack—from the autopsy of the first victim. If not for the extravagant display, it would seem the boy died of natural causes.'

Irshad hunched forward. 'Natural causes? Are you kidding me? Five-year-old boys don't just have heart attacks or die of natural causes!' he exclaimed.

'Not my words, but Dr D'Souza's,' said Simone and continued before Irshad embarked on another tirade. 'No trace evidence, no fingerprints left on the glass or the body, except a clear thumbprint left *posthumously* on the forehead of the first victim—the father's—and, hence, the arrest yesterday.'

Irshad stroked his chin. 'What else?'

'The Doll Maker is a woman,' Zoya jumped in.

Simone started chewing the inside of her cheek. This was exactly the kind of behaviour she abhorred. Zoya couldn't help but steal her thunder, could she?

'A woman?' he exclaimed.

'Yes, we have her on camera. It confirms the witness's account from the first murder.'

Zoya glanced at Simone for support. Simone kept looking straight at the superintendent.

Zoya stood up, took out her phone and squeezed past the chairs to Irshad. She tapped her phone a few times and started playing the clip of the Doll Maker blowing a kiss with her luscious pink lips at the mall camera.

Irshad watched with interest. 'A seductress, huh?' his lips curled into a wry smile when the video ended.

'Any suspects, besides the man you locked up yesterday for no reason?' he glared at Simone.

Simone shook her head.

Irshad leaned back in his swivel chair, his arms crossed, a faraway look in his eyes.

Zoya came back and sat down with a thump.

'There's something else,' said Simone.

'What?' asked Irshad.

'It looks like the killer is targeting little boys from single-father homes. Consistent in both cases.'

Irshad clasped his hands. 'Interesting,' he said.

'We are now looking into all children reported missing from single-father households within the last year.'

'That's good. But you'll still be a step behind the killer, Simone. Glean whatever information you can from such missing children reports, but I want you to find the next boy she *plans* to kidnap and be there to catch the killer in the act. I want results! I want her locked up before she murders again. Understood?'

Simone clenched her teeth. She wanted to lash out at the superintendent. *What about the Clipper? Forty cases and you still haven't shown results, sir!* She wanted to yell at him but better sense prevailed. She didn't move.

'Is that understood, Simone?' Irshad repeated.

Simone nodded. 'Yes, sir.'

'Good,' said Irshad. He glanced at his watch.

'What's our media strategy on the Doll Maker?'

Simone started, 'Complete transparency—'

'—withhold information, sir,' Zoya jumped in, again, much to Simone's annoyance. Simone balled her hands into fists.

Irshad eyed both officers, finally settling on Zoya. 'What do you mean, Zoya?' he asked.

'The media termed the first case as "the girl in the glass case". The identity of the victims and the fact that they were actually boys, was never revealed to the media. We stick to it. Keep the fact hidden.'

Irshad nodded.

Zoya went on. 'Also, we refer to the victims as *dolls*—makes us, the police, appear more humane, more empathetic. And, of course, a hefty cash reward for anyone who comes forward with information about the Doll Maker.'

'I like it,' said Irshad. He looked at his watch again. 'The press should be in the conference room downstairs by now.

I want one of you to come with me for the press conference. Umm . . . probably you, Zoya. Your experience and clarity should come in handy.'

Irshad looked at Zoya, avoiding Simone's glare. 'Okay, off you both go. I'll freshen up and see you downstairs in a bit, Zoya.'

Both women stood up, saluted and walked out, closing the door behind them.

'Simone, can I talk to you in private for a minute?' said Zoya.

'Go to hell!' Simone stalked away.

'Simone . . .' Zoya called after her.

Simone paid no attention. She zipped up her jacket and exited the crime wing with long strides. Her nostrils flared and her head throbbed, threatening to burst any minute. She needed to get away. She needed some air—some frosty smacks on the face.

Simone's phone rang and she answered it immediately. It was the NCRB inspector.

'What!' she barked into the phone.

'Hello, ma'am.' There was a cheer in his voice. 'I've got a match on the thumbprint on the twins' foreheads.'

Simone stopped. 'That was fast,' she said.

'Umm, yes, because I had a hunch about where to start based on the last murder.'

Based on the last murder? Simone held her breath. She knew what was coming.

'The thumbprints on their foreheads are from a single person—Mr Vijay Srinivas, their father.'

21

Ranveer's hands moved across the keyboard with the finesse and speed of a piano maestro, his mind focused, his goal one: to find the Doll Maker. Ranveer sat in his den, his man cave. Bose noise-cancelling headphones enveloped his ears, bombarding them with heavy-metal rock. He was moving his head back and forth with the tempo. Ranveer was in a zone, as one might say.

Ranveer was a gifted hacker, a supreme mix of talent and hunger that takes one from beyond mere proficiency to absolute mastery. It started in the fifth grade during the late 1990s, when Ms Bedi, the computer teacher, noticed him learning Java instead of playing solitaire like his classmates. She took special interest in him, brought him books, allowed him to use the school computers during recess, encouraged him when he faltered and when his father categorically refused to buy him a computer—'It's a fad, boy! It'll be gone tomorrow!'—Ms Bedi bought computer parts and helped him assemble his first personal computer. It was the first time a teacher had taken an interest in the reclusive, stubborn boy, who managed to pass in all other subjects only because of mercy and grace marks. He was a model child for failure, easy pickings for bullies, 'a lost cause' as the other teachers would say—until Ms Bedi saw flashes of his brilliance on a computer.

As a side project, Ranveer had built the school website. A local businessman saw his work and offered him a couple of hundred rupees to build a website for his new Internet café. *His first salary!* Ranveer was ecstatic. The only mistake he made was telling his father about it in excitement. *Son of a bitch doesn't want to study. He wants to make money*, his dad had growled. The scars on the back of Ranveer's hand still hurt where his old man had put out his cigarette as punishment. And, of course, dad kept his first salary. So, when a US-based enterprise emailed Ranveer and offered him a couple of hundred dollars to create a website, he knew what *not* to do.

Ranveer used the money to buy domain names related to big Indian enterprises—Tata Motors, Reliance Industries, Airtel, etc.,—who were still figuring out their online presence. Of course, company executives soon came knocking, seeking domain names in exchange for money. He obliged. He didn't have much use for the domain names except for the lakhs he earned in exchange. The lakhs, together with a fake identity, allowed him to refurbish his mother's ancestral farmhouse adjoining Van Vihar National Park in Bhopal, surrounded by evergreen deodar trees and untamed wildlife. The dilapidated farmhouse was locked up. He fixed it, built his *temple* with its crypts. On the day he turned nineteen, Ranveer ran away from home, leaving behind a fake note for his father that said—*Moving to Mumbai to pursue a career in Bollywood. Don't follow me!* He was certain nobody would follow him. Nobody would miss him. Neither would he miss them.

'Hello, Miss Doll Maker!' Ranveer whistled, as he watched the security camera footage of the Doll Maker blowing a kiss, her pink lips inviting, wet. He replayed the footage several times, each time more mesmerized with the Doll Maker's lips and her chiselled throat. How would it feel to slit her throat? Or pluck her carotid artery with a knife?

It had taken him less than ten minutes to find all the police files on the Doll Maker. A few more minutes to know that the police had nothing, absolutely nothing, on the killer. Sure, there were thumbprints on the victims' foreheads. He knew they were intentional. He was a killer himself. He recognized an artist when he saw one. The Doll Maker was good, really good. The Doll Maker's skill burnt deep, jealous holes in Ranveer's heart, like the cigarette burns on the back of his hand.

Ranveer rewound the video and pressed play again. The video showed the Doll Maker enter the corridor, lift the bandana covering her face and neck, and blow a kiss.

Suddenly, Ranveer hit the pause button.

Something in the video had caught his attention. *It cannot be,* he thought. He zoomed in to check, to be doubly sure.

He was right! It was right there!

Ranveer removed his headphones and shot up from his chair. His heart thumped loudly. He had something on the Doll Maker, something that even the police hadn't discovered so far. He was itching to share his findings with the police and to throw a wrench into the Doll Maker's plans. It would probably only slow down the Doll Maker, but how would it benefit the Clipper?

Ranveer started pacing and thinking. Was there a way to use the new-found information to not only slow down the Doll Maker, but also use it to leverage stardom for the Clipper?

It infuriated Ranveer that the Doll Maker had killed thrice in three days. Twins, this time. *The bitch!* he cursed. The limelight and the attention she was receiving from the media was unprecedented. The Doll Maker was a media darling, while the Clipper, just like his name, had been clipped away from the limelight.

All of a sudden, Ranveer stopped pacing. A realization hit him.

'Yes,' he muttered, bobbing his head slowly, deliberately. He understood the flaw in his planning. He had become too slow; not keeping up with the times. Nine years ago, when he started, a kill every three months was big news. But the Instagram generation had become hungrier for news and media outlets more generous in serving that news. The issue wasn't that the media loved the Doll Maker more. The issue was that the Clipper wasn't catering to the ravenous appetite of his fans at the rate they desired.

More news, that was what was needed.

Another kill, that was what was needed.

And it was needed right now.

22

Ranveer was trembling, his right hand vibrating like a rockstar's guitar strings. He grabbed it with his left hand, squeezing it tight, trying to stop the trembling. Soon, both his hands started trembling, as if the tremors had passed from one hand to the other.

He was sitting on the edge of the bed in the darkness of the hotel room. Neon lights—bursts of crimson red and fluorescent green—from dance bars across the street, dappled through the sheer drapes that sheathed the window. The room smelled of burnt plastic, probably cocaine, and sex, probably used condoms. Ranveer had chosen Hotel Desire for tonight, a seedy, derelict hotel off Bhopal's red-light district. The name itself was its claim-to-fame. It provided bed-for-cash on an hourly basis for one purpose only: romps in private.

Tonight was going to be different. A big bang, a big shock to the police and the media alike. No more hiding. No more games. Tonight would be ruthless, no holding back. His story would eclipse the Doll Maker. It would be blazoned across TV channels and newspapers tomorrow morning. Prime-time footage. Ranveer grinned at the thought, his chest puffed.

Even so, Ranveer was torn. He was being impulsive, a part of him protested. But it was a risk he had to take for fame, whispered another voice in his head.

Ranveer had jumped at the realization that he needed to kill more. And faster. There was no time to waste. It had to be done. Tonight. Time-pressed and with a strong urge to make an even bigger splash than the Doll Maker, Ranveer abandoned his usual criteria for a date—out-of-town and closeted transgenders—the criteria that had kept him safe for years. He logged on to G.B.T. and found the most expensive *date* willing to meet him at a five-hour notice. A prostitute, most probably. An escort, best-case scenario. But one couldn't afford to be choosy when time was of the essence.

Ranveer checked his watch. His date was ten minutes late. Ranveer got up and paced back and forth across the narrow space at the foot of the bed. Back and forth. His hands were clammy. Beads of sweat had started to gather on the top of his head.

Ranveer rushed into the attached bathroom, as big as a large wardrobe. He stared at his greasy face in the mirror. The pale green vein in his forehead throbbed incessantly. He flipped on the tap. Cold water sputtered out. Perfect, he thought. He splashed frigid water on his face. He wanted to feel the cold, the sting. He looked up at the mirror. His bloodshot eyes stared back. He smiled, as if lost movement had returned to a limb. He was ready.

Knock! Knock!

Ranveer took a deep breath. Waited.

Knock! Knock!

Ranveer took two steps to the door, unlatched it and swung it wide open.

'Hi, I'm Ariel! Are you Ripple?'

Ranveer stared at the woman. Stumped. He was instantly infatuated. Ranveer knew it was a man, beneath the sparkling, deep red, chiffon sari. But she was gorgeous. No wonder Ariel was one of the most expensive picks on G.B.T. He had seen her photos online, of course. But photos could be photoshopped. Here, in person, she looked exquisite, like Ariel, the Little Mermaid—the cartoon Ranveer had watched growing up. Her long, flowing hair was dyed a deep burgundy, matching her off-shoulder velvet blouse and low-waisted sari. A silver navel ring drew attention to her sleek, silken navel. Her gaunt face, textured with expensive but flawlessly applied make-up, matched her lean figure and small breasts. Ranveer was smitten. He immediately regretted coming to the hotel rather than meeting up at his own home. He could have taken his time, enjoyed her, kept her. Forever. But, alas, tonight was supposed to be different.

'Are you Ripple?' Ariel repeated.

'Ah, yes. Sorry. I'm . . . I'm Ripple,' said Ranveer. 'Please come in.' Ranveer extended his arm, showing her in.

Ariel smiled and waltzed in with grace, like a peacock. Her red bangles jingled as she entered. There were no exaggerated gestures, no loud exclamations—as Ranveer had come to expect from transgenders. Ariel was different. She was—there was no better compliment—a woman.

Ranveer latched the door behind him and strolled over to Ariel. She stood facing the window, with her back towards Ranveer, entranced by the array of neon lights.

Ranveer swallowed. His hands itched. His heart raced. He couldn't hold back, like a lion offered steak on a platter.

Ranveer brought up his right hand and touched Ariel's buttocks, from left to right, the soft chiffon sari against her supple and astonishingly ample cheeks. He gulped, squeezing her bums.

'Uh-uh!' Ariel turned around but didn't step away. 'Hold your horses, mister.'

Ranveer was confused.

Ariel swept her tongue across her top lip, slowly, seductively. 'Services will be rendered only after payment.'

Ranveer smiled. He liked her. She was a woman for sure, a woman with balls. He bent down and pulled out a black gym bag from under the bed. He unzipped the bag and dropped it on the bed. 'Five lakh for showing me a good night.'

Ariel nodded.

'And another ten lakh, with compliments, for showing me your *best* night.'

Ariel turned her head sideways, bit her lower lip and gave Ranveer a seductive smile. She stepped closer and brushed back her flowing waist-length hair, the bangles on her wrist jingling. 'That's very generous of you . . .' she breathed, biting her lower lip again, '. . . Ripple,' she whispered his assumed name like it was a secret, forbidden to be said aloud.

She caressed the sides of his arms and plucked at his emaciated biceps. She slipped her hands down, clutched his hands in her own and leaned in closer, her lips inches away from his. She pulled his hands behind her and let them settle on her springy backside.

'For tonight, I am yours. Only yours.' Her warm, minty breath tickled Ranveer's nostrils.

Ariel put her hands around Ranveer's neck, leaned in and kissed him on the lips, a slow, lingering kiss that ignited raw desire deep inside Ranveer. He kissed her back, harder, unrestrained. His loins throbbed. He knew she could feel him, as he could feel her.

Suddenly, Ranveer stopped. He was on a deadline, a mission. He couldn't afford to get carried away.

Just ten more minutes please, begged the blazing fire of passion wrenching his heart, like a kid in Disneyland.

'All okay?' Ariel asked.

'Why don't we take it to the bed?' suggested Ranveer.

Ariel smiled broadly. 'I'll go wherever you want to take me tonight,' she whispered, her voice husky, rough.

Careful what you wish for, Ranveer thought, smiling inwardly.

He bent down and picked up Ariel in his arms, like a new bride on her wedding night. Ariel squealed in delight. Ranveer walked around the bed and gently, as if she was a fragile sculpture, laid her on the bed, her head on a large, hard pillow, the hardest the hotel could provide—Ranveer had made sure of it. He lay down beside Ariel.

'So, Ripple, where would you like to start?' Ariel winked at him.

Ranveer's hand crept under the pillow. He felt the cold, sharp edge of the scalpel he had hidden there.

He smiled. He wasn't sure where he would start. But he knew where she would end tonight.

23

Irshad was slumped on the sofa in his office, his neck tilted at one end and feet dangling off the other. The sofa was meant for guests or senior officers. It was meant to be uncomfortable, to discourage his guests from overstaying their welcome. Irshad twitched, his neck ached. He didn't know how long he had been lying there with his neck bent at an odd angle. He squinted at the analogue clock on the wall. It was five past one. He had spent the entire evening on the sofa. Maybe, it wasn't that uncomfortable after all? Groaning, Irshad pulled himself forward carefully.

Irshad's phone started to ring.

He instinctively looked at the clock again, his mind automatically inventing an excuse in case it was his wife.

Irshad thrust his hand inside his pocket, fumbled around for the phone, and pried it out. The effort left him breathless.

It was an unknown number. Irshad declined the call. Probably a prankster at this time of the night!

Immediately, the phone started to ring again. Unknown caller. Who could it be at this hour? Maybe it was an emergency.

Or maybe, and this released a fresh dose of adrenaline into his veins, it was the inspector general, calling to reprimand him for his actions against a subordinate—the constable Irshad had suspended.

He sat up straight, cleared his throat and accepted the call, pressing the phone against his ear. 'Hello!' he said, his voice sharp.

The caller sighed loudly on the phone, as if a sense of calm had swept over the person.

'Irshad,' said a muffled voice, raspy and robotic, like his name was a statement, a finality.

'Yes, this is Irshad.'

'Oh, it is such a pleasure, an honour really, to hear your voice. Finally.'

'Sorry, who are you?'

The robotic voice laughed. It grated on Irshad's ear.

He was about to disconnect the phone, when the caller said, 'It has been nine years, Irshad. I'm sure we both need no introductions.'

Silence.

Irshad had a lot to say to the Clipper, a lot to ask. He had dreamed of this moment in his fantasies, in his nightmares and in his daydreams. He had even made a list a few years ago of the exact questions he would ask the Clipper. But, in this moment, words escaped him. A sweeping sense of relief mated with an agonizing sense of loathing swept through him. He was both excited and distressed—a duality that chained him tight, shutting his mouth.

But it was the voice that confused Irshad. It was deep, like a man's, but artificial, altered. Wasn't the Clipper a female, a scorned woman? But that was a theory, a conjecture, not reality, he reminded himself. *Oh my god! Have I been wrong all along*? he thought. The voice, even if altered, seemed definitely masculine. Maybe the altered voice was a way to obfuscate matters and make him second-guess himself?

'Well, I'm not sure about you, but I sure am happy to hear your voice, Irshad.'

Irshad shot up from the sofa. 'You, bitch! You have the audacity to call me. Me!'

Static crackled on the other end. The Clipper remained quiet.

'I'm going to find you. And I'm going to cut you into little pieces and feed—'

'*Shut up!*' the Clipper thundered.

Irshad pulled the phone away from his ear and put on the speakerphone.

'Listen to me, you old prick,' the Clipper's voice crackled in Irshad's enclosed office. 'Never, ever, call me a *bitch*. I'm the alpha, the dog that rips apart bitches. D'you hear me?' the Clipper thundered.

Irshad closed his eyes. He had been wrong, his theory now in a shambles. He had been chasing a woman. The Clipper was a man.

The Clipper continued, 'D'you want to find me, old man? Great! Come. I'll give you the address.'

Irshad stopped breathing, his senses suddenly alert, adrenaline gushing.

'Hotel Desire. Room 301. I have a gift waiting for you, Irshad. Come *now*, or the media might get the gift first.'

The Clipper ended the call.

24

Karan tossed and turned in bed. Sleep evaded him, like most nights. He sat up, checked his smartphone. 1.22 a.m. He sighed. He had less than four hours to wake up, rush to the printer and pick up next morning's freshly printed newspaper, smelling of ink and crisp paper. He was anxious. It was the first time that a report he had written would make its way to the front page. And he had the Doll Maker to thank for it.

Karan kicked off the covers. He felt hot though it was five degrees outside. It was no better inside despite the heater. Deep down, Karan knew it was the craving. The itch. He wanted a cigarette, a few soothing puffs of nicotine to calm his nerves and help him fall asleep.

Yeah right, he snickered. Half an hour ago he had tricked his mind—one cigarette and he would sleep like a log. He'd had three cigarettes and sleep was still playing hide-and-seek with him. He wasn't sure whether he was hiding or seeking. Either way, it didn't matter.

Karan guided his feet into the leather moccasins lined with soft fur, grabbed his pack of cigarettes and lighter from the bedside table, unlocked the French windows that saved him from the elements outside and went out into the balcony. The cold air hit him on the nose, numbing his sense of smell. He gasped. He flipped open the pack with shaky hands and lit a cigarette.

'Oh god!' he whispered after one drag, his eyes closed as if he'd just climaxed. 'Ha!' he snorted. It had been ages since he had shared a woman's bed. One year, give or take. He remembered her name. Anushka. He remembered her cat-like eyes, her curly hair that smelled of lavender each time they brushed his face, her chipped front incisor, her wicked smile and the tattoo of a raging fire, like the *lit* emoji, on her chest, exactly over her beating heart. Anushka. His wife. His ex.

He sent a puff of smoke into the chilly night. Took another drag.

It wasn't that there was a dearth of girls. Fans, mostly girls, followed him online, sent him love letters penned in exquisite calligraphy or erotic messages scribbled with lipstick. Some had even sent him naked pictures with their addresses. A few of those had followed up with suicide notes or notes proclaiming their undying love for him.

But there was something about Anushka that he couldn't forget. Couldn't move past. Couldn't forgive. She had come into his life like a tornado, lifted his world like a human cannonball shooting into the sky and then left him without wings a mile high in the sky. He had fallen hard but his hopes had been dashed. She was the one. The one who got away.

Karan sucked in a deep, balmy drag. The nicotine tingled his throat.

He had met Anushka during a panel discussion at Barkatullah University on 'The Rise of Digital Influencers'.

He had been a panellist. She, the moderator, a theatre student at the university, six years younger than him. He found her eyes attractive. Her eyes were just like his mother's eyes. He had asked Anushka out for coffee after the session. She had said yes. No fuss, no drama.

The drama was to come later. Anushka, he realized, got a kick out of creating scenes in public. For fun. For the spotlight. On their first date, she let the waiter know that he had given her coffee with full-fat milk instead of skimmed milk by pouring cold coffee on his gel-stained head. Right there, in the middle of the café, in full view of the other patrons. She had laughed and then taken a bow, like theatre actors do at the end of a play, and then walked out, her head held high. Of course, he had run after her. She was the spark he had been missing. Her immense zest for life, her daily adventures, her many public scenes—she called them improv, a sassy contraction for theatre improvisation—made him feel like he was on a non-stop nicotine high. They moved in after six months. He proposed to her six months later onstage, during the intermission of her favourite theatre play; she said an emphatic no in public but a resounding yes later in private. They had eloped, married in court and decided never to tell her parents. The two years with Anushka were like an unending roller-coaster ride.

Then, last year, something changed. The roller coaster slowed down. The improv vanished. She became quieter, something completely and horribly at odds with her very nature. She started spending more time with her theatre group—Vivaan Drama Works, a performing arts group. All-day workshops and late-night rehearsals, she'd say. He trusted her. He was a fool.

He started stalking her.

The first day he had followed her in disguise, nothing unusual had happened. Anushka went to a local college in the morning. Her group was conducting a theatre workshop. She had told him so. She hadn't been lying. After the workshop, the group dispersed and went their separate ways. Anushka came home. He was shocked, afraid. Had she noticed him stalking her? If she had, Anushka didn't mention it. She was already asleep by the time he got home and she wasn't pretending, at 8 p.m.! He was livid. Who sleeps at 8 p.m.? Definitely not the Anushka of old!

It didn't take long for the truth to surface.

He had made some excuse at work the next day and followed her again. Same pattern. Same workshop. Except, the group had gone to their rented studio, a two-storey building, after the workshop at 5 p.m. Before rushing off without a goodbye or a kiss that morning, she had told him that they were performing *The Phantom of the Opera* next month. He missed the old her. He missed her unrestrained kisses.

He had waited outside on a park bench with a direct line of sight to the front door of the studio. For six hours he sat there, his buttocks numb and sweaty against the rickety, steel bench. At 9 p.m., people egressed the studio, planted kisses on each other's cheeks and waved goodbye. Anushka wasn't one of them. He had waited another hour. And another. Finally, around 11 p.m., Anushka came out. Alone.

He was confused. Why was she alone? Was she depressed? Why couldn't she confide in him any more?

Anushka had strolled to the front gate, fished out her phone and called someone. Immediately his own phone had started buzzing. She was calling him. Luckily, his phone was on vibrate mode. He had answered. She told him the rehearsal was still going on and that she would probably come home in a few hours. She had disconnected the call before he could ask a question and had gone back inside the studio.

Karan was pissed off. He wasn't sure whether it was the hunger or the lies. The 'nice guy' in him had told him to walk away, to talk to her when she came home, to listen to her concerns, understand her and to mend the broken relationship. It was their marriage after all. Instead, he had decided to storm into the studio.

The front door was locked. He had walked around the studio to the back to check the rear door. It was locked too. He checked the windows. One window was unlocked. He had prised open the dusty window slowly and slipped inside the studio, finding himself in a messy storeroom. He had tiptoed to the door and opened it an inch at a time. The door opened into a large hall spanning almost the entire length and width of the ground floor. A single bulb in the centre of the ceiling illuminated the hall, which was empty. No sign of Anushka. It was then that he saw the stairs going up to the first floor. He had crept up, his ears alert. He heard a muffled voice. It was Anushka. He crept up further. The voice became louder, as if she was in distress and needed help. He had run up the last few steps and swung open the door to the only room on the landing.

The room was awash with the same yellow light as the hall below. A single bed stood in the middle. There was a man on the bed. His hands were tied to the bedposts on either side, his eyes blindfolded. Karan recognized the man. It was Vivaan, the portly 'uncle' in his late forties, the owner of Vivaan Drama Works. Karan had met him on several occasions.

He had advised 'uncle' on how to start and run the group's Instagram page.

Anushka sat on top of Vivaan. She was riding him, like galloping on a horse. Naked. Moaning.

Anushka had turned her head when Karan barged in. The surprise in her eyes soon turned into relief. She smiled and kept riding the horse.

Karan felt numb, his hands twitched, his legs quivered.

'You are welcome to stay and watch. Maybe that will turn your *slinky* on.'

He had stepped back, shocked, crestfallen. She had mocked him. She had created that nickname for his condition—*slinky*—a wonky, flexible spring, never able to stand up on its own, like his erectile dysfunction. Now she was mocking him, flinging the same nickname as an insult.

He had stepped back further.

And further.

And further, till he was out of the studio. Back home, depressed and forlorn, he smoked cannabis, snorted cocaine, injected chemicals he had never heard of and consumed pills in the hope of forgetting what he had seen. Nothing helped.

Karan took one last drag and threw the cigarette butt down the balcony. He shuddered and crossed his arms. It was getting colder. He turned around to walk back into the bedroom and saw his reflection in the French windows. Not bad, he thought. He wasn't depressed any more, at least not *that* much. He had redeemed his career, all thanks to the newspaper editor who had forced him to get help and get clean.

Maybe one more cigarette? he thought as he slipped his hand into the pocket of his dressing gown.

Suddenly, his smartphone started ringing, flooding the dark bedroom with its harsh light. Karan rushed inside and grabbed the phone.

It was an unknown number.

'Hello!' he said.

'Karan, my friend!' a deep, raspy voice said.

'Sorry, who is this?' Karan walked to the French windows and gazed at the gathering fog beyond his reflection in the glass.

A pause.

Karan was about to repeat the question when the caller said, 'The Clipper.'

Karan choked, suppressing a cough.

The gruff voice continued. 'I have a gift for you, my friend. Something for tomorrow's newspaper. Hotel Desire. Room 301. Go now. Thank me later.'

The caller disconnected the call.

25

Irshad slammed the brakes of his personal car outside Hotel Desire, a three-storey grey structure without paint. There were no frills, no extravagance. A neon sign on the building flashed the hotel's name, switching between fluorescent green and sleazy pink.

Irshad bolted to the front door and entered the narrow lobby. There were no security guards or doorman. It was a squalid building that had gone to seed and been converted into a makeshift hotel. The carpet in the lobby reeked of mould. A desk had been placed in a corner by the entrance to serve guests. A large sign over the desk proclaimed: *Cash Only*. Behind the desk, on the wall, was an A4 printout of the hotel's TripAdvisor 'Certificate of Excellence' and customer ratings— five stars! The guests were clearly delighted with the services or the lack of them, while they went about their illicit business in private. A bellboy sat slumped behind the desk, fast asleep.

'Hey!' said Irshad.

The bellboy didn't move; there was no change in the rhythm of his snores.

Irshad inched closer and banged his open palm on the desk. 'Wake up!' he shouted.

The bellboy lifted his head, his eyes dazed, his mouth drooling. He looked like a teenager, probably still in school, if he attended any. The boy wiped his mouth on the sleeve of his pullover, drool now sticking to the woollen fabric.

'Welcome to Hotel Desire. Your privacy is our priority. How can I help?' the boy droned on in a monotone.

'I'm the police, you idiot!' said Irshad, pointing to his uniform.

The boy shot up from his chair. 'Sorry, sir.'

'Give me the key to room 301,' Irshad ordered.

The boy hesitated, looking everywhere but at Irshad. 'Sir, a guest is staying in room 301. It's . . . umm . . . it's against our hotel policy to give the key to someone else.'

Irshad ground his teeth. 'You call this a hotel? Give me the key or I'll shut down this sex palace!' Irshad slammed his hand on the desk.

The boy, clearly flustered, mostly sleepy, pulled out a bunch of keys and plucked one out with trembling hands. He handed over the key. 'First room on the third floor,' said the boy.

Irshad took the staircase at the far corner, running up the stairs, taking two steps at a time. He was huffing profusely by the time he reached the third-floor landing. Irshad gulped in deep breaths. Early signs of ageing.

There were four rooms on either side of the stairs. Irshad walked to room 301 and pressed his ear to the door. There was no sound from inside. He knocked on the door once. He pressed his ear again against the door. Still no sound or movement. He knocked again, harder and longer this time. Same result.

'She's sleeping.' It was the bellboy. He had followed Irshad up the stairs.

'Who?' asked Irshad.

'The woman in the red sari. Super-hot. Like a model,' the boy smirked like a blithering idiot. Teenage hormones no doubt.

The boy continued, 'Sardar ji left an hour ago. Paid for the room until tomorrow noon. He said I should not wake the lady as she is really, really tired. Sardar ji winked at me when he said it.' The boy was grinning again, as if Irshad had not understood what that meant.

'Sardar ji?'

'The guy who booked the room. He left. Said not to wake—'

'Yeah, I get it!' Irshad raised his voice. He sighed, exhaling through his mouth in dismay. He turned away from the boy, knocked again and said, 'Police! Open up!'

There was no response.

Irshad used the key to unlock the room. The door swung open. A wave of a metallic smell, like a freshly killed deer, hit Irshad. He knew what it was. Blood. Copious amounts of blood.

Irshad took out his service revolver. 'Stay right there,' he said to the bellboy. 'If you hear shots, call the police.'

'But . . . I thought you are the police?' stammered the boy.

Irshad didn't reply. He walked into the room. It was pitch dark; the curtains were drawn. Irshad flicked on the switch at the entrance. Light flooded the stuffy passageway that led to the bed. He crept forward, his hand extended, gun at the ready. He half expected someone to jump on him from behind the wall. He edged closer to the bed, his eyes focused, his finger on the trigger, ready to shoot if the Clipper was hiding behind the wall.

There was no one in the room, at least no one alive.

Lying spreadeagled on the bed, like Leonardo da Vinci's 'Vitruvian Man', was a body. A woman. Her head was thrown back, nearly lolling off the bed, revealing a deep gash across the throat.

Irshad gulped, fighting back the urge to vomit. The stench was unbearable.

'Should I call the *real* police?' the bellboy shouted, his head inside the corridor.

'Shut up!' Irshad snapped. 'Go back to your desk downstairs and wait there.'

The bellboy withdrew his head, but Irshad didn't hear receding footsteps. The boy was still standing outside.

Irshad sighed and ignored the boy, focusing instead on the dead woman. Her eyes were shut, as if someone had pulled down her curled eyelashes, thick, lustrous and dark with mascara, like window blinds. Her raspberry eyeshadow shimmered. Red earrings, matching the colour of blood, hung silently from her bloodstained ears, as if in mourning. She had been beautiful in life, Irshad could tell. Blood had flowed down her neck due to gravity, drenching the long hair that swept the floor. The blood had pooled on the carpet but hadn't dried yet. She was wearing an off-shoulder blouse, her shoulders bare, pale and hairless, like her arms. Red bangles, like the ones women wear on *Karwa Chauth*, adorned her fragile wrists.

A sparkle attracted Irshad's attention—a silver ring on the woman's navel. Below the navel, the body was covered with a red sari, like a shroud. She was naked underneath, her skin visible through the transparent material of the sari. In between her legs on top of the sari lay a package wrapped in newspaper. Pasted on top of the package was a gift tag. It read:

To Irshad,
With love,
From,
The Clipper

On seeing his name, Irshad started to pant like a long-distance sprinter. *Calm down, calm down*, he told himself. He took a deep breath and released it. The pounding in his heart eased a little.

Irshad took out a pair of latex gloves from his pocket and put them on. It was best not to compromise the crime scene. But he wanted to be sure. He wanted to look under the sari. He didn't need to open the package. He knew what he'd find there. Carefully, he lifted the sari off the woman's groin and immediately covered her again. He squeezed his eyes shut and gritted his teeth.

She had been clipped.

He had been clipped.

Irshad was perplexed, not knowing which pronoun to use for the body. *He or she?* He decided to stick with 'it'—it was no longer a living being anyway.

'Fuck!' someone exclaimed behind Irshad.

Irshad spun around.

'I told you to—' Irshad stopped mid-sentence.

It wasn't the bellboy. It was Karan Kapoor.

Irshad knew Karan, the dashing crime reporter from the *Times of Bhopal*. He had met him, even got into a spat with him during several media briefings in the past.

'What are you doing here?' Irshad stepped forward, inches from Karan, physically blocking his view of the body.

Karan furrowed his brow. 'I got a call from the Clipper. He said he had a gift waiting for me here.' Karan leaned sideways and squinted at the corpse slain on the bed. 'The Clipper had always sent the testicles of his victims for nine long years. We never found the bodies. Looks like we have our first body in the Clipper's case. Big news for tomorrow.'

Karan looked at Irshad. 'Might I ask what you are doing here, sir . . . alone?'

Irshad crossed his arms. 'None of your business.'

Karan smiled. 'How convenient. I'm sure our readers would love to read about this twist in tomorrow's paper.'

Irshad sighed, dropping his arms. 'Okay, look,' he said, 'I got a call from the Clipper too. He gave me the hotel's name and the room number and told me to get here before the media. Guess he meant you.'

'Or that more mediapersons are on their way,' said Karan.

'Shit!' said Irshad. 'We cannot let this make it to tomorrow's newspaper.'

Karan chuckled. 'We? *You* cannot stop it, sir. It's big news. The concerned citizens of our city deserve to know the facts as they unfold.'

'Don't you understand? The Clipper has changed his MO! For nine years he followed a strict timetable and pattern. Forty-plus murders committed with precision. All *exactly* the same. And now, suddenly, he deviates from his routine. Becomes more aggressive. Takes more risks. Leaves behind a big clue—a body, probably a transgender person judging by the clothes and appearance. Why?'

Karan shrugged.

Irshad rubbed his chin. 'And he calls you, specifically. Why?'

'And you too,' Karan shot back.

'Yes,' Irshad nodded. 'You and me. Why?'

'Maybe, he wanted the body to be found, in time, by the right people.'

'Yes, the *right* people. I am the detective on the case. And you . . .' Irshad looked up, staring at Karan, 'you're the media person. You make him famous.'

'Doesn't answer why he has changed his MO.'

'It doesn't. But it answers one thing—he wants fame. The Clipper likes being in the news. Makes him feel like a star, a celebrity.'

Suddenly, a glint lit up Irshad's eyes. He perked up.

'Karan, I need a favour from you.'

Eyes narrowed, Karan stood akimbo.

'Can you hold on to the news for forty-eight hours? Please.'

Karan started shaking his head. 'Sir, I—'

'Listen to me! The news is yours, Karan, and yours alone. I will not let another mediaperson inside. Heck, only you know that the Clipper targets transgenders. It's fresh news in the case. Big news. All I'm asking is that you put a lid on it for two days. My hunch is that the need for fame is making the Clipper more aggressive and more careless. If we don't give him what he wants—fame—maybe he'll make a mistake.'

'That's one theory but I have a duty to report the incident. Like you said—it's big news. I cannot just sit on it for two days.'

Irshad sighed, rubbing his chin. 'What if I gave you even bigger news in exchange?'

Karan leaned forward, 'I'm listening.'

'You are reporting on the Doll Maker case as well, right?'

Karan nodded. 'Yes. In fact, I have a huge feature on the front page in the morning.'

'What if I gave you confidential information?'

'We *may* have a deal then,' Karan said with a sly smile.

'What if I told you that the three dead girls found in the glass cases . . .' Irshad paused, leaning in closer, and whispered. '. . . were actually little *boys* dressed as Barbie dolls.'

Karan inhaled deeply, relishing the information, his smile, broad.

Irshad extended his hand, 'Do we have a deal?'

Karan nodded and shook his hand.

26

Irshad paced back and forth, outside the hotel entrance, jacket zipped up and hands stuffed deep inside his pockets. There was a nip in the early morning air. He sniffled, his face dry and numb from the cold. He was waiting for the forensic technicians, whom he had called after Karan had left.

Karan had taken the bait, but Irshad wasn't sure if it was enough to hold off the reporter. Karan had agreed to wait for two days. Easier to update a news report on the Doll Maker than write a new one on the Clipper at 2 a.m., Karan had reasoned. They had shaken hands. It was a done deal. Irshad knew the deal would be honoured—it wasn't every day that a crime reporter got to deal with the superintendent of police in the hope for more scoops in the future.

Irshad only prayed that Simone and Zoya would never find out the source of the leak. He had compromised their case. If he had been at the receiving end of such treachery, he would have strangled the other officer. *Let's just hope it doesn't come to that*, he thought.

Irshad yawned loudly. He was weary, sleep knocking at his temples like a migraine. The espresso shot he had hurriedly consumed in the office, right after the Clipper's call, was wearing off. Maybe, it was his adrenaline crashing. Or was it the alcohol he had consumed earlier, gushing through his veins and trying to lull him to sleep?

'I need a drink,' Irshad muttered as he desperately tried to ward off the cold by walking around.

A car careened dangerously, its lights bouncing off a speed bump and stopped in front of the hotel. The mortuary van arrived right after the car.

Dr Marvin D'Souza stepped out of the car and walked towards Irshad. His team in the van alighted with their forensic kits and pulled out a collapsible gurney.

'Good morning, Irshad. Or is it still night?' Dr D'Souza hollered in his croaky, harsh voice, and vigorously shook hands with Irshad like he was meeting a long-lost friend. He seemed to have slept well.

Irshad's head pounded as if retaliating against Dr D'Souza's energy.

'So . . . a beauty queen lost her crown?' the doctor grinned.

'Not in the mood for lame jokes, Marvin,' grunted Irshad. He turned around, opening the front door. 'Follow me.'

'After you!' said Dr D'Souza without a drop in his spirits, like he was excited to see the body. Probably that was what it took to become a forensic pathologist. 'Come on, boys,' the doctor called out to his team.

'Nobody went up!' exclaimed the panic-stricken bellboy from behind the front desk. His ashen face was twitching, like the face of a non-believer who sees a ghost for the first time—the ghost of death.

Irshad had secured the crime scene. He had asked the bellboy to stand guard at the reception and keep anyone, except Irshad, from going upstairs.

Irshad nodded and walked to the staircase.

'I called Daddy. He is on his way,' squeaked the boy.

Irshad ignored him and kept walking. Clearly, it was a family business, with the son providing free labour at night.

Irshad led the technicians to room 301. It was the only room in the corridor with the lights on. He unlocked the door and shoved it open. The stale and sordid air rushed outside, as if trying to escape the horrors that lay inside.

'I'll get out of your way, Marvin,' Irshad spoke directly to Dr D'Souza, 'but first, if you don't mind, I want your preliminary assessment.'

'Why don't you go home and get some sleep, Irshad? Have one of your officers—' Dr D'Souza stopped. Irshad was glaring at him, his nostrils flaring. 'Okay, fine. Let's go,' said the pathologist.

'Thank you,' said Irshad.

Dr D'Souza took out a pair of latex gloves from his pocket and put them on. Then he put on a mask, pinching it in place over the bridge of his nose.

Irshad took out a handkerchief and covered his nose. He walked into the far end of the room and stood by the curtains.

Dr D'Souza followed him inside but stopped at the foot of the bed. He squinted at the corpse, with a deep slit on its neck, sprawled on the bed. He stepped closer to the body, making sure his thick black boots didn't disturb the blood on the carpet.

'Clean,' said Dr D'Souza.

'Sorry, what?' asked Irshad.

'The laceration across the throat. It's clean. Deep, but sliced clean. I bet it was a scalpel and not a kitchen knife.'

'Are you saying the killer is a trained medical professional?'

Dr D'Souza exhaled loudly, shook his head. 'No, I'm not saying that. You are saying that. All I'm saying is that the murder weapon is probably a scalpel and not a kitchen knife or a butcher's knife. Did you find one?'

Irshad shrugged. 'Nope.'

Dr D'Souza walked back to the foot of the bed. 'Seems there is no other wound above the torso,' he murmured to himself. 'Let's see what's hidden beneath the sari.'

Irshad tensed.

The doctor pulled down the soft fabric, revealing the nakedness and the missing testicles.

Irshad gulped and looked away.

'Yes, it's a man. He's been mutilated.' Dr D'Souza stared with interest. 'Seems post-mortem judging from the low amount of blood here compared to the throat.'

He covered the legs with the sari again and picked up the package wrapped in newspaper.

'What do we have here?' he said like it was a surprise gift that he was excited to open.

He smiled at Irshad. 'How come you didn't open the package this time? It's addressed to you, as always.'

'The mutilated body was enough for me. And, anyway, we both know what's inside.'

'That didn't stop you from opening the last forty packages,' Dr D'Souza glowered. Like most medical examiners, he hated it when the police tampered with evidence, more so if it was the police superintendent himself.

Silence.

With nimble fingers, Dr D'Souza removed the newspaper to reveal the usual black shoebox. He put the newspaper on the floor and raised the lid.

'A photo?' he exclaimed.

'What?' Irshad rushed over.

There were no testicles in the box.

Instead, there was a photo, grainy but coloured, at the bottom. It was a close-up of a screenshot of a woman's face—covered with a bandana but the lower half revealing pouting pink lips, like she was blowing a kiss at the camera.

It was a photo of the Doll Maker from the mall's security camera.

A heavy-duty marker had been used to draw a thick red circle around her angled throat. On the photo was a Post-it inscribed in neat, cursive handwriting:

What does Adam have, but Eve doesn't?
Answer the riddle. Thank me later.
Your friend,
The Clipper

Day 3

27

4.20 a.m.

Simone sat alone in the office waiting for Zoya and superintendent Hussain. Zoya had called her to say the boss wanted to meet both of them, *ASAP*.

Simone rocked her head from side to side, chewing the inside of her cheek. She was upset. Why hadn't superintendent Hussain called her instead? It was *her* bloody case. Not Zoya's. Hers.

Simone groaned.

She sat back and picked up the sheet of paper on her lap. The sketch of the Doll Maker—a vivid, computer-generated colour image. Simone had interrogated the school receptionist last evening; the *stupid* woman had let the twins leave with a stranger on the basis of a fake authority letter.

Simone raised the paper sketch to her nose and squinted at it, like a diamond merchant examining a stone for flaws. The sketch seemed oddly familiar, yet deceptively elusive. It showed a slender woman, probably in her late twenties with grey eyes and high cheekbones. She was wearing heavy make-up, a large maroon bindi and vermilion in her parting. A married woman? More likely a disguise.

'Humph!' Simone exhaled.

'Found something?'

It was superintendent Hussain, rushing into the office with a shoebox in hand and Zoya at his heels. Simone couldn't help but wonder if the two of them had spent the night together. A man married to his job and a divorcee looking to advance her career. Probably the reason why he always favoured Zoya.

'It's the sketch of the Doll Maker.' Simone stood up, extending the paper towards him.

'Not interested. Come into my office.'

Simone pursed her lips. She left the sketch on her desk and followed him.

'Good morning!' Zoya smiled at her.

Simone looked away and didn't answer.

Superintendent Hussain laid the shoebox on his desk and dropped into his swivel chair, which creaked under the sudden impact. It seemed he had aged five years since last evening. His hair was ruffled and his uniform in urgent need of ironing. The crow's feet around his bloodshot eyes seemed to have deepened. The grey in his stubble sparkled despite the dim light.

'The Clipper killed again last night,' he said as soon as both women sat down. 'Left a body for the first time—throat slit clean with a scalpel it seems. And then, he called me.'

Zoya's eyes widened. 'The Clipper called *you*?'

He shrugged. 'Yes, apparently we are "friends". And he wants to help.'

'Help?' said Simone.

He leaned forward in his chair. He removed the lid, took out the note and passed it to Zoya. 'Seems like the Doll Maker has stolen the Clipper's thunder. He wants to help us find her.'

'What?' said Simone. She snatched the note from Zoya. 'What does Adam have, but Eve doesn't?' she read the note aloud. 'What does it mean?'

'I don't know.' Irshad rubbed his eyes with the base of his palms. 'That's why I called the two of you.'

Zoya looked at the photograph of the Doll Maker inside the box; she was blowing a kiss. Zoya turned it around in her hand, like it was an expensive antique to be handled with care and examined it from all angles. She passed it to Simone and said, 'He has circled the Doll Maker's throat in the photo. I guess it means he wants to slit her throat like his victim's throat?'

Simone wasn't so sure. Why go through all this trouble just to threaten another serial killer?

Simone stood up and paced back and forth. 'In Genesis, what did Adam have that Eve didn't?'

'More self-control for one thing,' snorted Zoya.

Simone looked blankly at Zoya. 'What?'

'Well, as the story goes, Eve was easily deceived by the serpent in the Garden of Eden. She succumbed to temptation, ate the forbidden apple and later, made Adam eat the apple.'

'What do you mean *made* him eat the apple? He had a mind of his own, didn't he? You know, Zoya, you sound just like a male chauvinist!'

'Sorry, did I hurt your feelings, Miss Feminist?' Zoya retorted.

'Ladies!' Irshad banged his fist on his desk. 'Can we please focus on the issue here?'

'Sorry, sir,' said Zoya.

'Sorry,' mumbled Simone.

Irshad exhaled.

Simone said, 'Let's start over. So, what's the difference between Adam and Eve, man and woman. It should not—'

'What is it, Simone?' said Irshad.

Simone grabbed the photograph of the Doll Maker, her eyes narrowing. 'Oh, shit!' she said. 'It's like the Clipper's victims. The answer is the apple. That's what Adam has but Eve doesn't. An apple. Plain and simple biology.'

Zoya looked at Simone quizzically.

'An Adam's apple,' Simone yelled, excited.

Simone turned the photo over and jabbed a finger at the jagged protrusion in the Doll Maker's throat, encircled with red marker. 'The Doll Maker is not a woman. He's a man.'

28

Ranveer woke up happy. He felt good. He threw the quilt off and jumped out of bed. He was excited, like a kid on his birthday. He ambled downstairs to the living room, a bounce in his step, a song on his lips.

'Master of Puppets, I'm Pulling Your Strings!'

Ranveer swung his head back and forth, warbling his favourite Metallica song.

' . . . Twisting Your Mind . . .'

He strummed his fingers, as if plucking a guitar in his hand.

' . . . And Smashing Your Dreams!' He raised his pitch, his voice echoing in the near-empty house.

The song held a lot of meaning for him today. Made him feel like the man in charge, like he was the master, controlling every little movement of his 'puppets'—the police, the media and the victims. He was playing with them, twisting and turning their strings and smashing their dreams. Just like the song.

Ranveer stopped at the front door, violently bobbing his head one last time in tune with the song and threw open the door. Crisp morning air, chilly and weightless, greeted him. He embraced the frosty air despite the thin T-shirt and flimsy boxers. It invigorated him.

The veranda was shrouded in semi-darkness. The first rays of the morning sun peeked from underneath the horizon.

Ranveer strolled on the veranda and stepped out on the lush green lawn; the grass glistened with morning dew. The lawn ran the length of a tennis court, abutting the cemented driveway on one side and the rented cabin on the other. A gigantic mango tree spread its branches over the cabin, providing necessary shade from the harsh sun in the summers. In winters, however, it had an undesirable effect. But that was the tenant's problem, not his.

Ranveer's eyes searched for the treasure he had come to seize—the morning newspaper. Birds chirped from the mango tree, as if cheering and egging Ranveer on. He squinted, twirled on his heels, looking around. But there was no sign of the newspaper. Perhaps the newspaper boy was running late?

Ranveer's excitement was fast turning into impatience. He wanted to read about himself. He wanted to read about the spectacle he had left behind in Hotel Desire last night. He wanted to reclaim the glory that had been stolen by the Doll Maker. Most of all, he wanted to *own* the Doll Maker, like he owned his victims, maimed and preserved, forever.

Ranveer chuckled. His heart swelled, like it did when he first realized that the Doll Maker was his type. Queer. A beautiful man in a sari. Noticing *her* Adam's apple was a stroke of serendipity. But then he had spent years noticing, relishing and ripping away all signs of masculinity from his victims. Setting them free to be who they aspired to be—women.

Suddenly, a muffled cry erupted from the cabin, like someone shouting from under a blanket. Just as suddenly, it was gone. Was the tenant in trouble? Ranveer strained his ears. It was eerily quiet. Even the birds perched high in the mango tree had stopped chirping. Probably they had heard it too.

He walked a few paces to the cabin—a white wooden shed with a sloping roof, a single window facing the lake and a heavy oakwood door. A round vanity mirror as big as his hand was nailed to the door, like a courtesy to the visitor to check his or her appearance before entering the shed. Ranveer saw mussed hair and puffy eyes in his reflection. He raised his hand to knock on the door but stopped himself.

Complete privacy—that had been the deal when she had moved in a year ago.

She had reached out to him over email—an overly enthusiastic note that invoked their childhood friendship. They had been neighbours as children and their mothers were best friends. They had played together every evening— two five-year-olds running amok in the community park while their mothers sat gossiping on the bench. They had spun yarns of endless tales during sleepovers. They had held each other's clammy hands during those sleepovers too, afraid that the monster under the bed would rear its head, grab them with its claws and take them 'underground'— into a dark abyss from which, they believed, no one ever returned. They were kids. They were best friends, just like their mothers.

Ranveer didn't remember any of it. Nothing. The email had seemed like a scam. But as he read on, broken pieces tore through the fog that shrouded his memory.

She wrote how much she missed him after her mother passed away and her dad moved houses. Ranveer remembered it vaguely because he too had missed her terribly. She had vanished without a trace, without saying goodbye. It had broken little Ranveer's heart. He had cried for days, wetting his pillow, wetting his bed, afraid he would surely be chewed up by the monster now that she was no longer there to protect him. The nightly belting from his father had helped matters. He had stopped crying. He had stopped being afraid of the monster under the bed when he realized that there was a very *real* monster above ground, putting out lit cigarette butts on his skin— his father.

Towards the end of the email, she had begged him for help—for a place to stay. She was destitute, in between jobs, with no family to turn to. A month, maybe two, in a shed or a garage or a dog kennel, till she found another job.

Ranveer wasn't going to allow a stranger on his property. But then he had read the postscript—

PS: I'm on my knees, begging you. Help me for our mothers' sake.

Ranveer would have done anything for his late mother. Anything. May she rest in peace.

In a moment of rashness, he had emailed back a simple yes, but on one condition—complete, 100 per cent privacy. He would let her stay in his cabin if she promised to stay out of his hair and he would do the same. Period.

He had heard from the bedroom window as she dragged the trolley bag across the driveway. Ranveer had left the key on the doorstep. No hellos, no small talk. They had been friends as kids. They weren't friends now.

He had rarely seen her since. After a month, on the first day of every month, like clockwork, he would receive cash in a white envelope on his doorstep and an email from her with the subject line: 'Monthly rent delivered. Thank you!' Nothing more. He didn't need the money. He didn't need her. But the arrangement worked. So, he had let her stay. The least he could do for his mum.

Now, standing at her doorstep, his hand raised, Ranveer wondered if he should violate the condition of complete privacy himself.

There was a hefty thwack behind Ranveer. He turned around, just in time to see the newspaper bounce off the cemented driveway and land in the mushy shrubs that separated the lawn from the driveway.

'Idiot!' Ranveer cursed the newspaper boy who had hurled the newspaper over the tall gate like a grenade, with utter disregard for where it would land.

Ranveer strode across the lawn, the dewy grass dampening his hurried steps. He picked up the newspaper with his thumb and index finger, like he was picking up a rat by the tail. The newspaper was wet in patches where it had soaked the morning dew like a sponge.

Ranveer groaned. 'Idiot!' he swore again.

He flicked the newspaper roll left to right, as if it would help dry it. It didn't. Exasperated, Ranveer pulled off the rubber band tied around the newspaper and opened it. He was immediately stung by the headline on the front page. The byline said Karan Kapoor: *Serial Killer Murders 3 Young Boys in 3 Days.*

'Boys?' Ranveer murmured.

He had thought they were girls. Weren't they? Come to think of it, killing boys made sense. The Doll Maker was a man who liked to dress up. No wonder he was killing boys and dressing them up. Like himself perhaps. For some reason, the Doll Maker saw himself in those young boys.

Ranveer scanned through the article hurriedly. He wasn't interested in the Doll Maker's crimes or what the police said at the press conference or Karan's warning: *If you have young boys, keep them safe.* He was interested in *his* story, *his* crime, *his* moniker—the Clipper—blazoned across a headline.

It wasn't there on the front page.

He flipped to page two. Nothing.

Page three. Nothing.

He turned page after page, frustration building, till he reached the sports section on the last page. Nothing. No mention of the Clipper. No mention of last night.

Ranveer gritted his teeth, his eyes dazed, his mind clouded.

'I'm going to find you, Doll Maker. I'm going to rip you, one inch at a time . . . And I will let you heal again . . . And then rip you again. And heal. And rip. Heal and rip! Heal and rip! Till you beg me to kill you!'

Ranveer's fingers formed a fist, crumpling up the newspaper. He was shaking uncontrollably now. He wadded the newspaper tightly into a ball. Despite the chilly air, beads of sweat broke out on his forehead. He slammed the ball of paper into the damp grass. He jumped and stomped on the muddy paper ball, again and again. He shouted and screamed and howled.

And then he stopped.

Silence.

He realized he wasn't alone. He was too loud and too close to the tenant to hear him. She had probably already heard him.

He heard noises from the cabin. He walked closer, his mind making up excuses to explain his outburst. Then he realized it was his own property. *His* house. He didn't owe her any explanation.

He reached the door and saw in the mirror the dishevelled, sweaty hair sticking to his face. He stared at his reflection, making no attempt to smooth his hair.

'Sorry, I heard noises. I was in the back. Are you okay, Ranveer?' said Nalini.

It was her. The tenant. Her eyes groggy, her hair tousled like Ranveer's, as if she had just woken up.

Ranveer wasn't interested in small talk. He wasn't even sure why he had come over when he should have just run into his house. *Yes, that's what I must do*, he thought. *Get away!*

'Ranveer?'

Without a word, he turned around and started walking towards the house.

'Everything is fine,' he shouted as he retreated into his house. 'Go back to sleep, Nalini.'

29

Nalini closed the door.

That was weird. No face-to-face contact for a year and now, out of nowhere, Ranveer was standing on her doorstep, half-naked, shivering in the cold, looking like he was going to be sick.

Sure, it was his house. But he was the one who wanted complete privacy. And then he had come to the lawn to shout and scream. He did realize that she still rented the cabin.

Nalini shrugged. She understood the demons that drove Ranveer. After all, they both had one thing in common: violent, asshole fathers. The only difference was that his father had tortured him, while her father had tortured her mom.

The signs had been visible even as kids. She'd go to his house to play—his mom would invite Nalini only when his dad was away at work—and Nalini would find him in his room, sitting perfectly still, arms folded, chin lowered to his chest, staring at the mirror on the dresser, as if in love with his own reflection. She would chatter non-stop to compensate for his silence. She would run around the room shouting, 'Catch me, Ranveer. Catch me!' hoping he would shoot up from his chair and run after her, giggling, laughing, the dimples in his cheeks sparkling. He never did.

When nothing worked, which was always the case, she would sit cross-legged on the dusty carpet—even though she hated grime—prop her chubby elbows on her knees, her chin resting in her palms and stare at him, like she was admiring the vivid colours of a painting. His swollen, crimson lips, chipped front tooth, strawberry-coloured welts on his arms and legs and the angry scorch marks on the backs of his hands. Cigarette burns. He had told her once, while boasting how brave and strong he was and how he never even flinched as his father painted him red.

'Daddy! I want daddy!' cried the special little boy from the bed.

Nalini rushed to him. She did not comfort him but stood by the bed watching him squirm under the quilt. So helpless. So needy.

The boy tried to sit up but fell right back. Nalini had tied one of his arms to the bedpost lest he decided to run away in the night. Plotting and scheming would be unusual in a kid with Down's Syndrome. But fight-or-flight was the body's natural response. Nalini expected to win the fight but didn't want to take any chances.

The boy tried to sit up again and fell again. His forehead contorted, as he suddenly realized that he was tied to the bed.

'Daddy!' the boy started to bawl.

'Quiet!' Nalini whispered, as if lowering her voice would automatically make the boy lower his.

'DADDY!'

Nalini jumped on the bed. She climbed on top of the boy and put her hand over the boy's mouth. 'Shut up!'

The boy struggled, swinging his head from side to side, trying to shake off Nalini's hand. He screamed, but with a hand clamped over his mouth, it sounded like a groan.

Suddenly, he sank his tiny, sharp teeth into Nalini's little finger.

'Fuck!' Nalini screamed in pain. She pulled her hand away and spotted blood. As she sucked the finger, she could taste the salty, metallic tang of blood.

'Daddy! Daddy!' the boy continued to cry.

'You little piece of shit!' Nalini drew her hand back and slapped the boy, tight and hard, across the face.

The boy howled, covering his face with chubby arm.

'You want daddy, huh? You want daddy? Here I am!' Nalini's voice suddenly turned masculine—harsh and deep. The voice she had been born with. The voice of the man she didn't identify with.

'Your mommy gave birth to you, took care of you and died protecting you. And what did Daddy do? He hit her. He killed her. But you still want your daddy?'

She grabbed the little boy by the throat and squeezed it hard.

The boy flailed his limbs, choking, gagging and struggling for air.

Nalini roared like a deranged wrestler, her fingers crushing the boy's tender neck.

Suddenly, she stopped.

Her body went rigid. She climbed off the boy and collapsed on the bed, right next to him. She remained unmoving, unblinking. Alive, but deep in thought.

In the heat of the moment, she had become her father, the very man she had despised all her life. The man who had killed her mother and gotten away with it. The man who had banished Nalini to fend for herself when she was just a fragile little girl. The man of her nightmares; his murder, the highlight of her fantasies.

Nalini remembered the day her mom died as vividly as the seven murders she had plotted to redeem herself—1 June 1986. Her fifth birthday.

Smash! The breaking of glass.

Crack! The breaking of a skull.

Aieeee! The scream and the breaking of her heart.

Her dad was away in Indore. At a sales conference. He was a door-to-door salesman for Tupperware, an American multilevel marketing firm, selling plastic containers to bored and unsuspecting housewives. He had left his secure job as a police inspector and taken up direct selling, expecting to 'mint crores and crores' through Tupperware's shady pyramid schemes—enrol more people and get a cut from the sales of every person you enrol. But cracks soon appeared in the snow globe of his dreams. Sales targets became impossible to achieve, the pressure became suffocating and debts piled up. An occasional pint became a nightly bottle of whisky; an occasional slap became the nightly belting of her mom. Dad always used his old, police-issue belt—toughened leather with a heavy, metal buckle at the end—to thrash Mom, as if she was to blame for his life of drudgery and debt.

Dad was supposed to be at the conference for three days. He came back in one; thought he would surprise his *son* on his birthday.

It was before noon. Mom had dressed up Nalini in a baby pink, frilly frock with a red bow cinched around the waist. Mom said it was a birthday present 'for my beautiful daughter'. Nalini's heart had swelled with joy. Mom always called her 'daughter' when it was just the two of them. The daughter she had always wanted. The daughter she found in Nalini. As soon as she was dressed, Mom had applied a gaudy, pink lipstick on her tender lips. 'It's not every day that a girl turns five,' Mom had said. Nalini had licked the lipstick. She had tasted strawberries. And for the first time, she felt like a girl, a lady—like her mom.

They had sat beside the dollhouse in Nalini's room, mother and daughter, celebrating Nalini's birthday over a kitty party with dolls. All her Barbie dolls—usually kept hidden in her mom's trunk, away from the prying eyes of Dad—were invited. Mom had baked a cake—Black Forest cake—her favourite. Nalini had beamed with delight. It was the best birthday. Ever.

Until someone rang the bell.

Mom thought it was the postman or a salesman or the maid. She told Nalini to stay put while she went to shoo away whoever was interrupting their party.

It was a salesman indeed. Dad. Back home two days earlier than expected.

Sitting alone in her room, Nalini heard her mom say to her dad, 'You must be tired after the journey. Why don't you sit here? I'll get you a glass of water.'

'Where is the birthday boy?' Dad asked, while Mom fetched him a glass of water.

'Umm . . . I was just getting him ready.' Nalini heard the fear in her mother's voice. The same fear that reared its head right before she got smacked or belted or kicked. 'Here, drink some water. I'll bring the birthday boy out in a minute.'

Nalini wanted to show off her new dress to Dad. Mom had said that she looked beautiful. She wanted Dad to say it too. Surely, Dad wouldn't get mad at her? It was her birthday, after all.

'Daddy, Daddy,' Nalini had rushed out of her room.

He stood up from the chair, slowly, the wheels in his mind turning, his face ashen, like he had seen a snake in the house.

Mom's face was white with fear. Her head and shoulders drooped, as if surrendering to the wave of violence hurtling towards her.

It was on seeing Mom looking so hopeless and dejected that Nalini realized she had made a huge mistake by stepping out of her room. She realized that birthday or not, Mom would not be spared the thrashing.

Dad threw the glass on the tiled floor.

The glass splintered and shards bounced off the floor. One hit Nalini on her chubby leg.

'You filthy woman! What did you do to my boy?' Dad bellowed.

Mom fell on her knees, as if resigned to her fate.

Dad instinctively went for the belt around his waist. He tried to unbuckle it. His hands shook, his face convulsed. Luckily, or in hindsight unluckily for her, the buckle got stuck.

'Sonofabitch!' Dad roared in fury. He looked like he was having a seizure. He looked around, his eyes fluttering and searching. Finally, he spotted a bottle of whiskey. He grabbed it and ran towards Mom, who sat trembling on the floor, sobbing softly. He swung his hand back and rammed the heavy bottle on mom's head.

Nalini heard it. The sharp, unmistakable breaking of the bone. Her mom's skull.

Mom yelped like a puppy that's just been run over by a car and collapsed on the floor.

Dad dropped the bottle of whisky. The toughened bottle cracked but didn't break. The golden liquid oozed out of the cracks in the bottle and spilled over the white tiles, mixing with the blood seeping out from Mom's skull. Dad had rushed over and slapped Nalini across the face. She had started weeping, more because of her Mom's pain rather than the sting of the slap.

Dad seized Nalini by the throat, choking her. He yanked down her underwear, grabbed her balls, and squeezed them hard.

She had let out a loud, piercing scream.

'Do you feel the pain, boy?' Dad had asked her.

Nalini had bobbed her head vigorously, as much as his grip on her throat allowed her to, in the hope that Dad would let go of her balls.

Instead, he had squeezed harder, 'That's because you're a boy. You hear me? A *boy*!'

Nalini thought she would die. But suddenly, Dad released her from the chokehold and pulled Nalini into a rough embrace. His breath stank like the whisky puddle on the floor.

'Promise me, boy. You will never wear a girl's dress. Never. Ever!'

Nalini was stumped.

'Promise me!' Dad had yelled.

She nodded. She had kept her promise for more than twenty years.

Until last year.

Now, slumped on the bed next to the special little boy, Nalini pursed her lips, swallowing the lump in her throat.

She owed the boy an apology. She had turned into her father. She sniffled. This wasn't who she was. Her mom would have expected better from her.

Nalini turned sideways and hugged the boy.

'Mommy is so sorry, baby. Mommy is so sorry,' she whispered, her voice soft, feminine, like she had trained it to be. Tears streamed down her cheeks. She whimpered. The lump grew harder in her throat.

The boy lay still in her arms.

'Mommy loves you, sweetheart,' she whispered in his ear.

The boy didn't respond.

Nalini pulled away from the boy. Checked his pulse. There was no pulse.

'No, no, no!' she cried.

She jumped off the bed. Threw away the quilt that covered the boy's limp body. She pumped his tiny chest, trying to resuscitate him.

No response.

She tilted his head, lifted his chin. Put a finger under his nostrils.

He wasn't breathing.

She opened the boy's mouth, pressed her mouth against his and blew air into his mouth, hoping to pump air into his lungs.

Too little, too late.

The boy was dead.

Nalini fell to her knees. Her face grimacing in pain.

'Nooo!' She let out a deep scream.

She grabbed the boy's tiny, unmoving feet. She pressed her forehead against them and wept.

'Forgive me, baby. Forgive me.'

30

Serial Killer Murders 3 Young Boys in 3 Days

Simone read the newspaper headline again. She slammed the newspaper on her office desk, her blood boiling.

A few colleagues raised their heads, glancing in her direction in concern.

She wanted to lambast them; the lazy bums who had nothing better to do than enjoy an early morning show of 'Chhota Bheem'. She knew that that was what they called her behind her back. Her nickname. An ironical reference to her unconventionally tall figure and anger issues. She wore it like a badge of honour.

Simone buried her head in her hands. She was furious. She wanted to know who had spilled the beans to the press. Who told them that the girls in the glass case were actually boys?

Simone picked up the newspaper. She read the byline. Karan Kapoor. She exhaled loudly.

Picking up her phone, she dialled Karan.

The phone kept ringing. No answer.

Simone threw the phone on her desk in exasperation, attracting more glances from her co-workers. She wasn't even sure what the call would have accomplished. She wanted to shout at him, twist his arm and force him to betray his source, the traitor.

Simone sighed. She peered at the sketch of the Doll Maker on her desk. She gazed at the frail woman in the sketch, her features sharp, her nose small, her jaw angular. The woman seemed familiar, like a long-lost acquaintance you faintly recall but cannot identify even if she accosted you in the street.

But now they knew. It was a man in disguise.

What a waste! Simone crumpled up the sketch and threw the paper ball into the dustbin.

Her phone started to vibrate on the table. Simone lunged forward and grabbed it. The caller ID read: Karan Kapoor. Simone accepted the call, breathed into the phone but kept silent.

'Hi, Simo. You called? How can I help you?' There was a tinge of joy in his voice. Like he was trying hard to keep a lid on his excitement, the excitement of talking to her. Simone couldn't understand why.

'How did you know that the victims in the glass cases were boys?' Simone came straight to the point.

'A source,' Karan chuckled.

'I know your source is someone in the police department. Better tell me now, Karan. Don't make me do something you'll regret.'

'Ooh! Feisty. I like it.'

'I'm serious, Karan.'

He stopped chuckling. 'Empty threats count for nothing, Simone,' he paused, 'but it so happens, it's your lucky day today. If I tell you the name of my source, what new information about the case will you trade with me?'

'I'm not trading anything, Karan. I'm asking. Nicely.'

Karan burst out laughing at the other end. 'How about we discuss it over dinner tonight? I'm asking. Nicely.'

Simone was stumped. Was he asking her out on a date? Nobody had ever asked her on a date. Or was it simply a business dinner? An exchange of information over a meal?

'We can call it a business meeting, if you prefer,' he said, as if he had read her mind. The soft chuckle was back in his voice.

'I . . . I . . .' Simone stuttered, her mind in a whirl. This was a new territory for her. A small part of her was jumping with joy—a man had asked her out on a date. But the rest of her was revolted. It wasn't professional. It wasn't becoming of a police officer. Unless, like he said, it was a business meeting. Simply a meal.

'How about I pick you up at 7 p.m.?'

'No!' Simone squawked. She didn't want anyone in the department to see her on a date with a news reporter. Not that anyone would care. 'I have a car.'

Karan snorted. 'That works too. I'll text you the name of the restaurant.'

Simone nodded but didn't respond.

'And . . . Simo?'

'Yes?'

'I'm looking forward to our . . . date,' Karan chortled and disconnected the phone before Simone had a chance to point out that it, in fact, was a business meeting and *not* a date.

Or maybe it was? Her lips curled in a smile. She felt her face flush.

'You seem happy.'

Simone turned around, suddenly alarmed.

It was Zoya. She stood, hands in her trouser pockets, peering over Simone's shoulder.

'Mind your own business.' Simone shoved the phone into her pocket and swivelled her chair to face the desk again. She pulled out a document, attempting to look busy, hoping that Zoya would take the hint and leave her alone.

Zoya pulled an empty chair and sat down with a thump. The worn-out springs in the chair groaned in protest.

'I've been working on the profile of the Doll Maker. I think we have enough to narrow down the search. I want your opinion.'

'Yeah. Whatever.'

'Look, Simone,' Zoya whispered, inching closer to Simone. 'I can't help it if the superintendent favours me. I'm more experienced. And, quite frankly, I've got a better rapport with him.'

Simone scoffed, 'Well, cosying up to the boss definitely helps the rapport.'

A constable walked up to them.

'Sorry, madam *ji*,' he addressed Simone, 'here's the report you asked for.'

He handed Simone a slim, khaki file and left.

'Kids of single fathers,' said Simone, her voice composed, as if their verbal confrontation minutes ago had never happened.

'What?' asked Zoya, irritation in her voice.

'It's the list of kids reported missing in the last week by single fathers.'

Zoya gave Simone a quizzical look.

Simone said, 'Single fathers. And their thumbprints left on the kids' foreheads posthumously. That's the common link between all three murders. It's like the Doll Maker is blaming the fathers for the kids' deaths. Actually, not just blaming them. He's implicating them in their murders. He sees them as criminals. If not for their solid alibis, we'd have locked them up and shut the case.'

Zoya scoffed, 'Actually, we did lock up the first guy. The carpenter. Before he alibied out of jail.'

'So, you're saying that's my fault?' Simone crossed her arms.

'No, that's not what I'm saying. We were both party to that arrest. If anything, we'd both be at fault.'

Simone munched the inside of her cheek.

'What I *am* saying is we understand our killer and his psyche a little better. We know the type of kids he's targeting: kids with single fathers. And, we know, sort of, why he's targeting them.'

'Why?'

'The Doll Maker sees himself as one of the little boys he has killed. Most likely abused by his single dad as a child. He sees himself as the innocent and chaste Barbie doll. He dresses the little boys, like he dressed up as a kid or how he wanted to dress up. Either way, in his mind, he is relieving the boys of their suffering, preserving them as their most beautiful, flawless selves—like the Barbie dolls he always craved to be.'

'He's a eunuch?' said Simone.

'Could be a transgender person also. There's a difference.'

'How does any of it matter, Zoya? It might look cool in a Netflix drama like *Criminal Minds* but delving into his . . .

her . . . the Doll Maker's psyche doesn't help us. Facts and evidence help us. And that is why I asked for this.' Simone held up the slim file that the constable had handed to her. 'Knowing where the Doll Maker might strike next will help us stay ahead in the game.'

'I agree,' admitted Zoya, 'but there is room for both: fact-based investigation and behaviour-based profiling. Together, they work better,' Zoya snorted. 'Kind of like us. Poles apart. Contrasting personalities. But, I guess, together we work better,' Zoya smiled at Simone.

Simone looked away from her. She opened the file and pretended to read it. 'I'm sorry,' she murmured.

'You said something?'

Simone closed her eyes and exhaled. 'I'm sorry, okay?' she said aloud. 'I'm sorry for before. You were right. I can be an utter and complete bitch when I am mad. I have always been that way. When someone scorns me, my tongue automatically turns razor sharp. I can't help it.' Simone sighed. 'It's just who I've become. Not sure why. Not sure if I can control it or change it. But I know it.' Simone couldn't bring herself to look at Zoya.

Suddenly, she felt Zoya's hand, soft and gentle, on her forearm.

'Knowing is the first step to self-improvement, Simone. You can't improve if you don't know.' Zoya squeezed her forearm softly. 'You are young. You are rash. And, yes, you can be a bitch. But you are also much, much more. You are sharp, disciplined and painfully honest. Use that. Use the positives to overcome the negatives. And, if it fails, I am here for you. I can help. I *am* a trained psychoanalyst, you know,' Zoya gave her a knowing smile.

Simone pursed her lips, her eyes welling. Her heart swelled, like a weight had suddenly been lifted. She had never had a friend. Never knew companionship. But, today, in this moment, for the very first time, she experienced the soft embrace of friendship. Someone understood her. Someone saw her for who she could be, not just for who she was. It both broke and mended her heart.

She squeezed Zoya's hand, her grip firm and tight, as if latching on to hope, holding on to a wish that could fly away in the blink of an eye.

No words were spoken. None were needed when the flower of friendship unfurled its petals for the first time, revealing a blossom so lovely that all you could do was shut up.

'So, what does your file say?' asked Zoya, her eyes looking up at the khaki file Simone was holding.

Simone sniffled. She read through the single sheet of paper inside the file. 'Only four.'

'What?' asked Zoya.

'Four kids reported missing by single fathers in the last week. Three we know—the three murdered boys. The fourth was reported missing yesterday. A special kid with Down's Syndrome.'

'I think we've just found our next victim,' said Zoya.

Simone bit her lower lip and smiled, 'Even better. I think I know how to find *where* he'll strike next.'

31

Irshad woke up with a start, his eyes bleary, his head whirling. He shook his head to see if it would help with the dizziness. He checked the clock on the wall: 9.25 a.m. He had slept on this office sofa for more than four hours.

There was sharp rapping on his office door again.

He grimaced. To his hungover self, the knocking sounded like someone was drilling inside his head.

'Come in,' he muttered.

The door opened slightly and a young man pushed his head through the little space between the door and the jamb. He was probably in his early twenties, wearing fluorescent red glasses and hair coiffed into spikes with the help of a generous dose of hair gel.

'May I come in, sir?' he asked.

'I said come in!' Irshad shouted and frowned as his own loud words wreaked havoc inside his head. He clutched his head and sat still.

The young man walked in like he owned the place, a laptop in hand, and a smirk plastered on his face. He wore tattered jeans and a T-shirt that read: ERROR 404. Irshad didn't understand what that meant. Was the young man calling himself a conceivable error in family planning on the part of his parents?

'Good morning, sir! I am Pius from cyber crime. How are you, sir?'

Pius's impeccable white teeth gleamed in the morning light. He looked like he'd stepped out of a dental-clinic ad. Or even a hair-gel ad.

Groaning, Irshad pointed at the sofa and asked him to sit down. He had asked the superintendent of the cyber crime unit to send his brightest up for help with the Clipper case. Didn't expect the brightest to be so flashy. And young.

'Are you okay, sir? You don't look okay. I can come back later if you like?' Irshad didn't answer. 'Or can I get you a glass of water? Or maybe lemon soda?' asked Pius.

Irshad's brain cells protested against all the yapping.

'Stop talking for a minute, will you?' Irshad yelled. He shut his eyes and massaged his temples in an attempt to alleviate the bubbling headache. 'Yes, you can get me some water, please.'

Pius jumped up, put his laptop in the centre of the table and rushed out of the office like the building was on fire.

Irshad shook his head and chuckled. It seemed like Pius was either high on cocaine or coffee; the guy had way too much energy.

There was another knock on the door. 'May I come in, sir?' asked Pius, thrusting a glass of water through the door.

'Of course! You don't need to ask again.' Irshad was fast losing patience with the ball of energy whizzing around him. All he needed was some peace and quiet. He sighed. He had a feeling that it wasn't going to be an option as long as Pius was in the room.

Pius charged in carrying not one but two glasses of water. He thrust both in front of Irshad. 'I thought you need more water. You look like you need a jugful of water. But there were no jugs at the water station, only glasses. I also asked the inspector. He said—'

'Pius!' Irshad raised a hand. 'Thank you. Sit down. And stop talking.'

Pius smiled, his white teeth shining brighter than the office's wallpaper. He flopped down on the sofa, still brimming with enthusiasm.

Irshad was parched. He gulped down both glasses of water and smacked his lips. The headache eased a little. He felt better.

'Thank you,' he said again.

'You are most welcome, sir!' Pius grinned.

'And thank you for coming in on short notice to help with the Clipper case.'

'Oh, I am so excited, sir!'

'Oh, you are excited? I couldn't tell.' Irshad had meant to sound sarcastic. But his tone was flat and serious.

Pius perked up in his seat. 'Oh, yes, sir! This is my first time on a serial killer case. I've only seen serial killer movies. The suspense, the intrigue. Now I get to work on one in real life. So exciting! Only yesterday, I was—'

'I get it,' Irshad cut him off and made a mental note to not make offhand comments again, lest Pius went off like an untethered horse. 'Let's get started.'

Irshad stood up with a groan and walked to his desk. He picked up a Ziploc bag containing a smartphone, dragged his feet back to the guest sofa and slumped down.

'This phone belonged to the latest victim of the Clipper. We ran the victim's prints. He was a known escort. A tranny.'

Pius raised his hand.

'What?' asked Irshad.

'No judgement, sir. We are all equal. Full support to the LGBTQIA+ community.'

Irshad rolled his eyes. He carried on, 'The victim was arrested for prostitution a few years ago. No jail time and no police record since but I think the victim was still doing it under the radar. I want to know how. I want to understand how he was getting clients. I want to know how he got in touch with the Clipper. What did they talk about? Any clue, anything at all that can lead me to the bastard.'

'You want me to hack the phone?'

Irshad just stared at him.

'Easy-peasy! No sweat, sir,' said Pius.

He took the Ziploc bag from Irshad and fished out the phone. Pius connected the phone to his laptop using a USB cord and started tapping on his laptop.

Irshad lay back on the sofa, closed his eyes and took a deep breath. Sure, he was tired—his limbs ached, and his head throbbed—but he felt that he was closer to catching the Clipper than ever before. The Clipper had changed his MO, left behind clues that he usually didn't. Heck, this time, he left the whole body, replete with potential clues. Except, this time, he hadn't gifted the victim's testicles to the police. Maybe, it had been a keepsake for him? Irshad was convinced that there was a lair somewhere where the Clipper buried the bodies of his victims. All he had to do was nab the bastard and bury him alive in that lair. Irshad scoffed. He had been telling himself that for nine years. Nothing had come to fruition. But now he felt a wee bit more confident. He was getting closer. He could feel it.

'Done!' announced Pius.

Irshad's eyes shot open. 'What?'

'I'm in.'

Pius showed the phone to Irshad. The screen was lit up, the colourful apps on the home screen danced in the light, waiting to be tapped open.

'It's one of the old smartphone models. Easy to hack into. For me, at least,' nodded Pius proudly.

'Clearly,' snorted Irshad. He patted the young man's shoulder. 'Good job! Now, how was the victim communicating with the Clipper? We know they met at a seedy hotel. They must have discussed the date, time and place somehow. Let's start with the last dialled or received phone calls twenty-four hours prior to the murder. Can you give me a list of the numbers?'

Pius pressed a few keys on his laptop and said, 'Done!'

The printer in Irshad's office started whirring almost instantly.

Pius jumped up, went to the printer and came back with a printout. 'Here's the list of phone numbers and names as saved by the victim.'

'How did you connect your laptop to my office printer?'

Pius raised his eyebrows and chuckled. 'Sir, you do realize that hacking into a stranger's phone is a lot more difficult than connecting to a printer within the police department?'

Irshad was impressed. He hoped some of his own detectives showed the same amount of initiative.

'What next, sir?'

Pius's energy was starting to rub off on Irshad. He felt awake, driven, raring to go.

'Okay, let's divide and conquer. I'll check out the numbers on this list,' he pointed to the printout. 'I want you to start with the victim's online history. In all previous cases, as we didn't have the victims' mobile phones, we remotely checked the call and email history. Both checked out. There was nothing amiss. We concluded that the Clipper doesn't communicate via phone calls. Or emails. It was like the Clipper was communicating with his victims telepathically!'

'Ha!' Pius grinned. 'That's not possible, sir.'

'Exactly! So, how *does* he communicate?'

'There are numerous other ways to communicate. Assuming what you said is true and considering they were indulging in questionable activities; my guess is that the victims met the Clipper on the dark web.'

'Dark web? Where is that?'

Pius's grin broadened, 'Online, sir.'

'Okay, so let's look for the place on Google?'

Pius laughed out loud. 'Okay, let me explain, sir. There are many hidden places online, mostly illegal, which we cannot simply search on Google. You need to know the exact address and password to enter these places.'

Irshad must have looked dumbfounded because Pius said, 'Let me give you an example. It's like you've built an underground bunker that nobody is aware of and you padlock it so that nobody can open it without the key. For someone to access that bunker, they would need the exact coordinates of the place *and* the key. Now, you may decide to tell your wife about the bunker and give her a duplicate key so she can enter.'

Irshad nodded.

'Similarly, there are illegal websites selling drugs, murder-for-hire, pornography . . . you get the gist. You can't search for them unless you know the exact IP address of the website and the password that is given to trustworthy members only.'

'That's it!' said Irshad, his voice brimming with exhilaration. 'I think that's how the Clipper communicates!'

Pius's shoulders drooped, as if Irshad hadn't been listening to a single word he had said. 'Maybe so, sir. But we still don't know either the website address or the password.'

Irshad beamed. 'That's where you come in, my friend. Search the victim's phone. Search his browsing history.' Irshad bit his lower lip in anticipation. 'Take all the time you need but find the Clipper's bunker!'

32

'How do you know *where* to find the Doll Maker?' asked Zoya.

'I have a hunch. But I need to make a call first.'

Simone took out her smartphone. She opened the slim file with the other hand, found the phone number she was looking for and tapped in the digits.

'Who are you calling?'

'The father of the latest kid reported missing.'

'Why?'

Simone put a finger to her lips, shushing Zoya. She put the phone on speaker.

It started ringing.

'Hel—hello,' a man stammered as he answered the call.

'Is this Mr Goyal?' said Simone.

'Yes, that's me. Who are you?'

'I'm ASP Simone Singh calling to inquire about your son.'

'Oh, hello, ma'am! Did you find Kalpesh?' The sudden hope in his voice boomed inside the conference room.

Simone ran a finger down the list of missing children. 'Yes, Kalpesh. That's your son, right?'

'Yes . . . have you found him?'

Simone found it intriguing that the parents had named their kid *Kalpesh*—the god of perfection.

'Unfortunately, no. We have not found Kalpesh yet.'

'Oh . . .' his voice trailed off; his hopes dashed.

Simone continued, 'The investigation is still ongoing, Mr Goyal . . . I have one question for you though? It may help us locate your son.'

'Yes, yes, anything.'

'How did your wife die?'

There was a pause. Only the sound of static crackled through the speaker.

'What does that have to do with my son's disappearance?'

'It may help us, Mr Goyal. Please answer the question.'

He breathed in loudly over the phone, as if gathering strength. 'She died in an accident. A horrific accident.' His voice cracked.

'What sort of an accident?'

'We were doing *parikrama* in the temple. Offering prayers for the well-being of our son. Her pallu came in contact with a stray diya and . . .' Mr Goyal gulped aloud over the phone. He sniffled.

'. . . Her sari immediately caught fire. It was some synthetic material. I had *told* her not to wear that sari,' he was shouting over the phone now. 'It was too flashy and too shiny to wear at the temple.'

Simone closed her eyes and let out a sigh. She wanted to grab him by the shoulders and shake him. His wife dies and he finds her choice of sari culpable? Stupid, stupid man!

Mr Goyal regained his composure. 'Within seconds, the whole sari caught fire. People at the temple rushed to help. Eventually, we managed to douse the fire with water and rushed her to the hospital. But it was too late. She suffered serious burns and died the next day.'

Zoya slumped down, her head in her hands.

Simone exhaled.

'Do you know what still haunts me to this day?' continued Mr Goyal.

Simone kept silent.

'Her sari melted into her burnt skin, as if they were one and the same,' Mr Goyal said as he broke down, his cries booming off the speaker, his snuffles unrestrained.

Simone didn't know what to say. What was the right protocol to pacify a stranger in such a situation? She decided to ask the question she had called to ask.

'Can you tell me the name of the temple, Mr Goyal?'

The question silenced his cries, as if he suddenly realized that he wasn't alone.

'It . . .' He sniffed, gathering himself. 'It was Birla Mandir, the Vishnu temple on Arera Hills. I never . . .' He sniffed again. '. . . never went there again.'

'Thank you, Mr Goyal. That's all I wanted to know for now.'

Simone disconnected the call.

Both women sat in silence for a moment. They exchanged glances but no words were spoken and no gestures made.

Finally, Zoya said, 'I am guessing the temple has something to do with the Doll Maker?'

Simone clasped her hands and nodded. 'Yes, my hunch is that's where we'll find the Doll Maker. That's where he'll leave the next kid, dressed as a Barbie doll.'

'How do you figure?'

'In both the murder cases so far—the first kid found at the Bhopal Gas Tragedy memorial and the twins found at DB City Mall—the Doll Maker left the encased bodies at places where the mothers had died. Remember what the father of the first kid told us? His wife died of complications during childbirth because of a congenital birth defect due to the Bhopal Gas Tragedy.'

Zoya stared into space. She nodded slowly.

'And the twins. When I asked their father, he told me that the mother died after she fell from the top floor of DB City Mall.'

'Are you saying that the places chosen by the Doll Maker are not random? There is meaning behind these places?'

'Yes! Like everything else—the type of kids chosen, the encased Barbie dolls, the thumbprints of the fathers on the foreheads—everything is calculated and meticulously planned, including the locations where the Doll Maker leaves the bodies.'

'Your theory makes sense,' said Zoya. 'It's like the Doll Maker is blaming the fathers but venerating the mothers. Honouring them with innocent Barbie dolls. There is a method to the madness. A reason behind the rashness. That's what makes a psychotic serial killer more dangerous than a random one-off murderer.'

Simone shrugged. 'Not so sure about that. There is safety in randomness. Now that we have figured out his reasons and his processes, he is more vulnerable than ever before,' Simone smiled, 'and if we hurry, we just might catch him in the act.'

33

Nalini's eyes were flushed red. The tears had flowed non-stop, made her neck damp and pooled on her blouse. She wanted to cry. She wanted to shriek. But her dry eyes revolted; her parched throat rebelled.

Water. I need water, she thought.

Nalini whimpered. She let go of the boy's feet and picked herself up from the floor. Her shoulders drooped; her head wilted. The burden of murder dragged her down.

She trudged to the bedside table and picked up a flask of water. Just about to take a sip, she stopped.

She slapped herself across the face, a hard blow packed with pent-up rage, sadness and remorse. Her right cheek twitched in pain.

She walked over to the full-length mirror.

A clear handprint, pink with purple hues, slightly swollen, was visible on her right cheek.

She slapped herself again. And again. And again. Like a deranged woman, consumed by guilt, mad at her own existence.

Her cheek throbbed; the pain unbearable.

'Nothing . . .' she pointed an accusing finger at her reflection in the mirror. Her voice was deep and hoarse, like a man's. It was the voice she was born with. 'Nothing will make up for what you did, Nalini. Absolutely nothing!'

She moved closer to the mirror.

'You have never deserved anything but death. Dad was right to banish you. First you killed Mom. Then, Dad. And now, this sweet, little kid.' Her voice cracked.

'You were supposed to free him of his suffering, Nalini. Instead, you sent him to hell—squirming, kicking and gasping for the life he deserved.'

She jammed a finger at the mirror, as if jamming it in the chest of her reflection.

'You know, the day Mom died, I wish you had died instead.'

Nalini let out a shrill cry and fell to the floor.

'I know, I know,' she whimpered, her voice soft and feminine again. 'I wish the same.'

A fresh stream of tears flowed down her swollen cheek. All her eyes needed was a break to make more tears before the floodgates opened again.

Seconds turned to minutes. Minutes to an hour. Nalini stayed on the floor, her hair flopped over her face, her eyes ruddy and her right cheek more purple than pink.

Her head jerked up when a realization hit her.

'But I can still try. I can still give him an honourable send-off. I can still send him to his mother, as dignified and innocent as he was the day he was born.'

Nalini got up.

She would need to clean the body first. Get rid of all forensic evidence—her fingerprints on his neck, her skin cells under his nails while he had struggled and fought. She wasn't too concerned about the hair. It was a wig, bought by the dozen. But better safe than sorry—a mantra that had kept her in good stead so far.

Nalini walked over to the lavender-pink cupboards opposite the bed. She unlocked and opened all of them. The cupboards were stacked with the sundry items needed for her seven-day-redemption plan—disposable gloves, shower caps, hazmat suits, ski-masks, wigs, glue guns, a homemade mix of alcohol-bleach in spray bottles, make-up kits and shiny new glass cases.

Nalini pulled on a pair of disposable gloves, a shower cap and a hazmat suit, and got to work. She picked up the little boy and gently placed him on the floor. She removed his clothes and scrubbed his body with the homemade mixture of alcohol and bleach. She took out a glass case from the cupboard and cleaned every inch of it. Once done, Nalini stood up and breathed in the smell of clean—her favourite smell.

She threw away the gloves and changed into a new pair. The next part was sacred. She did not want even a speck of dirt on the Barbie doll.

Nalini opened her wardrobe and pulled out the clothes she had picked for her special baby doll—a red silk sari, already draped so that it could be put on like a pair of pyjamas, a green blouse with a bright yellow border on the sleeves, an ornate golden crown and matching bangles, a nose pin, a pendant and sandals. A Barbie doll dressed like Goddess Lakshmi.

For a moment Nalini felt giddy and contented. She imagined how beautiful the boy would look—as perfect as his name: Kalpesh.

Nalini dressed the boy while he lay rigid and unmoving on the floor. She opened the front door of the glass case. She picked up the boy and propped him inside the display case, against the built-in supports that kept the body upright.

The next part was the hardest. It always disturbed her. But, like the endeavour itself, it had to be done. She brought out the glue gun from the cupboard. It contained a stick of industrial-grade adhesive. She pinched open the lifeless eyes of the little boy and glued them open. The unpleasant, pungent odour of glue tickled her nasal hair. Nalini hunched forward and marvelled at how a thin line of glue reignited the last vestiges of life within the boy. He was back. He was alive. He was looking back at her, smiling with his eyes.

'I miss you, baby,' said Nalini. 'And I'm sorry for earlier. I didn't mean to. You know that, right?' She caressed the boy's pallid face.

Make-up time, she suddenly realized. The boy needed make-up. A lot of it. Especially for the marks she'd left on his neck.

Nalini applied a heavy dose of primer and foundation, and followed it up with dollops of blush, mascara and lip gloss. It helped. The boy looked more and more like she wanted him to—like a girl. Nalini put a wig of flowing, shoulder-length hair over the boy's head. The crown and the jewellery came next.

Nalini stepped back, delighted at her creation. Exactly the way Mom used to dress her up.

'*So* gorgeous!' she squealed, clapping her hands.

Mom would have been so proud, she thought.

'Now, for the finishing touch,' Nalini mumbled.

The thumbprint on the forehead.

She changed her gloves for the third time. It was essential for this step.

Nalini opened the refrigerator and pulled out a plastic box as small as a ring box. There was a Post-it note stuck on the lid. It read: *Number 4, Kalpesh.*

She opened the lid. Inside was a printed circuit board with a raised protrusion in the middle—the thumbprint of Kalpesh's father.

The task had seemed difficult to pull off during planning, but a quick Google search had given her the step-by-step method to create fake fingerprints. Step one was to source the original thumbprints. She had used a simple ruse: walk past the victims' fathers on the street, drop your laminated phone, keep walking like you're unaware of your loss till they call you out, pick up your phone and give it back to you. The least a gentleman would do for a careless woman in public.

The laminated film on the phone turned out to be a perfect surface for the thumbprints. She had dusted the thumbprint with powdered graphite from pencil lead, taken a high-resolution photo of the thumbprints and used a photo-editing software to flip the photo to create a mirror image of the print. The last step involved printing it on to tracing paper and then using a UV engraving machine she had bought on Amazon to create a physical print on a circuit board. Done! Thank you, Google, for the step-by-step instructions.

With utmost care, like holding a newborn baby, Nalini took out the circuit board. She bent down and stamped the forehead of the dead boy with the physical print.

She sighed. Her eyes moistened. The print represented all the trauma and malice that had pervaded the child's life since his mother died. Just like it had pervaded Nalini's after Dad killed Mom. An indelible dark mark left forever.

Nalini closed the glass case.

The little girl was ready to go to her resting place at Birla Mandir.

34

'No sign of the Doll Maker yet,' Simone said into her mobile hands-free device.

Static crackled on the police radio, before Zoya's voice boomed. 'Same here. Stay on high alert.'

Birla Mandir was a temple of marble and sandstone, with a towering maroon *shikhara* or mountain peak, standing sentinel atop the rolling, lush green Arera Hills. It offered visitors a panoramic view of the adjoining forest and lake beyond.

The temple had two entrances: an elaborate front entrance with a majestic arch that welcomed visitors into a central courtyard, which was as big as a football field, and a side entrance that linked directly to the heart of the temple, cutting down time for devotees not interested in a leisurely walk through the courtyard.

Simone sat in her Thar across the narrow street that linked to the temple's side entrance, while Zoya covered the front entrance. Five police inspectors in plain clothes patrolled the temple premises inside. The plan was to let the Doll Maker stroll in, as if nothing was out of place, and then nab the perp red-handed. Case closed.

The only question was—would the Doll Maker show up *today*?

Simone stood by her reasoning. The Doll Maker had proven to be a stickler for process, meticulous about detail. Simone was convinced that the location mattered to the Doll Maker. It was like a grand stage to unveil the next Barbie doll. And this was the stage to showcase the next murder. Right here.

But would he . . . or she? Simone decided to refer to the Doll Maker as he now that they knew his gender—would he come today? Or tomorrow? Or never?

Simone sighed. She stretched her arms and rotated her neck. For a moment she was entranced by the low-hanging clouds floating in front of her. She peered at the misty, green hill sloping down on her right. A group of devotees was walking up the narrow staircase that ran from the bottom to the top of the forested hill. Simone watched an old woman make the arduous climb, huffing and puffing as she reached the top, before smiling broadly, showing her toothless gums and then trudging across the street to the temple's side entrance. Simone had never understood what made people devote their entire lives to religion. What made them climb a thousand steps in their old age just to visit a deity of stone?

Simone's phone rang and she picked it up on the first ring. It was Dr D'Souza, the lead medical examiner.

'What is it, doc?' she came to the point. A lapse in concentration and she'd miss the Doll Maker.

'Hello, Simone. How are you doing?'

'Fine. Anything I can help with?'

'You sound busy, Simone. So, I'll make it quick.'

Simone rolled her eyes. *So, make it quick . . . don't tell me that you'll make it quick!*

Dr D'Souza said, 'We found the cause of death. We know how the Doll Maker is killing the kids.'

'Go on.'

'With no physical injuries, no signs of needle puncture marks and the kids being too young for heart attacks, it was clear that we were looking for deadly toxins.'

'What do you mean?'

'Poison.'

'But you said the toxicology report was clean?'

'Yes, I did. Which is why it was such a mystery to me. It had to be a poison, but it wasn't. So, we tested the three victims again. Once again, the tests were negative for known poisons. It didn't make any sense.'

Dr D'Souza was rambling now, narrating the story from the beginning. *Why couldn't people just come to the bloody point?*

'So, I did a bit of research on toxins which evade our usual tests,' said Dr D'Souza. 'And I found one. The kids were killed with plant-based poison from the suicide tree.'

'Suicide tree?'

'Yes!' Dr D'Souza sounded like an excited kid. 'It's a tree called *Cerbera odollam*, found in south India, mostly Kerala. It produces a sweet, juicy fruit. You would love it. But, its seed, ooh, that's a silent killer. One bite of the seed kills an adult within an hour; a kid, much faster. It goes undetected in regular tests unless you employ advanced and more expensive techniques.'

Simone stroked her chin. It was interesting information but didn't help her investigation. The Doll Maker showing up at the temple would help her investigation. Still no sign of him.

Dr D'Souza continued. 'Many years ago, there was a spurt in suicides in Kerala. A team of toxicology experts was brought in from France . . .'

Simone pinched the bridge of her nose. *There he goes again*, she thought as Dr D'Souza recounted the mystery of the suicide tree.

'At first, just like our case, nothing made sense to the French scientists. The only common link between all the suicides was the spicy food found in the stomachs of the dead. But then, who doesn't eat spicy food in our country?' Dr D'Souza chortled like he had cracked a joke.

I don't eat spicy food, Simone wanted to correct him, but didn't want the doctor to go off on a tangent and start another story about statistics on spicy food. She bit her lower lip and listened.

'They examined the spicy food found in the belly using high-performance liquid chromatography coupled with mass spectrometry—the incredibly advanced but expensive techniques I mentioned earlier—and found traces of the *Cerbera* plant. And, because they had funding, they ran the test on the autopsy tissue of more than 500 victims over a ten-year period and found that half of them had died from ingesting *Cerbera* seeds. The number was astonishingly and statistically too high for suicide rates seen in Kerala. And, you know what they realized?'

'What?' said Simone.

'Most of the presumed suicides were homicides. *Cerbera* is the perfect murder weapon. The victim dies naturally in his or her sleep. The plant doesn't show up in the toxicology report. And the killer walks away scot-free because nobody even realizes that it's a murder.'

Simone gasped.

'Interesting, right?' he said.

That wasn't why Simone had gasped. A white delivery van had come up the hill and turned into the narrow side street that led to Birla Mandir. It wouldn't have bothered Simone, except for two anomalies that told her something was amiss.

First, there was no branding or logo on the van, which was odd because no delivery company would let go of a free marketing opportunity. Look at Zomato or Swiggy or even Amazon; even their delivery boys carry bags emblazoned with the company's logo. But it wasn't completely unthinkable.

Second, the driver of the delivery van was a woman in a sari. Despite the mist, Simone noticed her shimmering pink lips and sunglasses from across the street. Who wears sunglasses when the sun is hidden behind grey clouds? Again, not unthinkable. But when Simone combined the two anomalies, her stomach churned.

The Doll Maker was here.

'Sorry, doc. I have to go.'

Simone disconnected the call.

35

Zoya's radio crackled.

'He is here. The Doll Maker is here.' Simone's voice boomed on the radio. 'All officers take note. He is coming through the side entrance in an all-white, delivery van. Dressed as a woman in a sari. Watch out for the woman dropping off a glass case inside the temple.'

Zoya pressed a button on her walkie-talkie to speak. 'You block the side exit, Simone. I'm going in through the front.'

The walkie-talkie crackled. Static. No response from Simone.

'Simone?'

'Yes, noted,' said Simone.

Zoya heaved a sigh of relief. One couldn't always trust a loose cannon like Simone to stick to the plan. They had decided to block the exit that the Doll Maker used. Zoya was to block the front entrance if that was used and Simone the side entrance. Simone had drawn the short straw. She had to stay put in her position, while Zoya closed in on the perp from the front entrance.

'I'm driving into the side street. Closing off this exit. No way is that delivery van getting out of here,' said Simone on the radio.

Zoya jumped out of the police van. She walked over to the front arch of the temple. She removed her shoes and touched the ground with her right hand before entering the temple, out of respect. Zoya was a devout Parsi. Sure, Birla Mandir was a Hindu temple, but a place of worship demanded respect.

'I've entered the temple veranda,' said Zoya into the radio. Her breathing escalated.

Temple bells clanged and echoed.

'No sign of the Doll Maker inside the temple,' said an inspector on the radio.

Zoya rushed across the cemented pathway in the open central courtyard, surrounded by lush green lawns on either side. She was panting, her heart racing.

'Do you have a visual?' Simone's voice came over the radio.

Many inspectors replied in unison, 'No.' 'Not yet.' 'No.'

Zoya stopped. Held up the radio and barked, 'Let's not scare him away with our radios, people. Talk only if necessary.'

Zoya hoped Simone got the message. It was near impossible to keep the woman away from the action.

Zoya glanced around the courtyard. It was late afternoon, but devotees thronged the temple. Probably for aarti. The number of devotees in the temple was higher today because it was a public holiday. Zoya was one such devotee herself. She wasn't complaining.

She stopped before entering the grand hall and glanced around.

No sign of the Doll Maker. No sign of a Barbie in a glass case.

She recognized two of her inspectors strolling along nonchalantly and talking to each other like two friends who met in the temple daily to discuss religion and politics—the nation's two favourite pastimes.

Zoya entered the inner sanctum of the temple and was immediately greeted by the sweet, intoxicating fragrance of incense and the piercing ringing of bells. She never quite understood the concept of bells—unless it was to inform God of your arrival. Like ringing a doorbell at someone's house.

It was colder inside the grand hall. The marble floor sent frigid darts up her feet despite her woollen socks. She shivered.

The hall was chock-a-block with devotees, who were dressed impeccably in vibrant rainbow colours. A dash of violet here, a pop of yellow there and bursts of red everywhere. She felt like she had walked into a wedding reception. Some devotees stood with their palms folded and heads lowered in prayers. The others sat on the floor, deep in meditation or in long negotiations with Goddess Lakshmi about, what else, money. Just seeing them sitting on the cold marble floor made Zoya shiver harder.

She walked in further, towards the beautiful idols of Lord Vishnu and Goddess Lakshmi. The idols stood together, decked in gleaming golden jewellery and satiny attire, wearing wide smiles and showering their blessings on all and sundry.

Zoya looked around the side entrance to the grand hall. Still no sign of the Doll Maker.

Zoya slipped to the front of the crowd, bowed her head and prayed. For a few seconds she forgot about catching the Doll Maker, about putting up with Simone's antics or about the promotion that had eluded her for years despite her track record. She thought about her son, Sunny. She missed him a lot. So much that it made her heart ache. She prayed that no mother should suffer the torment of meeting her son only once a week. She prayed that the motion she had filed in the high court against her ex-husband for Sunny's custody be accepted by the court. And, of course, she prayed for the good health and happiness of her son—the only ray of sunshine that shone through the grey cloud hovering over her since the past week. Zoya was depressed. As a trained psychoanalyst, she knew it. She knew she had to get help before the dark, tiny tentacles of deep sorrow mushroomed into the crushing hold of clinical depression. In that small window of happiness—the thought of Sunny soothing her ache—Zoya decided to see a psychiatrist tomorrow. It was time to reclaim her happiness.

Zoya raised her head and opened her eyes. Her vision was blurry with tears—of relief, of intent, of belief that tomorrow would bring joy.

Zoya quickly wiped her tears, pretending as if a dust particle was irritating her eye, as she was on duty. Three inspectors, her juniors, were inside the hall. She didn't want to show any sign of weakness in front of them. It was tough for men to cry but it was tougher for working women on duty.

Zoya shifted with the crowd to do a *parikrama* or circumambulation around the deities. Light dappled through the meshed windows built into the peripheral brick wall of the temple, creating a crisscross pattern of shadows on the walls of the shrine.

Where the hell was the Doll Maker? It had been close to ten minutes since Simone had radioed them about the Doll Maker's presence.

Zoya ambled across the circular pathway around the idols. Her eyes watched every woman wearing a sari like a hawk. Zoya was right behind the idols when her radio crackled with static. Zoya pulled it closer to her ear.

'He is inside,' someone hissed over the radio. Zoya recognized the voice of the inspector who was sitting by the side door, pretending to be deep in meditation.

She walked faster, unclasping the holster that carried her service revolver.

'Excuse me,' she said, trying to push past a coterie of old women walking side-by-side, faster than snails but slower than tortoises. 'Sorry. Excuse me, please,' she said again.

The women turned and stared at her with disdain but gave way.

Zoya heard them murmur something as she hurtled past them but couldn't make out what they were saying. She circled back to the front. Suddenly, she stopped in her tracks.

The Doll Maker, dressed in a red sari, hair in a bun, stood facing the metal railing that separated the crowd from the idols. A swinging door was built into the railing for the priest and temple staff to enter the area next to the idols.

The audacity, thought Zoya, as the Doll Maker unlocked the gate in full view of the devotees, pretending to be a temple staff member. From his profile, the Doll Maker looked like a woman. If Zoya didn't know better, there was no way she would have guessed that a crafty man was hiding behind 5.5 metres of chiffon.

A blue cooler with a white lid lay at the Doll Maker's feet.

Zoya's pulse raced. She inched forward. In her peripheral vision, she saw the inspectors follow her lead and move in. The plan was that she would nab the culprit and the inspectors would block any form of escape. It was all going according to plan. So far.

The Doll Maker swung open the gate, picked up the cooler and entered the space next to the idols. He didn't look around in fear even once. The perp was as cool as the chilly breeze flowing in through the temple's mesh windows.

Zoya kept her right hand on her holster, ready to pull out her revolver at any moment.

The Doll Maker tottered around the idols, heavy cooler in hand, towards the full-length, glass case built into the wall at the back.

Zoya entered the open gate and inched closer.

The Doll Maker laid the cooler on the floor, wiped his forehead with the back of his hand and bent down to remove the lid.

Zoya tiptoed to where he was hunkered down on the floor. He looked over his shoulder.

Zoya gasped.

A doll encased in a glass case lay snug inside the cooler. A beautiful little statue dressed like Goddess Lakshmi. The doll seemed so life-like, so real. Just as suddenly, Zoya realized—it *was* real. It was a dead little child.

She pulled out her revolver and jammed the muzzle into the Doll Maker's head. 'You are under arrest!'

36

Simone was tapping her foot on the car floor mat, her patience running out and anxiety taking over. There was total radio silence since an inspector had announced that the Doll Maker was inside the temple hall.

What was happening? Had they nabbed the perp? Or worse, had he escaped into the forest surrounding the temple? It was five inspectors and Zoya against the Doll Maker. Six against one. Highly unlikely that he'd be able to escape. But one shouldn't count their chickens before they're hatched.

Simone waited, chewing the insides of her cheeks.

Suddenly, in the distance, she saw the white delivery van crawling back from the temple. The driver seemed to be in no rush.

'Shit!' said Simone.

How was this possible? How did six officers miss a slender man in a sari?

Simone fastened her seat belt in a flash and started the Thar. One hand gripped the steering wheel, the other the radio. There was no way she would let the delivery van pass. Even if it meant ramming her Thar head-on into the oncoming vehicle.

She clicked the radio. 'Zoya! Come in, Zoya!'

No response.

Dammit!

'The Doll Maker is back in the van. Escaping. I repeat, he is escaping!'

The delivery van was less than 100 metres away.

The radio hissed.

'What?' It was Zoya. 'Impossible! We have the Doll Maker in custody.'

'I don't know who you have in custody, but the delivery van is hurtling towards me and the same person is driving it—a woman wearing sunglasses and a black sari.'

The van was fifty metres away and closing in.

'Shit!' said Zoya.

'What?' said Simone.

'The person we apprehended is in a red sari,' said Zoya. 'She resisted the arrest saying that she is one of the temple staff members who just received the delivery of this new idol of Goddess Lakshmi from a benefactor and that she was just putting it in place. She said we have the wrong person in custody. But every accused says that when caught, don't they?'

Simone's heart beat faster. In that moment, she knew that Zoya and the team had the wrong person in custody. She knew she had to stop the oncoming van at any cost.

The van was twenty metres away, picking up speed.

It was now or never.

Simone dropped the radio. She put the Thar in gear.

Ten metres away.

Simone twisted the steering wheel. The Thar turned sharply from the kerb, the driver's side directly in the path of the oncoming van.

For a brief second, the Doll Maker swivelled his head, his mouth opened in shock. He wore huge sunglasses. Despite the sunglasses, Simone knew he was looking at her with surprise and rage.

The Doll Maker tried to swerve but it was too late.

There was a loud crash as metal rammed metal. Bits and pieces of plastic and aluminium from the front bumper, and shards of glass from the van's headlights, flew in every direction like shrapnel.

The collision threw Simone sideways but the seat belt pulled her back. Her right elbow banged into the metal rim of the door, cutting her skin. She winced.

But, otherwise, the sturdy Thar had kept her safe.

She looked up.

The delivery van was a mess. The radiator grille and bumper had caved in and the bonnet had folded into a triangle on impact. Metal shards had flown into the windshield, riddling it with cracks. The airbag had deployed but looked like a crumpled football now that it had deflated. The Doll Maker sat stunned behind the wheel. The sunglasses had broken in half when his face had slammed into the airbag; one half of the sunglasses was dangling from the bridge of his nose. A deep gash had opened over his left brow.

Their eyes met.

It seemed to jolt the Doll Maker out of his momentary shock. He grimaced and flinched as he touched the cut over his brow. His lips trembled and his jaw twitched, as if he were mouthing obscenities at Simone. She couldn't hear what he was saying, which made her realize that she needed to get out of the Thar to arrest him. And pronto. She twisted and unclasped the seat belt.

The Doll Maker seemed to read her mind. He flicked the broken sunglasses off his face and removed his seat belt. He opened the van door.

Simone tried to open her door. It wouldn't budge.

'Shit!' she said aloud.

The Doll Maker, his movement constrained by the sari, pulled both legs up and climbed out of the van. Simone couldn't help but notice his white sneakers shining bright against his black sari fall. Even under pressure, his life under threat, he swayed with feminine flair, each gesture elegant, each movement deliberate. One couldn't tell, if unaware, that it wasn't a woman but a man.

Simone tried the door again. It budged slightly. She jammed her shoulder against the door and pushed it. 'Come on!' she yelled. The door opened a little more.

She looked up. The Doll Maker was hopping away from the crash site towards the T-junction where the side street met the main road. She shifted sideways in her seat, pulled up her long legs and rammed them against the door. Once, twice. The door flew open on her second attempt. The pungent smell of radiator coolant from the van wafted in. Simone wrinkled her nose.

The Doll Maker was about twenty metres away. Escaping.

Simone wriggled out of the Thar and dashed after him. She was taller and her stride longer. Her trousers gave her a distinct advantage over the Doll Maker's sari. She gained on him, her boots slapping hard against the asphalt road.

The Doll Maker looked back. His pupils dilated. He hopped faster, like a rabbit. Simone raced after him. The Doll Maker reached the T-junction. Traffic flowed in both directions on the main road.

Simone smiled. The rabbit was trapped between the heavy traffic in the front and her in the back. The few seconds he'd take to look in either direction before crossing the road was all she needed to pounce on him.

But the Doll Maker didn't stop; he didn't even slow down. He bolted across the street as if it were deserted.

Tyres screeched. Horns blared. Cars and bikes came to a sudden halt. Drivers swore at the sari-clad woman crossing the road without paying heed or attention to either the oncoming traffic or her own life.

'Lucky bastard!' Simone muttered, seeing the Doll Maker crossed the road unscathed.

The halted traffic started to move again.

'Shit!' Simone exclaimed as she reached the T-junction.

She slowed down. Waved down the traffic with her hands.

'Police! Stop! Police!'

A car nearly rammed her. The driver stopped, thrust his head out of the window and shouted, 'You crazy woman! D'you want to die?'

Simone didn't answer. She dashed after the Doll Maker, who was springing down the staircase that cut through the forested hill, connecting the city below to the temple.

The Doll Maker looked back.

A mistake. Simone smiled to herself. It would only slow him down.

The perp seemed to realize that there was no way he could outrun Simone if he took a straight path. He stopped and vaulted over the railing that separated the staircase from the dense forest. Within seconds, the Doll Maker was out of sight, hidden by the thick trees and towering bushes.

'Dammit!' cried Simone.

She too jumped over the railing and ran into the woods. Immediately, she was shrouded by a thick fog. It was darker here. The canopy of trees stood guard against the dull light attempting to get in. The fog didn't help. Simone stopped, letting her eyes adjust to her grim surroundings.

She heard branches breaking ahead of her, to the left. Bracing herself, she ran in the direction of the sound. She brushed past low-hanging branches and stepped on shrubs, the stamping of her own feet louder than any other sound in the forest.

Suddenly, she stopped. She wasn't sure whether she was still behind the Doll Maker or if she had veered off in a completely different direction. The perp was smart. What if he decided to retrace his steps back to the staircase, leaving Simone wandering around in the woods?

She strained her ears for any sound above the muted hubbub of the blaring horns from the main road. No sound. No sign of the Doll Maker.

Simone pulled out her revolver and swivelled around. She wanted to be prepared if he decided to ambush her.

A twig snapped a few feet away from her, behind a tree, its trunk as wide as the front fender of her Thar.

Simone ran towards the tree, both her arms stretched, her right finger on the trigger, ready to fire at a moment's notice.

Suddenly, a sharp blade pierced her right arm.

'Aieeee!' she screamed. Intense, scalding pain searing through her veins. The hand relaxed on instinct and the gun fell from her loose grip. Blood oozed out of her hand. Almost immediately, she felt the hard jab of something bony, pointy, like an elbow, into the side of her skull. She stumbled back.

Simone shook her head trying to regain her bearings.

The Doll Maker stood in front of her like a nightmare in black, his face covered with the sari pallu. A metal blade glinted in his hand—the blade he had jammed into her arm. It was pocket-sized, like a Swiss army knife.

Her hand was screaming in pain but this wasn't the time to indulge herself by giving in to the pain. She clenched and unclenched her hands into fists. The pain surged, as did her rage, invigorating her with its rampant drive.

The Doll Maker rushed forward and moved the blade in a slashing motion.

Simone, nimble like a fencer, stepped away from the piercing blow. Using his momentum against him, she kicked him in the back as he moved past her. The Doll Maker stumbled for a second before tripping over his sari and falling face down on the ground.

He rolled over and bared his teeth like a wounded lion.

'You bitch!' he hissed.

Simone was taken aback. It was the first time she had heard him speak. In her mind, he was a man, even though he dressed like a woman. But as the obscenity left his mouth, she realized that the tone, pitch and even the rhythm of his voice was exactly like a girl's voice. A little girl's voice. Soft, serene and soothing.

The Doll Maker stood up. 'I'm going to kill you!'

Again, he sounded like a young girl making empty threats at an adult. It was almost funny, except for the pocketknife that made the threat very real.

Simone bunched her hands into fists and raised them like a boxer.

This time the Doll Maker didn't charge at her. He strode, kept the knife lowered, as if waiting to thrust it into Simone's abdomen at the last moment.

Simone stepped back. He kept coming. She stepped back further. She wanted him to feel like he was in control. Wanted him to think that she was afraid. And then, when he was within touching distance, she shifted her body weight on to her back leg, raised the other leg in one swift motion and snap kicked the Doll Maker in the chin. She was taller, her reach farther. The Doll Maker was caught off guard. He went down in a heap.

Simone stamped her heavy boot on his knife-bearing hand. The Doll Maker squealed and screamed. He sounded like a little girl being beaten. It made Simone uncomfortable. She ignored her discomfort and stamped on his hand again, using the full force of her weight.

The Doll Maker shrieked, wincing in pain, and let go of the pocketknife.

Simone picked up the knife and pounced on him like a cheetah. She grabbed him by the throat and hollered, 'Who's the bitch now, huh?'

He writhed beneath her, struggling to free himself. But, Simone, who was heavier than him, sat like an anvil on his chest.

'Stop wriggling or I'll jam this knife in your throat!'

All of a sudden, the Doll Maker stopped moving. He wasn't wincing any more. He was laughing, his eyes glinting.

'Laugh all you want. You are going to jail for the rest of your life!' Simone released her grasp on his neck and unhooked the handcuffs clasped to her belt.

The Doll Maker started laughing hysterically, sounding like a girl gone bonkers.

'You find it funny?' said Simone.

Just as suddenly, he stopped laughing.

'No,' he hissed. 'I find this funny.'

Simone felt cold, hard metal on her midriff. For a moment, she was confused. Then it hit her. The gun. Her service revolver.

Before Simone could blink or move, a deafening gunshot rang through the woods.

Instant, unbearable pain engulfed her. She tried to scream but could only manage a throaty yelp. She clutched the left side of her belly. Felt her hand get drenched immediately. Blood. Her blood oozing out from the gaping bullet hole.

The Doll Maker shoved her aside.

Simone fell hard on her back. Her eyes fluttered. Her face contorted in anguish.

The Doll Maker stood up and adjusted his sari. He stepped closer to where Simone lay whimpering on the ground.

He raised the gun, aiming it at her head. His hand trembled incessantly.

The final shot, thought Simone. The shot that would kill her instantly. She braced herself. There was no escaping death.

'I'm sorry, Simo . . . Simone,' he said in his timid, girly voice.

He wiggled his quivering index finger into the trigger guard.

'I'm sorry,' he repeated. He was shaking uncontrollably now.

'Just do it, you little girl!' Simone spat the words through gritted teeth.

He stopped trembling. 'You see me!' There was relief and joy in his sweet voice. 'You see me for who I am—a little girl.'

He lowered his hand. And, without another word, walked away with Simone's gun.

The canopy of trees started to swirl. Simone felt dizzy. She found it hard to keep her eyes open. She knew she was losing blood fast, despite her hand pressing down on the bullet wound. She needed help. Immediately.

The phone.

The phone was in her trouser pocket. She had to call Zoya and tell her what had happened. Get help. She wriggled her hand inside the pocket and clutched the phone with her weak fingers.

Her head swirled like a merry-go-round. Her eyes fluttered.

Before she could call for help, Simone stopped moving.

37

'Simone . . .' Zoya whispered her partner's name like a prayer, her heart beating like a drum. She ran over to the inspector who had found Simone after many agonizing minutes since they heard the gunshot. Seeing Simone on the ground, a hand clutching her stomach, Zoya stopped short. Simone's police cap had fallen off her head, revealing her smooth, bald scalp.

Zoya gasped. She clasped the front of her khaki jacket for support. Simone had been shot and, from the looks of it, was probably dead. The thought hit Zoya like an arrow through the heart. She went numb and couldn't move. She couldn't hear the fuss being created by the police officers around her.

Zoya dragged her feet to where Simone lay, twigs breaking and crunching under her feet as she moved. She gulped and bent down.

Simone looked so peaceful, so innocent. As if she would wake up any minute and start laughing for no reason. Zoya shook her head and forced a smile. This was Simone—if she woke up, she would most probably start yelling at the people around her rather than laughing without reason.

Zoya inhaled deeply and held her breath. She picked up Simone's inert hand and checked for pulse.

'Is she alive?' asked an inspector.

Zoya looked up and said, 'For now.'

38

Nalini entered the outhouse, embracing the caress of the lemongrass-scented floor cleaner, and locked the door behind her. She didn't bother to turn on the lights. Didn't bother to clean the deep cut on her brow or the bruised left hand on which Simone had stomped or the blood that had seeped down and crusted over. Didn't bother to remove the heavy layers of make-up plastered on her face and neck. She sat on the edge of the bed, threw her head back and revelled in the free fall before her head hit the flat, hard mattress. She liked it when her head hit the mattress. It helped soothe the incessant thumping inside her head. She sat back up with a groan, closed her eyes and threw her head back again.

'Whee!' she shrieked before her head slammed down on the mattress.

She giggled like a little girl who has discovered a new game.

She sat back up and did it again. And again. Until her head throbbed with such intensity that pain and joy mingled together into a single emotion—solace.

She smiled. The close brush with the police aside, it was a blessed day. She was one step closer to her redemption.

Suddenly, Nalini sat up. She wasn't tired any more. She strode over to the study table beside the window and slipped into the kiddie chair. White light from the floodlight in the lawn outside streamed in through the window, illuminating the leather-bound folder on the table.

The redemption plan: seven days, seven boys. Four saved, three to go.

The plan had worked like clockwork so far, but a change was in order because of the hiccup today. A slight shuffle to make the police feel her pain.

Nalini opened the last page in the folder. The last child she had planned to save. It was supposed to be a fitting parting gift to the police before she bid a final goodbye to this pathetic life.

But now he had to be the next child she saved. The child who had lost his mother in the divorce.

'I understand your pain, Sunny. I'll save you.'

She bent down and kissed the photo of the child—Sunny Bharucha, son of DSP Zoya Bharucha.

Day 4

39

Irshad parked his car in the reserved lot and strode towards the office building, whistling a peppy song though he couldn't recall the lyrics.

At 6 a.m., the lush lawn in front of the entrance was lit by muted, pale yellow, street lamps. Not much was visible except the flood of fog that trickled into every vacant crevice of space.

Irshad breathed in the thick, biting air and immediately felt the insides of his nose go numb. His eyes watered. Nonetheless, he felt rejuvenated and giddy. It was a new day. A day full of promise; a day infused with hope.

They were getting closer to catching the Clipper, tightening the noose around his neck, inch by inch. He had high hopes of Pius. The young man had spent the entire day in Irshad's office, tapping away at his laptop, sipping Red Bull after Red Bull. *No wonder he is always zipping with energy*, thought Irshad. The boy was still working when Irshad had gone home with a bouquet of flowers for his wife. The bouquet had been slammed into the dustbin faster than he had had the time to explain his absence the previous night. Twenty-plus years and she still didn't understand the demands of his job. *Humph! Forget her,* he thought, *no point spoiling my mood early in the morning.* He started to whistle louder.

While Pius was busy trying to find the Clipper's bunker, Irshad had spent the day getting official records checked based on Ariel's call history. Ariel had received or made a total of nine calls twenty-four hours from her estimated time of death. It seemed surprisingly low for an escort, Irshad had mused. Four calls were from telemarketing companies; totally irrelevant and a complete waste of time. Two calls were from 'Mom', who actually turned out to be Ariel's mother. She had broken down when Irshad broke the terrible news to her over the phone. To spare her more pain, he had kept the gruesome details of the murder to himself. One call was made to 'Nivi', who turned out to be Ariel's sister. So Irshad had to repeat everything he had told the mother. He had to endure Nivi's wails and screams and curses as she blamed the police for Ariel's death.

Two calls were to and from 'Kareena', a fellow transgender person and Ariel's 'BFF', in Kareena's words. It had seemed the most promising lead so far. Maybe they worked together? Maybe Kareena could tell him how Ariel communicated with her clients?

Irshad had made the trip to Kareena's penthouse, which she shared with her partner. The partner was home, in his pyjamas, in the middle of a workday, so Irshad couldn't figure out what he did for a living except that he was rich enough to lounge around in a penthouse on a workday. The partner had sat tight-lipped throughout the interview, his arm around Kareena. The partner had glowered at Irshad as if the police superintendent was there to whisk Kareena away. As far as

Irshad could tell, the partner wasn't afraid of him; he was jealous.

After much coaxing by Irshad, and a gentle nudge from the partner, Kareena had come clean. She told him that she used to be an escort herself until a few years ago. That was how she had met her partner. A client-turned-lover. After she found 'true love'—at that moment, Kareena had gazed at the jealous partner and flapped her long lashes—she had adapted to the 'simple, yet meaningful life of a housewife'. It helped, Irshad noticed, that the partner could afford the heavy gold jewellery that Kareena was bedecked with on a lazy afternoon.

Kareena was Ariel's senior in college and she had introduced her to the escort business after Ariel was fresh out of college—without a job, without any prospects and 'willing to do anything'. Within months, Ariel had risen to become the most sought-after transgender escort in the business. It was a match made in heaven. Ariel, who identified as a woman, possessed everything that clients wanted: a gorgeous heart-shaped face, large hazel eyes, fair skin, and a svelte figure—all wrapped in a man's body. It also helped that she was young, rash and willing to do anything for money. 'Anything,' Kareena had stressed the word and smiled mischievously at her husband. Irshad didn't understand what she meant and fast-forwarded the conversation to the day of Ariel's death.

Kareena had met Ariel for their weekly high tea. Ariel worked at night and slept till noon, Kareena had explained. So high tea was the perfect time to meet. That day, the last time they met, Ariel was unusually excited about her date with a 'big money man' named Ripple. Naturally, an alias. Ariel was hoping that Ripple would like her and become a regular. He was offering her three times her usual rate—which itself was exorbitant considering that she was one of the best in the city. Ariel had even messaged Ripple during high tea, confirming the time and the place. She didn't want to be late.

Irshad's heart had started galloping at that moment. Ariel had messaged Ripple, most likely another moniker of the Clipper. How? He had called up Pius and asked him to do another check of Ariel's messages. But the search came back negative. There were no messages whatsoever—no SMS, no emails, no WhatsApp chats, nothing—between Ariel and Ripple. It was the same case with Ariel's deleted messages that Pius had managed to retrieve—although Irshad wasn't sure how.

It confirmed the initial hypothesis—Ariel was using a secret messaging service on the dark web. It also explained why there were no calls from prospective clients to a top-tier escort. Irshad had asked Kareena about it. But she shook her head and said she had always preferred a phone call from her clients when she was still in business. Irshad believed her. Why would Ariel, a top-rung escort with a criminal record, share details of a highly paid escort service with a tattletale like Kareena? BFFs or not, some secrets were best kept hidden, especially from the ones closest to you.

Now, as Irshad ran up the stairs to his office, two at a time, hope fuelled his strides and excitement filled his heart. He couldn't wait to wrap his fingers around the Clipper's neck.

Irshad entered the crime wing. Apart from the constable on night duty, not a soul was in sight. Irshad acknowledged the constable's half-hearted salute and strode into his office.

He pushed open the door.

Pius lay slumped on the sofa, legs dangling over the armrest. His laptop was still open on the table, humming like a hard-working bee, waiting for orders from its snoozing master. Empty cans of Red Bull, sprawled like Pius, occupied the remaining space on the table.

'Pius,' Irshad gently nudged the young man's shoulder.

Pius awoke with a start and sat up. He was drooling from the mouth and his eyes were bleary. The spikes in his hair had flattened. Wiping his mouth with the sleeve of his jacket, he said, 'Sorry . . . sorry, sir. I must have dozed off.'

Irshad smiled. Pius reminded him of himself. As a young officer in the police force, Irshad had spent many nights working late in the office. Often sleeping in his chair or on the visitor's bench outside.

'Why didn't you go back home, son?'

'I plan—' Pius covered his mouth to stifle a yawn. 'I planned to but then I found some clues on the message board that the Clipper uses. So, I kept searching and finished around 4 a.m. I thought I'll stay here and wait for you. But before I knew it, I was fast asleep.'

'I told you to take all the time you need. You should have gone home to rest. You could have start again today, refreshed and—'

'Sir,' Pius interrupted him. 'I finished.'

'Finished what?' Irshad was perplexed.

'Finished finding his bunker. I found the dark web service that the Clipper used to contact Ariel.'

40

Irshad stood stunned for a moment. 'You found his bunker?'

Pius pressed a key on his laptop and the machine came to life. 'That's why I was waiting for you here, sir. Come, I'll show you.'

Irshad sat down next to Pius on the sofa.

'Ariel was using Tor, which is an onion router. It encrypts and reroutes the IP address through multiple nodes, making it impossible to track,' said Pius.

'I didn't understand a word you said. Layman's terms please.'

Pius nodded. 'Sorry.' He pushed up his glasses. 'Basically, she was using a software to conceal her online fingerprints. That's why it took me so much time. I tried and tried, but in vain.' His eyes lit up. 'Then, it struck me. You had mentioned that Ariel has a police record from a couple of years ago. But she has been squeaky clean since she was booked. So, I realized that I should start my search from right after she was released on bail. She—'

'I didn't say she was released on bail.'

Pius looked at Irshad sheepishly. 'I checked police records in the system.'

Of course. Irshad bobbed his head.

Pius continued, 'She must have started using this website right after she was released. So, I crawled through her online history and read each and every comment, message and email she has sent since. It was easy once I found the username she had been using on all message boards and chat forums: Ariel_the_mermaid. Very creative,' Pius grinned, sarcasm lacing his tone, 'and rather stupid to use her own name, even if it was fake.'

'Anyway, I found this private chat on a popular escort service,' Pius scoffed, 'they should seriously up their encryption game, by the way.'

Irshad's face remained expressionless. He was in no mood for Pius's snarky side comments.

Pius took the hint and continued. 'The guy chatting with Ariel asked her out on a date. Or a "fun time" he wrote. Apparently, he was one of her most loyal clients. They had gone out many times before. After a few lovey-dovey messages, the guy started giving Ariel business gyaan on why she should be charging more for her services. Ariel stops him and tells him that it's not safe to discuss such matters on the escort service forum.'

Pius grinned, 'Smart woman, I must say. The chats are visible to the website owner and can be called upon as evidence in court by us,' he explained.

'She implores the guy to join a highly secure forum called G.B.T. Says all her clients have moved to the forum, except him. The guy says it's too much of an effort. Plus, he likes being different from her other clients so that she would value him more. When the guy doesn't relent after all that prodding, Ariel issues an ultimatum—join G.B.T. or never meet her again. The guy gives in finally and that's when Ariel, in a flash of stupidity, sends him an invitation to join the website.'

'What's G.B.T.?' asked Irshad.

Pius stabbed the keyboard a few times and a webpage popped up on screen. A single sentence was written in cursive script over a rainbow-coloured background:

Enter password to penetrate the sexy middle of L.G.B.T.Q.

A text box with a cursor flashed underneath the text.

'Gay. Bisexual. Transgender. That's what G.B.T. stands for,' said Pius.

'Okay, then what are we waiting for? Let's enter the password.'

'So . . .' Pius sighed and sat back on the sofa. 'That's where I'm stuck. I've found the bunker. But I don't have Ariel's password to enter the bunker. I tried a couple of options—her birth date, her passport number. etc.,—but I stopped, lest I alert the site administrator that I am trying to hack my way in.'

Irshad sat up and laced his fingers, his mind racing.

'Did you try the 'forgot password' option? We have her phone and email. We can reset the password with the code they send us. Like banks do.'

Pius shook his head. 'No such option here. These are illegal websites, sir. You better remember the password or get someone on the inside who can vouch for you to invite you again.'

'Can't you crack the password with one of those devices they show in movies?'

Pius guffawed, his shoulders jumping up and down. 'You've been watching too many movies, sir. Don't you think I would have done it already if I could?'

Irshad ignored the snide comment. Even if cocky, Pius was right.

Irshad sat in silence, staring at the blinking cursor on the screen. He had to put himself in Ariel's shoes. What password would she set? She wasn't that bright. Wasn't that stupid either.

'And, this is the first step,' said Pius. 'If this website is as secure as its cousins on the dark web, I'm guessing we will be asked to enter different passwords at every step of the way.'

More passwords? thought Irshad. *How would you remember so many passwords?* But that was life these days—a password for this and a password for that. Some you keep the same, some different.

That's when it struck him. Most people *don't* remember *all* their passwords. They write them down somewhere. They keep them secure in a file that contains all their passwords. At least that's what he did because his teenage son had told him to do it when he kept forgetting his passwords.

'How do you remember all your passwords, Pius?'

He smiled. 'The answer is in your question, sir. I *remember* them all.'

'That's because you are smarter than most of us. But what do the rest of us do?'

'What?' Pius scrunched his brow and sat up straight.

'Did you check for a file of passwords?' asked Irshad.

'File of passwords?'

'Like a note or a document where she had saved all her passwords.'

Pius's jaw dropped as realization hit him like a snowball in the face on a winter morning. 'Yes! You may be right! Why didn't I think of it?'

Irshad chuckled and patted his back, 'Because you are too smart for your own good.'

Pius frantically searched Ariel's phone. Within minutes, he was smiling. 'Found it! It was in the notes app.'

Irshad's stomach was filled with sudden anticipation.

'Guess what her password is?' chuckled Pius.

'What?'

'The same as her username!'

Pius reopened the website and entered the password: Ariel_the_mermaid. As soon as he pressed enter, the rainbow-coloured screen faded and, suddenly, burst into thousands of pieces of confetti, like someone had broken open a pinata. A message, also in rainbow colours, appeared on screen:

Hi, sexy! How can I satisfy you today?

'Gotta give it to the creators of this site,' said Pius. 'Puts you in a good mood from the start!'

The welcome message moved to the top of the screen, and tiles and tiles of graphic listings appeared underneath it. For a moment, Irshad felt like he was shopping on Amazon except, instead of detergents, there were gents for rent. Most listings had pictures of men scantily clothed in lacy thongs or sheer stockings or transparent negligees, offering a whole gamut of services— from fetish play to orgies with dominatrices.

Irshad looked away, ashamed. In his long police career, he had learned to bite violence, chew it like bubblegum and swallow it if needed. But this was new. Something different. Something more unpalatable than violence. He felt like a voyeur, like he was cheating on his wife, somehow, even though he was straight.

Pius noticed his gaze fixed on the wall. 'You okay, sir?'

Irshad took a deep breath. 'Yes . . . yes.'

Pius shook his head. 'You clearly haven't seen a porn site before.'

'As a matter of fact, I haven't.' Irshad looked back at the screen. 'Can you access her chats with past clients?'

Pius clicked an envelope-like symbol on the top right corner. The screen refreshed and asked for another password. Pius checked Ariel's notes app and typed in her password for accessing her inbox on G.B.T. The screen refreshed again, revealing the inbox.

'We are in!' exclaimed Pius.

There were some unread messages on top, mostly from new suitors judging from the subject lines.

'Click this one!' Irshad pointed to the last read message.

It was from Ripple. Irshad's heart started to beat faster. It was the last message in a long email chain:

Hey Ariel!

Thank you for agreeing to meet at the last minute.

   No, I wasn't kidding—willing to pay three times your usual charges. GST included. ☺

   Let's meet at Hotel Desire. 9 p.m. sharp. Please be on time. Thanks!

   PS: Is it too much to ask if you can wear a sexy sari tonight?

Pius clicked a button and Ariel's reply to the last message popped up:

   Yay! I'm excited about our date tonight, Ripple! XOXO

   PS: For your generosity, you get to keep my sari tonight. Free of charge! ☺

Irshad shook his head, reading the seemingly innocuous exchange of emails. Ariel had no idea of the bloody turn that her life was about to take; no clue that the Clipper would keep more than the 5.5 metres of the garment that clothed her.

Pius yawned, 'So, what now, sir?'

What now? The question nibbled at Irshad. This was the closest he had ever come to catching the Clipper. The Clipper suddenly felt within his reach. An email away.

He smiled. *An email away*, he chewed on the thought in his mind. It made sense. It was the only way to catch the sonofa—

Irshad turned to the young man sitting next to him. 'You know, Pius, with a little help you could look quite convincing as a woman.'

'Sorry?' Pius raised his brow.

'What feminine name sounds like Pius?' Irshad rubbed his chin.

'What do you mean, sir?'

'Pisces!' said Irshad and smiled knowingly as Pius. 'What do you think of Pisces as your undercover name?'

41

The situation was getting out of hand.

Another day. Another kid dead.

Ranveer was in the room of mirrors—the empty basement with mirrors for wallpaper—with that day's newspaper in his hand. Barefoot, he paced back and forth across the cold, stone floor. Frigid prickles from the cold floor pierced his numb heels and ran up his femur like agonizing bolts of electricity. For him, walking barefoot on cold stone was meditative. It helped him think clearly.

The Doll Maker had made headlines again. *Again! Four days in a row!* Ranveer couldn't fathom how incapable the Bhopal Police would need to be to let a serial murderer run rampant, killing a child a day. His mind boggled.

Suddenly, he felt claustrophobic. Tremors took control of his body as a flood of emotions inundated him. He flicked his right hand, as if to shake it dry. His breathing accelerated. Panic gripped him.

And then, abruptly, he started sprinting across the long basement. His limbs sliced through the heavy air in the basement, propelling his body forward. He reached one end of the enclosed room and ran back. And did it again. And again. Until every ounce of energy was spent, every bit of emotion expelled. Finally, exhausted, he dropped on the floor, heaving like an exhausted animal after a hunt.

He had underestimated the Doll Maker, the *bitch!* He had spent the better part of his life controlling transgenders like the Doll Maker. And now, a transgender was controlling him. He had to regain control. Again.

Do I even have to do all the detective work for the police? he thought and stood up suddenly, the movement leaving his head whirling. He didn't care. He had to find his competition before his competition ripped him apart. He snorted. *Ripped?* That's what he had done to unsuspecting transgenders all these years. The irony wasn't lost on him. It felt like some sort of twisted karma. He didn't like it. Not one bit.

Ranveer walked the length of the room and then dashed up the stairs, two stairs at a time. He strode to his study, sat down and booted up his laptop.

The police must have missed something.

He hacked into the police system and pulled up the murder book with daily entries from the detectives-in-charge. Simone and Zoya. *Pathetic! They should have put a man in charge. Now, I need to do their jobs for them.*

He also pulled up footage from all public and private security cameras in the vicinity of Birla Mandir, the latest scene of the crime. *I just need one clear headshot and the facial recognition software will do the rest.* Of course, it's the first thing the police detectives *should* have done as well. So, he wasn't quite sure what was taking them so long apart from the general apathy that pervades the Indian police.

Ranveer spent the next hour going through every inch of video footage. The clearest footage was from a CCTV camera mounted above the side entrance of Birla Mandir. However, the Doll Maker was wearing sunglasses; her face hidden behind her sari pallu. *A nice touch*, thought Ranveer. The eyes were most important for a facial recognition software. Without them, he was grasping at straws.

He sighed when he was none the wiser even after an hour of probing.

Next, he turned his attention to the latest police reports and findings. There was nothing new in them either, except one section which surmised the reason why the crime scenes—the Bhopal Gas Tragedy Memorial, DB City Mall and Birla Mandir—were chosen by the Doll Maker: that was where the kids had lost their mothers. *Interesting*, he mused. *Maybe, I just need to find the next victim to know where he will leave the next Barbie in the glass case and ambush him there?*

He shook his head. It wouldn't work if the police knew about the next victim as well. He could tell that the police were catching up; they were only one step behind the Doll Maker now. They had been waiting for him at Birla Mandir. He knew that from the latest report that Zoya had typed up. The Doll Maker had narrowly escaped after shooting one of the detectives. Simone. He shook his head again. *Should have put a man in charge*. A man like him.

Ranveer was running out of patience. *How do I find him?* The little tremors returned in his right hand. He clenched and unclenched his hand, noticing thick green veins pop through the scars on the back of his hand. *Be patient*, he told himself. *There is always a way. Always.*

Ranveer dragged his chair forward. Took a deep breath and decided to comb through each and every document again. He reread the reports and watched the footage again. Nothing, even after another two hours.

Then, in one of the folders, he saw an image file titled: *Sketch*. His pulse raced. His hand quivered faster. He had missed this file earlier. How? *Had it only just been uploaded in the system? Was it a sketch of the Doll Maker?* It would be difficult to run facial recognition using a sketch, but one could hope. He double-clicked the file.

Right then, his phone chimed. A message. He recognized the tone. Someone had sent him a private message on G.B.T. and the service had in turn sent him a secure, garbled notification. He had subscribed to the notification service, lest he missed a message while planning a date with his victims. Who was messaging him? He wasn't planning a date with anyone. Curious, he looked away from the laptop screen and reached for his phone.

He logged into the secure website and opened his inbox. There was one message from someone named Pisces. Seemed like an escort from the profile photo, which depicted a typical Bollywood scene of yore. Pisces was wearing a low-waist sari in the picture, the fabric gleaming and fire-engine red. A matching bralette covered her flat, shaved chest. She was ogling at the camera, her eyes wide in surprise behind red-rimmed glasses, her lips in an 'Oh!' as her hands held the pallu which had 'accidentally' slipped off her shoulder, revealing her modest cleavage.

Ranveer bit his lower lip. Even though the photo was clearly staged, it aroused him. Maybe it was how she looked so innocent in the photo, or maybe it was the red sari. Either way, he wasn't complaining.

He tapped open the message.

Fear gripped him instantly. Beads of sweat formed on his forehead as he read through the message:

Hi Ripple!

I'm Pisces. Heard a lot about you from my friend, Ariel. She couldn't stop raving about you before your date!

I know she is my friend and everything, and I might be going behind her back by doing so, but I was wondering if we could get together sometime? I've been told by clients that I 'blow' them away with just my tongue ☺!

Message me! I'll let you keep more than my sari!

XOXO
Pisces

Ranveer shot out of the chair. A bead of sweat trickled down his temple.

Shit! Shit! Shit! This is what happens when you pick a random escort and don't follow the selection criteria! he lambasted himself.

Ranveer ran a hand through his lustrous hair and massaged his head, trying desperately to calm himself down but in vain.

Does she know I killed Ariel? She says Ariel 'is' my friend. So, probably not. It gave him some respite.

He marched back and forth, his mind in overdrive, his hands shaking. What troubled him most was the last sentence—*I'll let you keep more than my sari!* That was more or less what Ariel had told him in the postscript of her last message. It was proof that Pisces, or whatever her real name was, knew about their email exchanges. She wasn't lying. It wasn't a joke. It was a loose end that needed to be tied.

Suddenly, he stopped pacing.

Yes, Pisces must be killed. Heck, she was even asking for it, although, granted, she hadn't realized what she was asking for.

A lopsided, wicked smile stretched across his face.

And then, *never again*, he promised himself. Never again would he stray from the criteria that had kept him safe for nine years. No more random escorts.

He picked up his phone and typed a quick message to Pisces:

Hi Pisces,

I don't get blown away THAT easily. ☺ *Prove me wrong and I'll make it worth your while!*

How about I pick you up at 9 p.m. tomorrow from Hotel Desire?

He smiled. He loved this game.

Ranveer switched off the phone and looked at the laptop screen. He immediately froze. The sketch of the Doll Maker was open on his laptop.

He swallowed hard, forgetting to breathe for a moment.

He recognized the Doll Maker. She was his childhood friend. She was his tenant. She was Nalini.

42

Simone stirred. She moaned.

Something small, soft and stubby was brushing back and forth across her shaved head, like someone was incessantly scratching her head with a teddy bear. It was both soothing and irritating at the same time—calming when the teddy moved in the direction of her non-existent hair, and vexing when it moved against the hair, as if trying to pull her sprouting hair from their roots.

Simone groaned loudly, hoping the constant brushing would stop. It didn't.

Her face twitched in annoyance. She opened her mouth to speak, but no words tumbled out. She was parched, her throat clogged, it seemed.

'He he!'

She registered a loud, unsuppressed giggle.

Simone tried to open her eyes but the effort was too taxing for her. Simone's head swirled; dizzy due to the after-effects of whatever drug she had been given. Who drugged me? And why? The answers eluded her.

'He he! He he!' The giggles went on.

Simone took a deep breath and smelled coconut oil. She ignored the fragrance and turned the full focus of her wobbly mind on opening her eyes. Her eyelids fluttered; her groan grew louder. Finally, she opened her eyes to a world of white—cotton-coloured ceiling with twin tube lights showering ivory light, salt-coloured walls and two empty porcelain-like plastic chairs that sat next to the bed. In between the chairs was a tiny table. On it stood proudly a colossal bouquet of red roses, twice the size of the table.

'He he!'

She tilted her head in the direction of the sound. It was a chubby little boy, probably five years old. His hair had been parted to one side and slicked in place with oil, most likely coconut, the source of the smell that pervaded the room. The boy wore black rectangular spectacles, a size larger than his cute, beak-like nose could withstand. He kept pushing his glasses back in place with one hand, even as he stood on his toes next to the bed, his other hand outstretched, rubbing his palm back and forth on Simone's head, giggling merrily.

Simone's displeasure melted away on seeing his happy face. But who was he? She had never seen him before. She moistened her lips and said, 'Hel—' Her throat jammed up.

The boy peered at her from above his glasses. 'Hello!' he said excitedly.

Simone cleared her throat, 'What . . . what are you doing?'

'He he!' the boy glanced away, his focus back on her shaved head.

'Why are you rubbing my head?'

The boy nodded with unfettered enthusiasm. 'You have no hair, auntie!'

Simone tried to smile, but her facial muscles remained still, failing to register the emotion.

The boy moved his palm from the back of her head to the front. 'Is sooo soft!' Then he moved the palm back. 'He he! Now is tickling my hand! He he!'

'What's your name?' she asked.

He bit his lower lip and shook his head. 'Guess!'

Simone sighed. 'I don't know.'

'Okay, I give you hint. It starts with "S" and ends with—'

Suddenly, the door creaked open. The boy jumped up in surprise.

'Sunny! What are you doing?'

Simone recognized the voice. Zoya.

'Nothing, Mumma. Nothing.' The boy ran and jumped on one of the plastic chairs, his feet dangling like he didn't have a worry in the world. Come to think of it, he didn't.

'I told you not to disturb auntie. Did I not tell you?' Zoya scolded her son.

'It's okay,' Simone forced a smile, 'we were just chatting.' Her voice came out hoarse and croaky.

'Oh, Simone!' exclaimed Zoya. 'You are awake!' She rushed to Simone's side and gently held her arm. 'You gave us such a scare last evening.'

Suddenly, it all came back—the collision with the Doll Maker's van, the chase, the struggle and the gunshot. As if on cue, a frisson of pain rippled through Simone's stomach. She whimpered.

Zoya hurriedly poured water from a steel flask into a plastic cup. 'Here. Drink some water. You'll feel better.'

Simone tried to bend forward and groaned as her stomach erupted in pain.

'Let me.' Zoya came to her assistance. She tilted her head forward and put the cup close to her mouth. Simone took a sip of water before reclining back again.

'I'm so glad you are still alive, Simone,' said Zoya as she shut the flask. 'God is kind.'

Simone snickered. She didn't believe in God. She believed in doctors and she was sure that it was to them she owed her life.

Zoya continued. 'The doctor said you were lucky the hospital was a stone's throw away from where you were shot. We found you in time. And luckily, you were still breathing when we took you in.'

Simone knew the statistics. There was an 85 per cent chance of survival from a gunshot wound to the stomach *if* and *only if* one was still breathing when brought to the hospital. It meant the bullet had missed all major organs in the abdomen. Else, she wouldn't be alive. Probably, in addition to the doctors, she did owe it to sheer dumb luck.

'How long was I out?' asked Simone.

'Close to twenty-four hours. How do you feel now?'

Simone glanced at Zoya. 'Like I was shot in the stomach.'

Zoya laughed out loud. 'Well, that's a first,' she said.

'What?'

'Miss Simone making a joke.'

Simone rolled her eyes, 'A lame joke.'

'A joke, nevertheless. Maybe this incident will show us a different side of you. A new and improved Simone,' Zoya winked at her.

Simone shook her head, 'I highly doubt it.'

'Mumma, can we gooo now? Please, please, please,' Sunny interrupted, swinging his legs even faster, as if to drive home the point about his impatience.

'Sunny, we'll go in a few minutes. Be patient.'

'But I'm bored.' Sunny pouted, crossing his arms and lowering his chin. The legs stopped swinging.

'Okay, you can play with my mobile phone in the meantime.' Zoya plunged her hand into her trouser pocket and took out her smartphone.

'Yes! Yes! Yes!' Sunny was grinning again, his legs swinging faster than before. 'Give me!' he said, his hands outstretched, 'I know how to unlock it.'

Zoya offered him the phone and he pounced on it.

Zoya turned back to Simone. 'I don't usually give him the phone for more than one hour a day.' She smiled, but Simone caught a whiff of pain in her forced smile. 'Call me selfish, but I meet him only on weekend nights after police duty. What little time we have together, I don't want him to spend it with that stupid phone,' Zoya bit her lower lip.

Simone lifted her arm and caught Zoya's hand. She squeezed it tight. There was no better way of telling a mother that she understood her pain, her agony of being separated from her only child.

Zoya squeezed Simone's hand in return. She chuckled, 'You know, I really think we have a new and improved Simone with us.'

Simone smiled weakly, 'Don't bet on it. It might be the drugs running through my system.'

For a few minutes no one spoke. Only the music from Sunny's mobile game kept silence at bay.

'By the way,' said Zoya. 'Your grandma was here the entire night and the whole day today. I came an hour ago and had to force her to go home to freshen up. She didn't want you to be left alone for even a second.'

Simone nodded. 'Sounds like my grandma.'

Zoya nodded too, 'Super tough, yet caring. She didn't shed a single tear when I called her over last evening. Kept praying for your recovery. Said she was sure you'd survive. Lo and behold, you did!'

'Yeah, yeah,' Simone said in a mocking tone. 'It was the prayers that saved me.'

Zoya narrowed her eyes. 'I think you might be right after all. The drugs seem to be wearing off, revealing the *nice* old Simone again.'

Simone sighed and looked away. 'Who sent the flowers?' she looked at the bouquet of red roses, changing the topic.

Zoya was grinning again. 'A secret admirer.'

'Who?' Simone was confused and curious. She didn't have any secret admirers that she knew of. Heck, she didn't even have admirers.

Zoya walked over to the bouquet and plucked out a tiny greeting card propped between two roses. She read the message inscribed on the card:

Dear Simo,
You missed our date yesterday! Get well soon . . . so you can make it up to me! ☺

There was no name on the card. Simone pursed her lips, suppressing a smile.

'So, who is it from?' Zoya raised an eyebrow.

'It's not what you think. I was supposed to meet Karan—he's a journalist—for a business meeting yesterday evening. It's just harmless flirting. That's all.'

Zoya shook her head, grinning. 'Simone, my dear, a guy will not send you *fifty* red roses if it is just harmless flirting. He likes you.'

'Nah!' Simone dismissed Zoya's theory with a feeble wave of the fingers. 'You forget. No one really likes me.'

'Okay, we should be going now. It's past Sunny's bedtime,' Zoya said politely.

'No, Mumma. I'm not sleepy!'

Everyone chuckled at his cute indignation, except Sunny of course, who was quite serious about not being sleepy.

Zoya said, 'Yeah, yeah. Not sleepy because you want to play games.'

'Yes!' said Sunny, his gleaming front teeth on full display.

Zoya shook her head and looked at Simone. 'We'll go now. I'll come back tomorrow to check in again.'

'Thank you, Zoya,' said Simone.

'What are partners for?' Zoya replied. She peered down at Sunny, 'Okay, say bye to auntie, Sunny.'

'Bye!' Sunny waved his hand.

'Tell Simone auntie to take care and stay safe.'

'Take care and stay safe, auntie,' repeated Sunny in a monotone.

'You too, Sunny,' said Simone. 'Take care and stay safe.'

43

'Mumma, open fast! I want to pee!' said Sunny, stomping his feet.

'I know, I know!' said Zoya, unlocking the door. 'I asked you at the hospital, but you said you didn't want to go then. Now give me a second!'

Zoya pushed open the door and Sunny dashed past her.

Zoya stepped into the house and locked the door behind her. She sniffed. The house smelled like a blooming garden of lemongrass.

She shrugged. Maybe the maid had used the new floor cleaner she'd bought to mop the floor. *But was it lemon or lemongrass scented?* She shrugged.

Zoya dropped her keys in a bowl, decorated with little rainbows, on top of the shoe cupboard right next to the main door. She took off her boots and slipped into comfortable moccasins. Her feet felt like they had stepped on a cloud.

'Mumma!' cried Sunny from the washroom.

'What is it, Sunny?'

'I made a boo-boo!' he shouted, as if proud of what he had done.

Zoya shook her head. She knew what it meant. The little fellow had peed all over the toilet seat and floor despite standing on a stool kept there for his convenience.

'Sunny Bharucha, how many times have I asked you to be careful!' she hollered back and walked over to the attached toilet in Sunny's bedroom.

Sunny's shoulders drooped. 'Sorry,' he whispered.

Zoya sighed. How could she be angry at her chubby bundle of cuteness?

She ruffled his hair. 'You have to be more careful next time, okay? Now, wash your hands.'

He nodded and pulled up his jeans. The glint in his eyes was back. He pushed the stool to the wash basin and stepped on it. He turned on the tap and washed his hands, while Zoya got busy cleaning the mess he had made.

Once done, Sunny pushed his glasses back, and said, 'Now can I play on the mobile phone? Please.'

Zoya stood akimbo, towering over him. She didn't say a word. Just stared at him without blinking. It was her stern look. Sunny knew not to push her buttons after receiving that look. He immediately wilted like a leaf in autumn.

'It's past your bedtime, Sunny. Open your wardrobe and pick out the jammies you want to wear tonight. I'll be out in a minute to help you change.'

Sunny dragged his feet the entire way to his bed.

Zoya finished cleaning her son's mess, washed her hands and went to Sunny's room. He was sitting on the edge of the bed. The wardrobe remained shut, no jammies in sight.

Zoya sighed. Walked over and sat next to him.

'Because you were such a good boy at the hospital today, tomorrow you can play for two hours on the phone, instead of one.'

'Really?' Sunny perked up, like his namesake.

'Yes, really. But now, you need to change and go to sleep.'

He nodded, jumped off the bed, ran to his wardrobe and picked out his favourite Spider-Man jammies. Zoya helped him change and tucked him into bed.

'Comfortable?'

He nodded, pulling the quilt close to his chin.

'Now go to sleep, okay?'

'Tell me a story, Mumma.'

'Sunny, it's too late for stories. Go to sleep if you want to play on the phone tomorrow.'

He smiled. 'Okay, Mumma. Goodnight, Mumma!'

'Good night, sweetheart. Sweet dreams,' Zoya tousled his hair and kissed him on the forehead.

She switched off the lights, closed the bedroom door behind her and walked into the kitchen. They had had pizza on the way home but she was hungry again. She opened the refrigerator and scanned the scant items on display. After much thought, she opened the freezer and took out a tub of chocolate chip ice-cream.

A well-deserved treat for Saturday night, she thought. She couldn't pinpoint what she had done to deserve it, but who cared.

Zoya took out a spoon and ambled over to the living room. She flopped down on the two-seater sofa and turned on the television. *Netflix time*, she thought, bobbing her head twice in excitement. She wasn't one of those police officers who brought work home and spent nights mulling over case files. Like Simone. She believed in letting the mind and body recuperate after a hard day at work. No point in dashing through life like it was a marathon. That was the recipe for a quick burnout. Much psychological research had been done on the topic, and she wasn't going to argue with the science of the mind.

Zoya decided to watch a rerun of her favourite show, *Criminal Minds*. She propped her feet on the centre table, opened the tub of ice-cream and thrust the spoon in deep for a big mouthful.

'MUMMA!' Sunny's shriek ripped through the apartment.

Zoya sprang to her feet, dropping the ice-cream tub on the centre table. The spoon fell on the floor with a sharp clang. Zoya hurried into Sunny's room, her heart beating, her mind flipping. What had happened to Sunny? He was not the kind to scream. He would come out and wake Zoya if needed, but never had he screamed like this before.

Zoya flung open his door and switched on the lights.

'Sunny! What happened?' Zoya shrieked.

The little boy was hiding under the quilt. Zoya hurled the quilt aside and saw Sunny curled up in a ball, shaking, his forehead creased, as if in pain.

'Mumma!' he jumped up and wrapped his arms around Zoya's neck.

'What happened, Sunny?' Zoya asked again, rubbing his back.

'The monster was whispering to me, Mumma!'

'Monster? Where, Sunny?'

'Monster under the bed!'

Zoya sighed. This wasn't the first time that Sunny had complained about the monster under the bed. Zoya had convinced herself that it was just a phase. Every child at one time or another was afraid of the dark or a monster in the dark. But he had never screamed or been so scared of the monster under the bed.

'There is no monster under the bed, son.'

'There is!' Sunny hugged her tighter. He whispered in Zoya's ears, 'She was whispering like this.'

'She?'

'Yes, it's a little girl monster. She whispered my name. *Sunny.* She said she was my friend. She said, "*Come with me, Sunny*". She said, "*I am going to keep you safe, Sunny*".'

'She said that?'

'No! She *whispered*, Mumma! Like this!' he was whispering again.

'Okay,' Zoya pulled away from him. 'Let me check under the bed and catch the girl monster.'

'No, Mumma, no!' He grabbed Zoya's pullover with his chubby fingers.

'Don't be afraid, Sunny. Mumma is a big girl, right?'

He nodded slowly, but with trepidation.

'So, Mumma can catch the little girl monster. You stay on the bed, okay?'

He shook his head with vigour even as he tightened his grip on Zoya's sweater.

'Okay, you hold my hand while I look underneath.'

It seemed like an agreeable compromise to him. He grasped her hand, digging his tiny nails into her skin.

Zoya pulled aside the bed cover hanging over the side, bent down and surveyed the floor under the bed.

It was spotless. No toys, no balls of hair and dust bunnies, no girl, no monster.

Zoya took a deep breath, her nerves relaxed. The lemongrass smell was stronger here. Zoya made a mental note to compliment the maid on her squeaky-clean work. If only the maid kept the rest of the house as clean as the underside of Sunny's bed. Well, one can hope at least, she thought.

'Come here, you little monster! You had the audacity to scare my Sunny? Let me teach you a lesson!' Zoya raised her voice in mock assertion. Watching Sunny from the corner of her eye, she pretended to grab something from under the bed and put it inside her trouser pocket.

'There you go, sweetheart,' Zoya stood up. 'I've caught the little monster and I'm going to flush her down the toilet.'

Sunny crossed his arms and lowered his chin to his chest. 'I'm not *stupid*, Mumma. I did hear the monster whispering.'

Zoya exhaled loudly. 'Okay, smarty-pants. Let me show you what's under the bed.'

'No! I don't want to see!' he jumped up and hugged Zoya again.

'Sunny, you are a big boy now.'

He didn't seem convinced.

Zoya picked him up, knelt on the floor and put him down. Together they lowered their heads and scanned the clean flooring underneath the bed. Out of curiosity, Zoya extended her arm and brushed a finger against the floor. It came back clean—no dust. She bobbed her head, approving the maid's work once again.

'Satisfied now?' she asked Sunny.

The boy looked glum. Unsure about what to say. Or what to believe.

'But it was there. I'm telling the truth, Mumma.'

'I believe you, baby.' She picked him up and tucked him in the bed. 'But the monster is gone now. You saw for yourself. So, there is nothing to be afraid of.'

Sunny didn't respond. Didn't move a muscle.

Zoya sighed. 'How about this? You try and sleep. If the monster comes again, you can sleep with me tonight. Okay?'

Sunny perked up. 'Okay, Mumma,' he said, his eyes gleaming.

'Now lie down and close your eyes.' Sunny did as instructed and Zoya pulled the quilt over his chest.

'Goodnight, baby.'

'Goodnight, Mumma!'

Zoya walked towards the door. Just as she was about to turn off the light, she noticed that the wardrobe door was ajar. *Sunny probably forgot to shut it properly when he took out his jammies*, she thought. She strode over and shut the wardrobe. She switched off the lights, shut the bedroom door and went back to the living room.

Zoya picked up the spoon that had fallen down, went to the kitchen, tossed it into the sink and took out another one. Picking up the tub of ice-cream, she slumped on the sofa again. She was glad for the onset of winter—the ice-cream had only melted slightly. Zoya browsed the last-watched episode of *Criminal Minds* and played the next one. While the video buffered, she twirled the spoon inside the tub, sat back and scooped out a dollop of ice-cream.

About ten minutes into the episode, her eyes started to droop with the heaviness of sleep. *I should go to bed*, she thought. *Maybe after this episode*, she convinced herself.

Suddenly, she heard the faintest of creaks from inside the house—like a door opening. Her eyes shot open. *Was I imagining it?* she thought. Possibly. She tried to concentrate on the video.

Then, she heard the creak again, like someone had closed a door.

She pressed pause on the remote. Jumped up.

Silence. The only sound she heard was the ticking of the clock on the wall and the incessant chirping of crickets and cicadas in the veranda outside. She crept closer to Sunny's room, her ears alert to pounce at even the faintest of noises. Was Sunny right about the girl monster?

Then, she heard it. The whispering. The soft mutterings of a little girl. Coming from Sunny's room.

Her heart jumped into her throat. She gulped it back down.

'MUMMA!' Sunny's scream tore through the closed door.

'Shit!' mumbled Zoya.

She dashed to Sunny's room and flung open the door.

She gasped. The quilt had been thrown aside. Sunny was not in bed.

'Sunny!' she screamed. She switched on the lights and dashed to his empty bed, forgetting her police training for a moment as her motherly instincts took over.

She heard a hiss behind her.

She turned. All she saw was a woman in a black sari wearing dark sunglasses and gaudy pink lipstick before she swung a cricket bat at her. Before Zoya could raise her hands, the bat rammed her nose.

Zoya fell. Her eyes flickered. Her head lolled like a car spiralling out of control. She couldn't breathe through her nose. It was clogged with blood and broken cartilage. She gulped in deep drags of air through the mouth.

She blinked rapidly to move past the tears and fight the dizziness. She had to get up. She had to save Sunny.

Zoya sat up.

Bam!

She heard the crunch in her skull before unimaginable pain swarmed her brain.

Sunny—was her last thought before darkness engulfed her completely.

44

Nalini swerved her white hatchback into the driveway and turned off the ignition. The engine gave one final yelp before shushing completely, letting the sound of wild crickets and cicadas echo through the night. She slumped back in the seat with a feeble sigh, her hands dropping into her lap, releasing the tension that had built up in her shoulders since she had decamped with Sunny.

Sunny. The thought of the boy stiffened her again.

She turned around in her seat and saw the boy sprawled on the back seat, fast asleep. She relaxed. The sedative was strong enough to keep the boy knocked out till morning. *By then, it would be too late.*

She was jolted out of her reverie by the jarring sound of the front gate sliding back into place. Her work tonight wasn't finished yet. She slipped out of the car, opened the back door and scooped up Sunny in her arms. She let his head rest on her shoulder, placing one hand under his bottom to support his weight. She kicked the car door shut. After a brief struggle with Sunny in her arms, she finally managed to lock the car.

She lumbered across the damp lawn to the cabin, the single floodlight by the driveway casting a long shadow on the dewy grass. Her eyes flicked sideways to the house. Ranveer's house. As always, it was shrouded in darkness, like the owner was forever in mourning. A wave of relief swept over her. She was thankful for the privacy, grateful to live out her last few days in peace.

She choked back a flood of tears. *Three more to go*, she reminded herself. *Then, finally, I can be with you, mother.* She looked up at the night sky, the full moon hidden behind flimsy clouds.

She stopped at the front door of the cabin. Her dishevelled and grimy appearance was reflected in the mirror on the door. The Band-Aid on her brow had turned crimson and needed to be replaced.

Suddenly, she saw a shadow at the edge of the mirror. Her heart jumped. She swung around sharply. No one. She stood still, while her eyes kept roving across the lawn and the unlit house. No movement. Nothing.

She exhaled loudly and turned back to the keypad and entered her password. The door opened with a sharp ding. She stepped inside and let the door bang shut behind her, knowing that even trumpets would not wake Sunny in his current state. Without turning on the lights, she trudged to the bed and laid Sunny down on the mattress.

Nalini stood there in near darkness and watched the boy sleep. She ruffled his hair.

'One more day, sweetheart,' she said to the boy, 'and you'll eternally be this peaceful.'

She pulled a quilt over Sunny, bent down and kissed his forehead.

Nalini walked to the bathroom and tapped the light switch. It didn't turn on. She switched it off and on again. Didn't work. *That's odd*, she thought. She had changed the bulb a few months ago. It was too soon for another change. *Perhaps there's some issue with the circuitry.*

Nalini left the bathroom door open to let in the muted floodlight, which struggled to sweep in through the window. She unclipped her hair extensions and put them aside. Next, she opened the medicine cabinet built into the wall and extracted some cotton pads and a make-up remover. Within minutes she had stripped off her make-up, revealing the male she was born as.

I need a shave. Again, she thought.

She turned on the tap and splashed water on her face. It felt nice. Like Mom used to do when she removed Nalini's make-up when she was young. She doused her face with water again, revelling in the few seconds of tranquillity.

She looked up into the mirror, water dripping from her brow.

There was a sudden movement behind her. Like a shadow flitting in and out of the mirror.

She spun around and looked behind her.

Nothing. No movement, no sound.

She shook her head. *I'm becoming a scaredy-cat*, she mused.

She turned back to the mirror. And there he was, staring back at her, his eyes dark, his countenance fierce, his arm outstretched, pointing a gun at her head.

'I've been waiting for you for a long time, Nalini,' said Ranveer. 'Or should I say Doll Maker?'

45

'He is *my* son! Don't take Sunny away from me! Please, Abbas. Please!' Zoya clung to her husband outside the courthouse, tears streaming down her cheeks.

'Step aside, Zoya. People are staring. Don't create a scene!' he hissed. 'The court has ruled. I have full custody of Sunny now.'

'I beg you, Abbas. Please don't do this.' With a thump, she fell at his feet, clutching his leg and embracing it tightly. 'I'm his mother. How will I live without him? Please . . . I beg you,' she said, her voice cracking.

Abbas bent down and grabbed her arm. She felt a painful prick as his long, uncut nails dug into her skin. 'You should have thought of that when you filed for divorce, Zoya. Now, get lost!'

He tried to push her away. He stood up, exasperated and wiped away the beads of sweat on his forehead with his shirt sleeve.

Zoya didn't let go of him. Her wails only got louder.

People started to gather around them, mostly for the entertainment value rather than to intervene, as if it were a street show.

Abbas sighed. He had a reputation to protect. He squatted and whispered in Zoya's ears, 'Look, I'm not taking Sunny away from you. You still have visitation rights on weekends. Heck, I'll even send him over to your house myself on weekends.'

Zoya calmed down a little. Her wails turned to sobs.

'Now, stop behaving like a child and get up. Or I won't hesitate to go to court and take away your visitation rights as well!'

The threat worked. Zoya shook her head. 'No, please don't.'

'Then you better let me go. Now. Before I change my mind.'

Zoya let go of his leg.

Abbas smoothed the wrinkles on his trousers and walked away even before Zoya could push herself upright. Her cheeks burnt in the afternoon sun. She didn't cover her face, didn't move into the shade. In that moment, pain felt like an understanding and empathic friend who hugs you and holds you tight even when the people around stare and judge and snicker at your plight.

In the distance, she saw Abbas jump into his chauffeur-driven BMW. Sunny, in the back seat, clung to the back glass, crying, trying to reach out for his mother with his chubby, little hands while the nanny tried to prise him away.

Instinctively, Zoya extended her arm, her fingers reaching for Sunny, her heart aching to hold him tight.

'Sunny . . .' she whispered.

The car started to move away. Sunny flapped his arms in desperation, his face contorted in anguish.

'Sunny,' she raised her voice and began running after the car.

The car gained speed and, within seconds, Sunny was whisked out of sight.

'Sunny! Sunny!' she screamed.

She opened her eyes.

The bedroom light stung her pupils. She grimaced and closed her eyes again.

'Sunny,' she mumbled. And realized that she had been dreaming.

She gasped, gulping in air through her mouth. She couldn't breathe in through her nose. *Why?* Her head was on fire, like she had locked horns with a raging bull. She lifted her hand and pressed a finger into the back of her head.

'Aieeee!' she moaned in pain.

Her finger felt moist. *Sweat?*

She opened and shut her bleary eyes, trying to adjust to the harsh lighting. Soon, Sunny's room came into focus. His bed, his toys, his open wardrobe.

Just as suddenly, it all came back to her. The wardrobe door left ajar, the monster under the bed, the cricket bat smacking her face and the intruder.

'Sunny!' she howled and sat up.

The pain inside her skull spiralled. She clenched her teeth and wheezed loudly. But the very thought of Sunny being in danger propelled her to her feet. She floundered out of the bedroom, like she was wading through mud.

'Sunny!' Her voice bellowed in the stillness of night.

No response.

'Sunny!'

Using the wall as a crutch, she stumbled into the living room. It was dark and much colder here. The only source of light, bleak and dull, was the street lamp outside.

No sign of Sunny. No sign of the woman in the black sari.

Zoya turned to the front door and stopped. The front door was open. The chilly night breeze burst in, unhindered.

It was then that it hit her. The black sari. The gaudy pink lipstick. A missing five-year-old boy who had lost his mother. The Doll Maker had kidnapped Sunny. Based on previous cases, Sunny had twenty-four hours before he turned up dead in a glass case.

46

Nalini stood paralysed in front of the mirror, staring at the reflection of the gun's muzzle inches from her head.

'I trusted you, Nalini,' hissed Ranveer. 'I gave you a place to stay when you came to me last year, destitute and starving. I honoured our childhood friendship, despite no contact whatsoever since we both were five. But . . .' he paused, 'you betrayed me.'

'Betrayed you?' Nalini found her voice.

'You took away what was mine, what has always been mine.'

Nalini didn't understand. A roof over her head—for which she paid regular rent—was the only thing Ranveer had provided. What was she missing?

'What did I take away, Ranveer?' said Nalini, her brow furrowed in confusion. 'Yes, I'm the Doll Maker. Yes, I used your premises to put my little boys to sleep. But not once did I interfere with your life. Just like you had asked. So, I ask you again, what did I take away that was so precious that you are standing here, holding a gun to my head rather than turning me in to the police?'

Ranveer gulped. Nalini saw his Adam's apple move up and down as he swallowed hard.

'Fame,' he whispered. The gun quivered. His hand started trembling in desperation.

'Fame?'

'For nine years, the people of Bhopal talked about me, wrote stories about me, feared me. Nine. Long. Years. But then you came along. Within days you took away what I had worked *so* hard to achieve as the Clipper. And now, no matter what I do, they seem to only care about the Doll Maker.' He hissed her moniker like it was a curse.

The Clipper? The words whirled and tumbled inside Nalini's head. She vaguely recalled reading about the Clipper. *Where?*

Suddenly, her eyes widened as she remembered the heinous crimes hidden behind newspaper headlines.

Ranveer snorted. 'See. It took you a while to even remember me. Slowly but surely the Clipper is fading from memory. All thanks to you.'

'You . . . you are the Clipper?' Nalini grabbed the bathroom sink to steady herself.

Ranveer smiled smugly, 'The one and only.'

Nalini stood tall. 'Go ahead, then. Shoot me.'

Ranveer stopped smiling and narrowed his eyes, 'I'm not kidding. I *will* pull the trigger.'

'Do it.' Nalini locked eyes with his reflection in the mirror. 'I was going to do it in three days anyway. Saves me from committing suicide. One less sin to take to Mom.'

Ranveer brought his other hand up to steady his gun-bearing hand. 'Suicide? You're going to just walk away from all this fame?'

'Ha!' Nalini shook her head. 'One person's fame is another's bane. You're most welcome to take back your precious fame, Ranveer.'

Ranveer steadied his finger on the trigger. 'If that's what you want, so be it.'

He pulled the trigger. A resounding gunshot reverberated in the tiny bathroom, its echo both piercing and numbing.

The mirror shattered. A thousand shards flew unfettered, leaving behind a single, skewed piece still attached to the top of the frame.

'You can't kill me, Ranveer. At least not without killing yourself.' Nalini stared at her reflection and giggled. Her soft, girly laughter sounding more ominous than infectious.

The face in the mirror turned dark, stopped laughing and pointed the gun at its own reflection in the mirror. 'What do you mean?' said Ranveer's manly voice.

'You still don't get it, do you?' the voice was Nalini's again. 'I am you. And you are me. We're different. And yet, we're the same.'

'No! We are not!' Ranveer raised the gun and fired again. *Bang!*

The last remaining piece of the bathroom mirror splintered.

He looked around. Nalini was gone.

A nervous laugh slipped through his mouth. 'I killed you,' he whispered. He laughed wildly like a man possessed. 'I killed the Doll Maker!' he howled, his voice ringing in the constricted space.

Suddenly, a voice nagged him, like another person was speaking inside his head. It was Nalini's voice. *Where is the body?*

He stopped laughing. He shook his head and massaged his eyes, trying to remain alert. His gaze swept the floor around him. The voice was right. *Where is Nalini's body? Am I going crazy?*

He bolted out of the bathroom and ran out of the cabin, leaving the door open. He stopped in the middle of the lawn, bent down, hands on his knees, trying to catch his breath. He was wheezing, as if a bout of an asthma attack had gripped him.

He saw his shadow on the ground—a long, dark silhouette marked by the lonesome floodlight. He gulped, forgetting to breathe for a moment. The shadow was wearing a sari. His hands felt the soft touch of chiffon on his knees, and suddenly, he knew. He knew what Nalini meant. *I am you. And, you are me.*

He started to shake uncontrollably. He had never worn a sari. But . . . Nalini had always worn one. Even as kids. When Dad would be away at work, Mom would insist on inviting Nalini. Always. She would dress her up in chiffon saris, drink tea from toy cups and dance with dolls. She adored Nalini like the daughter she had always wanted, but never had.

But, after that fatal day—when Dad came home early, found Nalini and slammed a whisky bottle into Mom's head—Ranveer had stepped in to protect Nalini. Every night Dad would come to his room in a drunken rage with a cigarette in hand, its orange embers seared like a vivid dream into his memory. He would ask Nalini to hide while his dad grabbed his balls and reminded him that he was a boy. *A boy! Not a sissy girl*, Dad would roar, his speech slurred, his breath stale. And if Ranveer's heartrending screams weren't enough as Dad crushed his balls, he would jam the burning cigarette into the back of Ranveer's hand, telling him *never ever* to invite Nalini into the house again. Ranveer never did. Till Dad died last year—suicide, said the cops—and there was no longer a need to protect Nalini. But now that he thought about it, his mind perfectly clear, he couldn't shake off the uncanny similarity between Dad's suicide and the deaths of Nalini's dolls.

'Was it suicide or . . .' Ranveer braced himself and asked the sari-clad shadow, '. . . did you kill Dad?'

No response.

Then Nalini's girly giggles filled the silence, 'I had to. For us. For you.'

'You didn't *have* to!' he yelled at the shadow, his voice raspy, his tremors wild. 'I had taken care of the situation.'

'By running away from home?' said Nalini.

'You are a fine one to talk! I protected you for months before you ran away.'

'You didn't protect me, Ranveer,' Nalini's voice became shrill, like a little girl yelling, 'you jailed me! Locked me away. Just like Dad told you to. It took me years, but I finally broke out of the prison you built around me.'

'If I hadn't, Dad would have killed you.'

'And you.'

'What do you mean?'

Nalini chuckled. 'You still don't get it, do you? We are two souls in one body. I die, you die. Simple.'

Ranveer held his head with both hands, his mind whirring too fast to speak.

Nalini waited, letting it sink in.

Ranveer looked up with a jerk, his hands falling to his sides. 'And . . . you said . . . you were going to commit suicide in three days.' He pointed an accusing finger at the shadow on the ground, 'You were going to kill both of us!'

Nalini's head drooped in sadness. She nodded, slowly.

'I miss Mom,' tears started flowing from the corners of her eyes. 'I miss Mom *so* much!' she sniffled. 'Mom used to say that we pay for our sins on the very earth where we commit them.' She looked at the shadow on the ground, tears streaming down her ruddy cheeks. 'So, I am paying for my sins, Ranveer. Saving little boys tormented by their fathers, deprived of their mother's love. I am *saving* those kids, Ranveer. Penance for my sins. Before I can meet Mom again.'

Ranveer was unmoved, his face stoic. 'That's why,' he murmured to himself.

'What?' asked Nalini, crying, her voice cracking.

'That's why I was infuriated, almost demented, itching to find you. And stop you. My body—*our* body—sensed the danger it was in. And, once again, like it has always done, it called to me for help, to step in and protect us while you ran away and hid like a coward.'

'No, please, no,' Nalini fell to her knees. She was sobbing uncontrollably now. 'Let me go to Mom. Please.'

Ranveer stood up. He was seething with renewed purpose, with unflagging fury.

In that rage, he knew how to send Nalini back to the jail she had come from. He had done it once. He could do it again. All that was needed was the fear of Dad coursing through his veins.

He pulled apart his cardigan. The buttons broke away with an audible *twitch*, flying aimlessly before soundlessly dropping on the grass. He removed and threw away the cardigan like it was on fire.

'What . . . what are you doing?' A cold shiver of fear ran down Nalini's body.

Ranveer didn't reply. He pulled away the pallu of the sari, unfurled the pleats, and peeled away the soft fabric wrapped around his legs.

'No!' Nalini tried to stop Ranveer, but her feeble attempts were no match for his deranged intensity.

The blouse and the petticoat came off next.

Nalini shivered, standing in the frigid cold in her undergarments, before Ranveer stripped those away too.

'I'm taking back control!' he hissed. 'Sending you back to where you came from!'

'No! Please, Ranveer!'

Stark naked, Ranveer ran towards his house, away from Nalini's shadow. He had regained control of the body. It was his to save, his to wrench away from the hell Nalini was planning to send it to.

He burst inside the house, locking the door behind him and switched on the lights. Instantly, he came face to face with his multiple reflections bouncing off the mirrors that lined the walls of the living room.

'Wait! Listen to me for one second, Ranveer,' said the reflection of Nalini.

Mirrors! The realization hit him like an unsuspecting bird crashing into a window. That's how he had always communicated with Nalini, without knowing that she was living inside his own body like a parasite.

The parasite must be expunged.

'Get away from me!' he roared at the reflection.

He peeled his gaze away from the mirrors and fixed it on the floor. He ran for the staircase and dashed upstairs, taking two stairs at a time, to his bedroom.

He was panting. Breathless. Sweat buttered his armpits.

He rushed to the bedside table and pulled open the drawer. A pack of cigarettes.

He swallowed hard, knowing what came next.

He snatched the pack, his hands shaking, and ripped it open. A few fell on the floor. He took one out and snapped open the lighter. He flicked it. The lighter didn't ignite.

'Come on! Come on,' he howled.

He flicked it again. A flame burst through, dousing his face in orange hues.

He lit the cigarette, his hands shaking violently now. He gulped.

You are a boy! Not a sissy girl! Dad's hoarse voice clamoured in his head.

'Goodbye, Nalini,' Ranveer screamed.

He jammed the burning cigarette into the back of his hand.

Day 5

47

Her home, the last vestige of innocence, her locus of solace, had become a crime scene. Zoya stood at the entrance to Sunny's room, arms crossed, shivering, fingernails piercing the skin of her upper arms through the sheer sweater. Despite the technicians and the inspectors milling around in the room, it felt empty. Sunny was gone. Missing. Kidnapped.

Night had given way to the wee hours of the morning. It had been hours since the technicians arrived. So far, they had unearthed nothing more than what she already knew. It had been hours since an alert message had been sent to all traffic police on beat duty. But no one had seen Sunny. Or a woman in a black sari with an abducted kid. The description was too wide and her hope dim. She was running out of patience and ideas to find her son.

'Anything? Did you find any fingerprints? Any evidence? Anything?' she shrieked at the personnel gathered in the room.

Everyone stopped working and looked at Zoya, either with pity or exasperation. She had been riding them hard all night, asking them to double-check and triple-check everything. She had even heard one of them say in jest that Simone had had a bad influence on her.

Dr D'Souza, the lead medical examiner, cleared his throat and said, 'Carry on, folks . . . Zoya, a word, please?' He walked out of the room, a grim expression on his face, like when people are about to deliver bad news but words elude them.

'Let's talk in the living room, shall we?'

Zoya slumped on the sofa. Her arms remained wound around her chest, fingernails digging into her skin. To her, it was a small penance for not keeping her child safe; punishment to keep the gnawing guilt at bay.

'How's your head? Fine?'

'Fine.'

What kind of a question was that? Of course, I'm NOT fine. But it had nothing to do with the throbbing head wound. She had allowed the medics to clean the wound and bandage it, but she had flatly refused to go to the hospital. It was still her case, her crime scene. It had just become more personal. And time-bound.

'Good, good,' Dr D'Souza pushed up his glasses.

Zoya started to tap her feet on the floor, waiting, impatiently for the doctor to get to the point.

'Zoya, we all understand that it's a difficult time for you. You are hurt—'

'I said I'm fine!' Zoya interrupted.

Dr D'Souza nodded and continued. 'Yes . . . but, I can't even begin to understand what havoc Sunny's disappearance must be wreaking on you.'

Zoya bit her lip, her foot started tapping faster.

'I really think you should get some sleep and—'

'Did you find anything in the room? Anything that can help me find Sunny?'

Dr D'Souza sighed and moistened his lips. 'Unfortunately, not much. The assailant was most likely wearing gloves. We found black fibres, probably from the sari, but it won't help us nab the guy. Our best bet is the hair strands we found under the bed. We have sent them for DNA profiling and matching with our database. But, as you know, it'll take some time and—'

'And what?'

'If it was a man wearing a sari, I think it's also possible that the hair strands are from a wig . . . I just don't want you to get your hopes up.'

'Anything else?' Zoya said without any expression on her face.

Dr D'Souza shook his head.

'Okay. Then I think your work here is done.'

The old man nodded and stood up, his knees creaking in protest. Within ten minutes, the lead technician wrapped up the work and left with his crew.

Zoya remained motionless on the sofa the entire time, her mind numb, her body jittery. There had been no ransom call so far. No message from the Doll Maker. Nothing. Which only confirmed her worst fear: by the end of the day, Sunny, like all the other little boys, would be found dressed like a Barbie. Dead.

Zoya jolted upright on the sofa and started pacing back and forth.

Suddenly, there was a knock on her fully open door. It was one of the constables on sentry duty outside her house. Zoya didn't know why she needed protection, but superintendent

Hussain had insisted. So, she had agreed to the increased vigilance at her house in exchange for staying on the case.

'Madam *ji*, this parcel came for you.' He handed Zoya a thin rectangular box wrapped like a birthday gift. It even had a bow tied around it.

Zoya took the box. It wasn't her birthday. Nor was it Sunny's. *Who'd send a gift to her?*

Her heart raced. She opened the bow and ripped apart the wrapping paper.

She gasped.

It was a Barbie doll inside a transparent, plastic box. There was a note stuck on the box.

She flipped open the tiny card. It said:

I'll return your Barbie doll very soon. Till then, you can play with mine.

48

Simone sat up in bed. She scrunched her nose as pain erupted in her midriff. The painkillers were starting to wear off, but she forced herself to fight through the pain rather than risk a lifelong addiction to pain killers. She had heard of more cops addicted to post-operative drugs than she cared to emulate.

While Grandma immersed herself in prime-time entertainment, Simone's mind whirred back to the curious case of the Doll Maker. She had come close, very close, to catching the man hiding behind dollops of make-up and the pallu of his black sari. She had him pinned to the ground. With nowhere to escape. But the lucky bastard managed to grab her gun at the right moment and slipped away. Come to think of it, he could have shot her in the head. He didn't. Why? *You understand me*, he had said, when she called him a little girl. He even apologized for shooting her. *I'm sorry, Simone*, he had said. *How did he know my name?* He was probably following his own case, trying to keep up with the police.

There was something oddly familiar about him. Like she knew him from somewhere. An acquaintance or a schoolmate, but long forgotten.

Suddenly, her eyes flew open. *He hadn't said 'I'm sorry, Simone'. He had said 'I'm sorry Simo . . . Simone.'*

'Shit!' she mouthed.

Grandma turned to her instantly. 'What happened, *bachu*? Are you okay?'

Simone was silent for a moment. The realization heavy on her mind. *How was it possible? He cannot be the Doll Maker!* The man she had encountered in the woods didn't look anything like him. Sure, he had the same build and a similar jawline, although she couldn't be absolutely sure. The colour of his eyes was different. *But that can be changed with lenses*, she answered her own doubt. The sari-clad man in the forest had long and lush hair. *But those could be hair extensions*. And how did he manage to speak so convincingly like a little girl?

'Simone?' Grandma got up from the chair. 'Is the pain unbearable? I can ask the doctor to increase the dosage.'

Simone glanced at her grandma. 'No . . . no. I'm okay. I just need to make a call.' She turned, ignoring the pain that erupted in her belly and reached for her smartphone lying next to her pillow.

'It's work-related, Grandma. I just remembered something and need to make a call. You carry on with your serial,' she said, as she furiously stabbed the phone with her fingers. She found the number she was looking for and stabbed it one final time to make the call.

The call went unanswered.

'Fuck!' said Simone.

'Simone, language!' said Grandma.

Simone apologized meekly and dialled the number again.

'Pick up. Pick up,' murmured Simone.

This time the call was answered.

'Zoya?' said Simone.

'Simone, I don't have time right now,' Zoya's voice was on edge, 'unless it's about Sunny and how I can find—'

'I know who he is!'

Zoya quietened for a moment. 'What do you mean?'

'I know who the Doll Maker is.'

'Who?'

'I'll tell you, but you'll have to smuggle me out of the hospital first. Because I'm not going to miss the moment when we catch the sonofabitch.'

'I'm on my way. But tell me, who is the Doll Maker?'

'The only person who calls me *Simo*. Karan Kapoor!'

49

Pius stood at the entrance of Hotel Desire. He checked the watch on his mobile phone. 8.55 p.m. *Five minutes before the Clipper arrives*, he thought.

He rubbed his smooth, hairless arms, hoping it would stave off the biting cold. Didn't help. *Should have insisted on a shawl at least*, he thought. When he had asked superintendent Hussain for a cosy sweater to cover the flimsy sari he was forced to wear, the police superintendent had reprimanded him and said—*you are not a homely girl being given away in marriage. You are an escort. Show some skin. And, please, act like one!*

Pius sighed.

He jumped in place, like he was skipping a rope, his earrings and bangles jingling with the motion. He stopped immediately when the six-inch stilettos wobbled as if he was on stilts.

'Dammit!' he cursed.

The hotel receptionist looked at him curiously. Pius looked away quickly, afraid his face would betray his thoughts.

The receptionist was a policeman in disguise. So were the two autorickshaw drivers waiting for passengers at the entrance and the couple snogging in one corner of the front courtyard. All police personnel undercover. All were waiting to pounce on the Clipper when he arrived. Superintendent Hussain, along with a few police inspectors, was in the surveillance room inside the hotel, monitoring the feed from spy cameras fitted around the hotel.

What was I thinking? Not for the first time Pius chided himself for agreeing to go undercover as a transgender escort. When the superintendent had floated the idea yesterday, it had seemed 'cool'—yep, that's what he had called it. *Idiot!* he scolded himself again. He couldn't remember what made him agree. Was it the charm of an adventure in the field compared to the monotony of sitting in front of a laptop each day? Was it to impress a superior? Or, simply, did he think it'd be fun?

'Fun, my foot!' he murmured, the stinging in his heels surging at the thought.

'Stay focused, Pius!' Hussain's voice boomed through the minuscule earpiece plugged deep into his ear.

Shit! He had forgotten that superintendent Hussain was listening through the microphone planted inside the sequined brooch that pinned his pallu in place.

'Sorry . . . sorry, sir,' he whispered.

'Don't answer back!' Hussain exploded on the earpiece. 'The Clipper might be around. If he sees you talking to yourself, he'll know you're wired.'

Pius nodded hastily. Blew a white plume of breath, hoping the Clipper would arrive before his heels gave up.

It had taken a team of quickly assembled make-up artists and hair stylists an entire day to prepare Pius for the role he was essaying tonight—Pisces, the bubbly transgender intent on showing the Clipper the steamiest night of his life, right before the police nabbed the perp . . . or, and this sent a frightened flutter into the pit of his stomach, the Clipper killed him first. *No, I should have never agreed to this*, he thought, breaking into a cold sweat.

'Excuse me, madam?'

Pius jumped in surprise. A grey-haired man, in tattered and putrid-smelling overalls, had crept up on him without him noticing. The man held out his hand. Initially, Pius thought that the man was a beggar asking for alms. Then, he noticed a phone in the man's hand.

'Yes . . . what do you want?' said Pius. He didn't try to sweeten his manly voice with feminine fervour.

The old man was taken aback by his voice, for his eyes widened in surprise.

A compliment for his team of stylists, mused Pius. The get-up was working. He could pass as a woman till he opened his mouth.

'Are you Pisces?'

Pius was about to say no when he remembered that that was his name tonight.

'Ye . . . yes,' he stammered.

Was this the Clipper? An old, withering, homeless man?

'This mobile is for you,' said the homeless man, stretching his arm further, holding out the phone.

'For me?' said Pius.

'Yes, your boyfriend . . .' the man pointed to the street behind Pius, 'gave me the phone and asked me to give it to you.'

Pius turned around. The street was deserted. There was no one watching or waiting.

'Did he say his name?'

The old man scratched his scraggly beard. 'Ah, yes! Mr Ripple.'

Pius's heart started to pound. The Clipper was here. Somewhere close, watching, secretly.

Gingerly, Pius took the phone from the old man like it was a ticking bomb. He realized that a burner phone was how the Clipper wanted to communicate with him. *Smart.* The Clipper had asked for Pisces's mobile number in a subsequent chat on G.B.T. The police had rejoiced and put a tracer on his phone, thinking that a call from the perp would be easy to trace. They were wrong. It was a ploy. Best case, the Clipper was just being careful. Worst case, he knew about the trap the police had laid and was toying with them. Pius swallowed; the thought sent a cold shiver down his spine.

The burner phone started to ring.

Pius looked around, hoping to see the Clipper nearby holding a phone to his ear. There was no one except the undercover cops, alert and watchful.

Pius cleared his throat and accepted the call.

'Hi!' he whispered the word like he was moaning while making love. Superintendent Hussain wanted him to act like a sexy escort yearning for love. So be it.

'Pisces?' said a gruff voice.

'Yes, darling. I've been eagerly waiting for you.'

The man on the phone snorted. He didn't mince words and came to the point, 'I want you to cross the hotel's courtyard and walk to the street. Now.'

'Umm . . . but . . . I thought you were coming to pick me up here?'

'Just a precaution. Now, do as I say. And don't disconnect the phone.'

Pius stood frozen for a brief moment.

Seeing no way out, Pius started sashaying towards the street, his stilettos clicking against the concrete courtyard, his tenuous hips swaying like a fashion model on a runway—exactly like he had been taught in the little time he had to prepare for the act tonight. Pius stared at the undercover cops as he walked past the autorickshaw drivers, hoping they'd follow him. They didn't. They sat there watching him walk away, confusion dripping from their alarmed faces.

'Don't worry. Do as he says. You're wearing a GPS tracker.' Hussain's voice buzzed in his earpiece. It comforted Pius to know that the police superintendent had understood. Unconsciously, Pius touched the hair clip that not only held his fake hair extensions in place but also a GPS-tracking device.

He crossed the street, just as a black Maruti Suzuki Swift pulled up right next to him.

'Get in the black car!' the Clipper's urgent voice boomed from the burner phone.

Pius controlled the urge to look back at the safety of the hotel surrounded by cops. It'd be a dead giveaway, so he composed himself, slid into the front seat of the car, and shut the door.

'Hello, ma'am! I'm your Uber driver for today,' a middle-aged man, missing a front tooth, gleamed at Pius.

'Hello,' said Pius.

The driver did a double take on hearing Pius's voice. 'Oh . . . sorry,' said the driver. 'Sir or ma'am, what do you prefer?'

'Tell the Uber driver to shut up and drive!' the Clipper hissed on the phone.

'Let's go, please,' Pius said to the driver politely. 'I'm in a hurry.'

The driver nodded. He turned up the volume on the radio, which was crooning the Lady Gaga and Bradley Cooper number, 'Shallow'. The song was one of his favourites, but Pius was in no mood to sing along. The driver stepped on the accelerator and sped away from Hotel Desire.

Pius breathed in deeply and stole a quick glance back at the receding hotel in the side-view mirror. He wrung his hands to stay calm. If anything, his nerves only intensified. His only thought—*I have been kidnapped. Willingly.*

50

'Ask the Uber driver to stop here,' the Clipper's urgent yet serene voice filled Pius's ears.

'Umm . . . you can drop me here,' Pius relayed to the driver.

'Here? But the address says—'

'Yes, here!' said Pius.

'Okay.' The driver shrugged his shoulders, turned on the flashing blinkers, and parked the car by the kerb on a busy main road. The vehicles behind honked incessantly showing their displeasure at their sudden stop, before veering away.

'How much?' Pius asked, unsure who was paying for the ride.

'Already paid with card, ma'am. Thank you for riding with me. And, if you don't mind, can you give me five stars on the app please?' He flashed a broad, disarming smile.

Pius smiled back and nodded.

'Pisces, get out of the car. Fast. Drop the phone on the road and get into the Mercedes-Benz behind it,' the Clipper said on the phone before disconnecting the call.

Pius lowered the phone from his ear. He peered into the side mirror and spotted a red SUV come to a stop right behind his Uber ride. He swivelled in his seat, grabbed the front of his unruly sari, and stepped on to the paved shoulder along the road.

'Shit!' His face immediately scrunched into a painful grimace as his feet hurt. The pain, although unbearable, reminded him to stay in character. Tonight, he was Pisces, a transgender person. He adjusted his sari, like he had seen sari-clad women do so often, making sure his movements, even if exaggerated, were both delicate and deliberate.

Pius braced himself as the cold breeze tickled his bare arms and sashayed down the kerb to the Mercedes. Its passenger window rolled down as he approached the car.

'Throw the phone and get in!' said the slender man at the wheel. Dark aviators rested above his gaunt cheeks and chiselled jaw. His shoulder-length hair had been slicked back with gel. He would have looked like a rich man's chauffeur, except that he was wearing a tuxedo, ready for the Oscars, it seemed. *Definitely looks like a movie star*, thought Pius.

Pius dropped the phone and let it shatter against the asphalt. He pulled open the SUV door and slipped into the front seat.

'Seat belt, please,' said the man.

Pius did as instructed, the tiny hairs on the back of his neck tingling, his mouth suddenly dry.

Without saying another word, the man locked all the car doors and swerved the Mercedes into the moving traffic. He was a pool of calmness—there was no sense of urgency or hurried movements. It was completely at odds with the Uber dash that Pius had just experienced.

It was then that Pius noticed strange circular scars on the back of the man's hand while he manoeuvred the steering wheel. *Does he have a skin disease or something?* he wondered.

'Hi, I'm Ripple,' the man said in a hushed tone.

Pius swallowed hard. He was sitting right next to a mass murderer. He was locked inside a moving car with a serial killer. Nowhere to run to escape from the Clipper.

The Clipper took a sharp right turn.

Pius moistened his lips to speak, but the Clipper continued, 'I'm sorry about before. It was a necessary precaution.'

Pius cleared his throat. 'I understand, darling. If anything, it made this date even more exciting. Like an adventure.'

He took another right turn, his eyes focused on the rear-view mirror.

The Clipper smiled. 'I like your voice.'

'My voice?'

He nodded, his eyes on the road. 'I like that you embrace your manly voice, without trying to sound like a woman.'

He took another right turn.

'Oh . . .' Pius wasn't sure how to respond. 'Thanks!' he said, finally. 'I hope you like the sari. I specially picked it out for you tonight.' Pius flashed his long, fake eyelashes at the Clipper.

The Clipper ran his tongue over his lips. Pius saw a glint in his eyes. 'I'm sure I would like to take it off you.'

The Clipper took another right turn. His eyes kept switching between the rear-view mirror and the road ahead.

'Umm . . . aren't we on the same road where you picked me up from?' said Pius, looking around, confused.

The Clipper sighed. 'Yes. I took four right turns and came back to where we started from.' He glanced at Pius for a moment, his lips creasing into a tiny smile. 'Just making sure you weren't followed. One can't be too cautious given the business we're indulging in. I'm sure you appreciate that.'

'I do,' said Pius, trying to sound merrier despite the realization that the police weren't on their tail. He was on his own, left to deal with a serial killer. His breathing intensified. Superintendent Hussain hadn't said a word into the earpiece for a while now, aggravating his nerves, which were already on edge. Maybe the earpiece was out of range? He hoped the GPS tracker in his hair clip was still working.

Suddenly, the Clipper veered off the main road and entered the dark woods near Bhopal national park.

Beads of sweat appeared on Pius's forehead as question after question hammered at him. *Where is he taking me? Is he going to kill me deep in the forest? Will anyone find my dead body? Would I feel pain when he clips me? Of course, I will!* He answered his own question and folded his hands together, as if praying in a temple.

'Is everything okay, Pisces? You look scared.'

Pius let out a nervous laugh. 'Yes,' he admitted, 'I'm scared of venturing into the forest at night.'

'Don't be!' snorted the Clipper. 'I'm here to protect you.'

Pius covered his mouth, his bangles jingling, to prevent himself from snorting back at the Clipper's empty promises.

The Clipper stepped on the accelerator, swerving the SUV on a gravel road.

'I was thinking we take the party to my farmhouse tonight. It's near the park. It's in the middle of nowhere, actually. A perfect combination of privacy and pleasure. You'll like it, I'm sure.'

Pius rubbed his hands together. He wasn't sure he liked this at all. Again, and not for the first time tonight, he chided himself for agreeing to go undercover. He was no James Bond. His skills were limited to facing an unethical hacker with a laptop, not a cold-blooded killer with stilettos.

They travelled on the gravel road for ten minutes before Pius saw a two-storey building, surrounded by a wall of concrete, emerge within a clearing of trees.

'Wow! It's magnificent. You live here?' Pius asked, buttering his tone with sham excitement.

The Clipper beamed, as if proud. 'It *is* grand, isn't it?' He slowed down and pressed a button on the steering wheel. The thick, ponderous front gate slid sideways automatically, allowing the car to enter the driveway.

Pius noticed a single floodlight irradiating the lush, sprawling lawn next to the driveway. A brick structure, like a cabin, stood at the far end of the lawn. It was pitch black inside the main house. Engulfed by fog, it towered like a sinister ghost against a backdrop of deciduous trees.

'Home sweet home,' said the Clipper, turning off the ignition. 'Stay. I'll help you out, Pisces.' The Clipper jumped out of the SUV and slammed the door shut behind him.

For a moment, Pius thought he was trapped inside the car. The sudden stillness was suffocating. But then, the Clipper strode around the vehicle and opened the door for him.

'Come, my lady,' said the Clipper, extending his hand and bowing slightly, like a medieval knight.

My chivalrous killer in shining armour, thought Pius. It did nothing to assuage his strained nerves. *Where were the police?* The question gnawed at him as he held out his finely manicured hand for the Clipper. The red nail polish adorning his fingernails shimmered against the heavy beams of the floodlight. Pius let the Clipper help him out of the car.

The Clipper locked the car and wrapped an arm around Pius's waist. 'You are freezing! Let's get you inside.'

Pius nodded, both thankful and apprehensive about the suggestion.

They walked towards the house. The Clipper's hand dropped a little and came to rest on his buttock.

Pius wanted to slap his hand away but decided against it. *I'm an escort*, he reminded himself. He tilted his head closer to the Clipper's and whispered, 'Would you like to give them a little squeeze?'

The Clipper beamed heartily like a kid handed the keys to a candy store. He stopped, pulling Pius closer, right there on the veranda, both hands grabbing and squeezing his bottom. 'You mean, like this? Or . . .' he pinched the cheeks harder, '. . . like this?'

Pius squealed, more from pain than delight.

'Ha!' the Clipper chortled.

Suddenly, the muted scream of a child tore through the stillness of the night.

'Who was that?' said Pius, abruptly turning towards the source of the noise: the cabin.

'I don't—'

Another scream.

'Do you have a kid?' Pius asked, confused if the Clipper was hiding a wife and a kid he didn't know about.

'No, that's my tenant's kid. A single mom. Why don't I make you comfortable inside first and then come back to check if everything's all right with the tenant?'

The Clipper nudged Pius towards the front door without waiting for an answer. Pius complied.

The Clipper paused and tapped a password into the keypad attached to the door. The door opened with a sharp ding, like gears meshing, somewhat like the doors in five-star hotels. 'Welcome!' he stretched his hand, gesturing Pius to enter first.

Pius smiled and stepped inside the dark house. Warm, trapped heat immediately rushed out, caressing his face. It felt good, even if for a tiny moment.

The Clipper clapped his hands once and soft yellow lights came on.

'Smooth jazz!' the Clipper said aloud, like he was speaking to the empty house. Immediately, the sound of soft, melodious saxophone started emanating from varied corners of the house. Total surround sound.

Pius twirled in place, entranced. He had always dreamed of a house like this. He knew he could build an intelligent house with his coding skills. All he needed was what most people desired—money, enough frigging money!

As he gyrated, Pius felt like he was being watched. Like many eyes were on him. Then, all of a sudden, he realized— there were mirrors everywhere! A standing mirror at the entrance, floor-to-ceiling mirrors for walls—except the glass windows in the front—and a mammoth mirror on the ceiling instead of a chandelier. Everywhere he looked, his reflection peered back, copying his every move, watching his every step. It disturbed him a little.

'Why don't you make yourself comfortable in the living room? I'll have a chat with the tenant and be back in a sec,' said the Clipper as he half-turned towards the door.

'Sure, Clip—' Pius bit his lower lip, suddenly realizing his faux pas. *Ripple, not Clipper.* His heart jumped into his mouth.

The Clipper turned fully towards Pius, his face devoid of expression. 'Sorry?' he hissed.

Pius gulped hard. He raised his arms and started adjusting his hair clip. 'I mean this hair *clip* is so annoying. . . you go ahead. I'll wait for you here.'

Pius held his breath, hoping his improvised excuse had worked.

The Clipper stood for a few seconds, unmoving, silent. 'Right,' he said finally and walked to the front door.

Pius let out a sigh. The Clipper had bought his excuse. He had come *this* close to breaking his cover.

The Clipper hummed in tune with the jazz music reverberating around the house. He tapped his fingers on the door keypad.

Suddenly, the sound of gears grinding together overshadowed the soft jazz. Hard metallic shutters rolled down, covering the floor-to-ceiling glass windows. Pius twisted in place and saw similar shutters roll down every window visible from where he stood.

Pius clasped his clammy hands. He was trapped.

The Clipper faced him. He pulled out a revolver from the inside pocket of his tuxedo. He pointed the gun at Pius and smiled slyly. 'On second thoughts, let's get this party started, shall we?'

51

'Karan Kapoor? The journalist?' Zoya stopped in her tracks.

'Don't stop. Keep walking,' Simone hissed, lowering her police cap to hide her face.

They didn't speak another word till they marched out of the hospital doors. The plan was simple: keep your head low and walk out like two policewomen leaving the premises after a regular visit. The police uniform had helped. It was a police hospital after all. The nurses were used to seeing khaki all the time. They hadn't even given Simone another glance as she marched out of her room with Zoya.

Simone slowed down to a crawl and clutched her stomach as soon as they were in the parking lot.

'Sure you want to come along?' asked Zoya.

Simone bobbed her head repeatedly. 'More than anything . . . let's just get in the car.'

Zoya wobbled ahead, unlocked the police van, opened the passenger door and pushed back the seat into a reclining position.

'Thanks,' said Simone. She held the grab handle above the seat and pulled herself in even as her gut revolted.

Zoya ran around the van and jumped in. 'Where to?' she asked.

'Near Bhopal national park.'

Zoya narrowed her eyes, 'I thought we were going to Karan's house?'

'That's where he lives. I asked an inspector to get me his address from the system while you were on the way.' Simone pulled out her phone, typed the address in Google Maps and showed it to Zoya. 'Let's go get the bastard who has your son.'

Zoya paused for a moment, the reminder of Sunny's disappearance pulling her into a trance. She bit her lower lip, her hands crushing the steering wheel. 'What if my boy is already dead?'

Simone held her arm. 'He isn't. We are going to save him. But we need to hurry.'

Zoya nodded, her head bobbing with conviction.

Within seconds they were out of the hospital parking lot and in the evening traffic. Zoya turned on the police siren on the van. There was no time to waste, especially not on traffic.

'Are you sure it's Karan?' asked Zoya, as the van zoomed ahead above the speed limit.

'Yes . . . more or less. There was something familiar about him when I caught him in the woods near the temple. I couldn't put a finger on it then because of the get-up, the sari pallu covering his face and the make-up. And then, he had called me "Simo". Only one person calls me that—Karan. I know it's a hunch or maybe it's a coincidence. Not enough to—'

'It's enough for an arrest,' Zoya quickly added.

Simone knew it wasn't enough for an arrest but she wasn't going to argue with a mother whose only child was missing and who was tearing the city speed limits.

She exhaled; her thoughts full of the only person who had ever asked her out on a date. Karan. The dashing reporter. The almost famous Instagrammer. Oh, how giddy she was when he had asked her out. How ecstatic she was to see the bouquet of red roses he had sent her at the hospital. No one had ever sent her flowers before . . . well, no one had ever shot her in the gut either.

'I think we should call for backup,' Zoya wrenched Simone away from her thoughts. 'Just in case,' she shot her a quick glance and nodded at her injured belly.

Zoya was right.

Simone picked up the police radio in the van and asked the dispatcher to send a backup team near Bhopal national park.

'So much police activity near the national park tonight. What's happening there?' asked the dispatcher as soon as Simone was done giving him Karan's address.

Simone and Zoya exchanged puzzled looks.

'What do you mean?' asked Simone.

'There are three other police teams near the park right now. And superintendent Hussain just asked for more backup ASAP. Wait a minute . . .' the dispatcher went silent, leaving Simone both confused and anxious. *What was the superintendent doing near the national park with so many personnel?* It was unusual and completely atypical of superintendent Hussain, who rarely approved of more than two teams, even for arresting a perp with a warrant—the lead team and the backup. Nothing more.

'. . . it's the same address!' the dispatcher's voice burst through the radio.

'What?' asked Simone.

'Superintendent Hussain just asked for backup at the same address as yours. Do you still need backup if another team is already on its way?'

Simone was thoroughly confused now 'No, leave it. Thanks.' She switched off the radio.

'What is the boss doing at Karan's place with so many teams?' Zoya bombarded her with questions immediately. 'Has he figured out that Karan's the Doll Maker?'

'But then, why weren't we . . . or at least, you . . . informed?' Simone shot back.

Zoya took a sharp turn at the intersection, bringing the road adjoining the park entrance in full view.

The flashing red-and-blue lights were the first thing that caught Simone's attention. Police vans. Two of them. Parked near the park entrance, which was blocked with police barricades. *What the hell is happening here?*

'Guess we'll have our answers soon,' said Zoya, as if she'd read Simone's mind.

Zoya brought the van to a halt near the entrance. She lowered the window.

'What's happening here? We need to access this road ASAP!' she shouted at the two constables patrolling the barricade.

One of the constables strode closer to the van and saluted Zoya. 'Don't know, madam *ji*. Superintendent Hussain's ordered us to block all roads close to the park.' He stole a quick glance at his comrade and lowered his voice, 'We heard there was an undercover operation underway. They are catching him red-handed in his house now.'

'Catching who?'

'You know, the serial killer who has been terrorizing the city for so long.'

'The Doll Maker . . .' Zoya murmured the name to herself.

'No, madam *ji*. The Clipper.'

'What!' both Simone and Zoya said in unison.

'I guess superintendent Hussain called you here,' said the constable. 'Let me clear the way for you.'

Without waiting for a response, he retraced his steps and called out to his comrade to help clear the barricade.

'Two killers in the same house?' Simone thought aloud, while Zoya put the van in gear and zoomed into the unlit road along the park.

'Does Karan have a sibling?' asked Zoya.

'Don't know,' Simone shrugged.

'Come to think of it, both the Doll Maker and the Clipper are two sides of the same coin, sharing one thing in common.'

'Which is?' asked Simone.

Zoya exhaled. 'Transgenders. The Doll Maker demonstrates proclivity, while the Clipper shows aversion to trans people. One dresses up little boys as beautiful dolls, the other kills dressed up dolls. If you ask me, they are brothers. Probably both experienced severe trauma as kids. Tough to come out as transgender in a society that views it as a disease.'

'Are you justifying their actions?' asked Simone.

'Really? Is that what you think I am doing—justifying their murderous actions? I am analysing, not justifying. You do realize that one of them kidnapped my son? My only child who might already be dead!' Zoya's voice faltered. Suddenly, the stoic façade she had built splintered. Her face twisted in pain, and out poured loud, harrowing sobs.

She stopped the car.

'Zoya, listen to me,' Simone grabbed her arm. 'Sunny is alive. We are going to find him and bring him home safely. D'you understand me?'

Zoya shook her head, tears streaming down her flushed, chubby cheeks. No words came out of her choked throat.

Simone continued. 'I'm sorry for what I said. I just meant that there are no excuses, no justifications for the murder of innocents. I understand you were psychoanalysing. I'm sorry for being insensitive.'

'What if I can't hold my baby any more, Simone?' Zoya was looking straight ahead at the dimly lit road, uninterested in a single word Simone was saying.

'Zoya, look at me,' Simone squeezed her arm.

Zoya sniffled and pursed her lips. She faced Simone, but her eyes kept roving the floor of the van.

'You will get to hold Sunny again. I promise . . . but right now we need to hurry. We need to get to Karan's house. Every ticking second is precious.'

'Yes . . . sorry . . . yes,' Zoya nodded vigorously, as if shooing away the clouds of doubt that had enveloped her. She stomped her foot on the accelerator and the van lurched forward, shearing through the growing fog.

No one spoke for a few minutes. Soon, the tar road turned into gravel. Zoya didn't take her foot off the accelerator. The vehicle dashed over the bumps, big and bigger, each bump stabbing Simone like an icicle in her belly.

In the distance, a two-storey house lit by a single floodlight came into view.

'Uh-oh! I think we have a problem.' Zoya slowed down and brought the van to a stop about 200 metres from the house. The road was blocked by two police vans similar to theirs.

Standing in the headlights, staring at them, his arms crossed, was superintendent Hussain. He was wearing an odd expression . . . as if he was pissed.

52

'Take off your clothes,' hissed the Clipper, his hand steady and outstretched, as he pointed the gun at Pius.

'Umm . . . sorry?' said Pius.

'You heard me. Take off *all* your clothes.'

Pius hesitated. Removing the brooch on his sari meant the audio feed to superintendent Hussain would be interrupted. His best bet was to buy more time and hope the police would break into the house after, somehow, getting past the wrought-iron shutters that now barricaded every door and window.

'Now! Or I won't hesitate to shoot.'

Pius decided to play along. He bent down and removed the most irksome part of his attire—the stilettos. He stepped out of the heels and stood barefoot on the cold marble floor. It was comforting, like a soothing ice pack for his twitching feet.

'Come on, hurry up. Remove the sari and any other weapon that you might be hiding underneath it.'

Pius had no choice. He unpinned the brooch and let the pallu fall, revealing his non-existent bosom.

'I think you are mistaken,' said Pius, untucking the sari from the petticoat. 'I'm not carrying any weapons. I came here—'

'You came here to entrap me. You are either the police or working with the police. You thought you could catch me like a worm trying to bait a small fish. Well, let me tell you, I'm the shark that rips apart sissy worms like you.'

The Clipper paused and snorted, as if chuckling at a joke that he had cracked in his mind. 'Actually, this is better. The higher the stakes, the higher the risk. If I come out of this alive—which I plan to—the media will fall in love with me all over again. The Clipper will be the talk of the town again. And the Doll Maker, a mere wrinkle in the past.' His lips curled into an unkind smile.

Pius removed the petticoat and blouse and stood hunched in his undergarments.

'What part of *all* your clothes did you not understand?'

Pius controlled his chattering teeth. He glanced at the main door as he removed the last vestiges of his clothing.

'No one is coming to help you, missy. And if they try, they will have to raze this house to the ground with a wrecking ball or a bomb to enter. This house is built like a bunker. Custom-made. Exactly for a day like today. By the time the police find a way to enter, I'll be long gone. And you . . . well, let me show you your final resting place.'

Pius gulped. For a moment, he was thankful for the tracking device in his hair clip. At least superintendent Hussain would be able to find his dead body.

'Let's go to the basement, shall we?' the Clipper jerked the revolver in the direction of the staircase.

Shivering, his arms hugging him, Pius walked down the stairs. As he descended the stairs, each step sent frigid chills up his hairless legs and spine. He shuddered. The very idea of body wax seemed stupid now.

A soft, melodious hymn—coming from the basement—reached his ears. He descended further. The Clipper right behind him. The gun inches from his head. The music grew clearer with each step.

'There is a switch on your right,' said the Clipper. 'Turn it on.'

Pius did as instructed.

The basement was instantly flushed in bright, white light. Pius stepped off the last stair and stopped, his mouth agape, marvelling at the spellbinding sight before him. The entire basement, about the size of a football field, was completely and immaculately empty. Grey tiles spanned the floor. And mirrors, lots and lots of them, covered the four walls of the basement like wallpaper. It was a room of mirrors.

'Keep moving. To the centre of the basement.'

Pius dragged his feet. It was colder here. Even the soft hymn failed to calm his nerves.

In the middle of the basement, a single white tile stood out in a sea of grey.

'Step on the white tile. And then step back,' said the Clipper.

Pius did as asked and stepped back. A sound blasted below him. The white tile and the eight grey tiles surrounding it shifted downwards and moved across, together as one large block, revealing a makeshift staircase that led into the darkness below. A heavy smell of disinfectant rose from below.

'Welcome to the temple,' said the Clipper. 'Bow your head and enter.'

Pius bowed his head in mock deference. His instincts told him not to descend into the crypt. *There is no coming back*, he thought. This was his last chance. *Fight or die*. He bunched his hands into fists. He was not going down without a fight.

But, before he could turn around and land a punch, two strong hands pushed him from behind. He lost his footing and fell into the crypt. His screams were soon shrouded by darkness.

53

'What the hell are you doing here?' Irshad asked Zoya as she stepped out of the police van.

'Looking for my son,' Zoya matched Irshad's tone, surprised that she had it in her to stand up to a senior officer.

Irshad stared back at her without saying a word. He came closer and looked inside the van.

'And you brought Simone? She is supposed to be in the hospital, recuperating.' He glared at Zoya.

'I brought myself, sir!' Simone shouted from inside the van. She undid her seat belt and, with sheer willpower, tried to climb out of the van. Zoya ran to help her out. Irshad followed.

'Okay, what is going on here?' said Irshad, exasperated.

'Simone figured out who the Doll Maker is. It's Karan Kapoor, the reporter.'

'Karan?'

Both Simone and Zoya nodded in tandem.

'But that doesn't answer why you are here. I'm in the middle of an undercover operation. I do not have time for whatever you are here to talk about.'

'We didn't come here to see you, sir,' said Simone.

Irshad's eyebrows snapped together, bewildered. 'But the constable at the blockade in front . . .' Irshad pointed towards the entrance of the national park, '. . . radioed me and said you are here to see me.'

'We've come to arrest Karan and . . .' Zoya paused and breathed in, '. . . and rescue Sunny. We are as surprised to see you here as you are to see us.'

'Karan, the Doll Maker, lives in the same house as the Clipper—that one!' Simone pointed to the marble building.

'You know about the Clipper?'

Simone smiled. 'The same constable at the blockade in front told us.'

Irshad shook his head and looked away at the dark woods surrounding the house, thinking, chuckling. 'So, we have two serial killers in the same house. Guess it's our lucky day, ladies. Let's go and—'

'Sir! Sir!' an inspector ran towards them, waving his hands in panic.

'What happened?'

'We just lost Pius's location.'

54

Ranveer smiled as the transgender's screams turned to deep, agonizing moans. He had pushed Pisces—or whatever her real name was—ten feet down on the stony, ragged floor of the crypt.

Ranveer stepped on a grey tile adjacent to the open crypt. With a whirring sound, the tiles moved back into place, closing the secret entrance to the crypt. There was no way to open the crypt from inside. Pisces was locked inside. Forever. As was his temple filled with fond memories. He was going to miss it. But he could always build another. In another city, possibly another country.

But, for now, he had to get away. He wasn't sure how much time he had before the police came calling. *Soon, very soon*—he was convinced.

Ranveer gripped the revolver harder. He began walking towards the other end of the basement. There were three exits from the enormous underground space. One was a staircase that connected the living room upstairs with the basement. The second, a tunnel close to the middle that connected the basement wall to the cabin. And third—built for escape, just in case of a day like today—was a tunnel that connected the opposite end of the basement to a bushy, unexplored location deep in the national park. It was the third exit that interested him tonight.

Ranveer walked with confidence. He felt in control. His hands steady, devoid of the little shivers that usually plagued him in such stressful situations. It was a good sign. It meant he had full control over his body. No more struggle, no more infighting with scaredy-cat Karan who shared the same body. Ranveer had always been aware of Karan, his alter ego. Karan was the first one. The original. The faint-hearted. The one who had created Ranveer. Whenever under duress, Karan, like a terrified puppy, would go and hide somewhere deep inside, shivering, panting, screaming for help. Ranveer would step up. After all, he was the strong one. The saviour. Sometimes it was to take a beating from the school bully. Mostly it was to take the belting from Father or kicks in the ribs or cigarette burns—whatever took his father's fancy on that particular day.

But, last night, it had come as a shock when Nalini proved that she was his alter ego too. Ranveer knew her, of course. They were childhood friends who had lost touch. But last year, out of the blue, he had received an email from nalini.kapoor.1992@gmail.com. He'd immediately known who it was from. The year—1992—was their birth year. She'd implored him to give her shelter. He'd relented and agreed to rent out the cabin. But how did he miss the signs that she, like Karan, was also his alter ego? There were always signs when he switched on and Karan switched off. They were two different beings with different tastes in clothing, hairstyles, cigarettes and even sexual partners. Sometimes, when he'd switch on, he would be wearing a fluorescent orange T-shirt—he hated colours, unlike Karan. His shoulder-length hair would be tied in a ponytail like Karan preferred but he liked his hair free-flowing and parted in the middle. Or he'd wake up in the middle of the night and find himself spooning a naked woman. For all their vices, and unlike Karan, he preferred men.

How did I miss the signs with Nalini? he wondered. The signs, if anything, should have been clearer. He would have noticed if he had woken up wearing a sari or lipstick or jewellery or a bra.

Unless . . .

He stopped walking. He bunched his hands into fists. His nostrils flared. *Unless Karan was hiding Nalini, keeping her a secret. From me. From the saviour. Why?*

'Ranveer . . .' said a voice in his head. It was Karan.

The hand holding the gun started to tremble.

He circled in his position, eyeing his reflection in the mirrors on the basement wall.

'I'm sorry, Ranveer,' whispered Karan.

'Why did you hide Nalini from me?' Ranveer stepped closer to the wall and raised the revolver at his own reflection.

'I think you know why . . .' murmured Karan.

Ranveer stared hard at his reflection, his hand was shaking uncontrollably now. 'It was you! We had sent Nalini away after Mom died. Father didn't approve of her. But you brought her back last year when Anushka, your wife, left you for another man. I remember you were depressed and heartbroken and an utter and complete mess. Nothing helped. Not drugs, not psychiatrists. Until, out of the blue, Nalini came back and you perked up. I thought a childhood friend was helping you grieve, helping you tide over the clinical depression that had engulfed you. Not for a moment did I realize that it was all a ploy, so that . . .' Ranveer went numb. Words deserted him. The sudden realization wrapped its tentacles around his quivering body.

Karan said, '. . . so that she could do what I was too afraid to do myself,' Karan bit his lip.

'Commit suicide,' Ranveer finished the thought.

Karan lowered his head nodding.

'You coward!'

Bang! Bang! Bang! Ranveer shot thrice at the mirrors on the wall. Glass splintered and crashed on the floor.

Karan dropped to his knees, huffing deep, harrowed breaths.

'Stop it!' said a shrill, girly voice. Nalini. She stood tall and flicked stray strands of hair behind her ear. 'Can't you see what you are doing to him?'

She threw the revolver away.

'You, bitch!' said Ranveer, through gritted teeth. 'Go back to where you came from!'

He punched himself on the nose. He fell back, head first, on the floor.

Nalini sat back up. A thin trail of blood trickled out of her nose. 'Ha! That's exactly what Karan and I want—you out of our lives.'

'I am his saviour! I have stood up for him, taken beatings for him and even killed for him. What have you ever done for Karan?' Ranveer drew his hand back and slapped himself, hard, across his right cheek.

Nalini touched her throbbing cheek and winced. She raised her chin and glared at Ranveer, staring back at her in the mirror. 'Yes, you are valiant and strong and did so much for Karan. But I'm going to do what you could never do: end it. Once and for all.'

Ranveer stood transfixed, unsure of what to say. He shook his head, blinked furiously. 'Is that what you want, Karan?'

Karan nodded; his head bowed down. He couldn't face Ranveer's glare in the mirror. 'I am done. I am just *so* done with this wretched life.' His voice broke. 'I tried. I really, *really* tried to carry on after Anushka left me. But no matter what I do, I can't shake that image of her in bed with Vivaan, riding him like a horse, her head thrown back, laughing at me, calling me "slinky". She never rode me. Never. Because she couldn't. She said she understood my condition. She said we would make it work. She said she loved me. Lies! All lies.'

Karan sniffled and wiped away tears with the back of his hand. 'Did I deserve such humiliation? Maybe I did. I wasn't good enough for her. I know. I wasn't the man she deserved. If I think about it, I wasn't the man she ever wanted or desired or craved.'

Ranveer rolled his eyes. 'Why are you bringing this up again? I thought we took care of the bitch and the old man she was fucking?'

'Mind your language, Ranveer!' Karan glowered at him in the mirror, his eyes bloodshot, his hands balled into fists. He stepped closer to the mirror and jammed a finger in the broken glass, as if jamming it in Ranveer's chest. 'Never, ever talk about my wife like that.'

'Your ex-wife.'

Karan's nostrils flared. He wanted to punch Ranveer. Break his nose. But he knew he'd only be hurting himself.

Maybe, that's what he wanted—more pain to relieve the pain he was feeling.

Ranveer said, 'What changed, Karan? You and I, together, took care of her. It was supposed to help you get over her . . . and whatever shit this is.'

'Yes . . . yes,' said Karan, a faraway look in his eyes. 'I had thought that slitting her throat with a scalpel would ease the pain, the humiliation, the hurt. But it didn't. In fact, I miss Anushka more with each passing day. I cannot go on like this—alone, miserable, desperate. I can't see her or feel her or look at the glint in her eyes. She's gone. Forever. Because I butchered her.'

A fresh stream of tears poured down his cheeks.

'Repentance—is that what this is?' Ranveer screamed at Karan.

Karan looked up. 'I've been repenting since the night you grabbed Anushka's hair, handed me the scalpel and convinced me that it was the only way to break free.'

'So, now it's my fault?'

Ranveer shoved him back.

Karan stumbled, before steadying himself.

'No, Ranveer. It's *our* fault.' He peered at Ranveer one last time in the mirror. 'And I'm taking both of us down.'

Karan closed his eyes.

Look at me, you coward! said a voice in his head.

Karan kept his eyes squeezed shut. It was the best way to drown out Ranveer's voice and break his grip over him.

You need me to protect you! shouted Ranveer in his head.

Karan didn't reply. He inhaled deep, calming breaths trying to calm his nerves and let the rage fizzle out.

We don't need you, Ranveer. We don't need your protection any more, echoed Nalini's voice in his head.

Karan started counting. 'One . . . two . . . three . . .' It's what Mom had taught him to do to calm himself down. Ranveer, who thrived on rage and misery and discontent, hated it. A wave of serenity washed over him and swept him away and by the time it slowly and gently lowered him on to firm ground, Ranveer had lost control over the body.

Karan smiled and opened his eyes. It was just him in the basement. And Nalini.

'We don't have much time before Ranveer fights his way back. What next, Nalini?' asked Karan.

Sunny. The little boy, said Nalini's voice in his head. *We must relieve him of his misery and pay for our sins. Send him to heaven. And then, we follow.*

Karan nodded. He turned on his heels and walked briskly to a mirror in the middle of the wall. He pushed it and slid it aside to reveal a secret door built into the wall. He felt a pang of guilt for his betrayal. Only he and Ranveer knew about the two secret tunnels from the basement—one that opened in the middle of the jungle and this one, that opened inside the cabin. They had sworn never to reveal it. Ever. To anyone. Karan had just broken that promise by showing it to Nalini.

He opened the door and stepped into the tunnel and closed it behind him. Quickly, he removed his tuxedo, his shirt, his shoes, his pants and his underwear. Nalini wouldn't need these clothes for what was to come next. He stood there in darkness for a moment and let the stale, frigid air of the tunnel wash over his naked body.

'Let's finish this, Nalini. Once and for all.'

55

'Shit!' said Irshad.

If they'd lost Pius's live location, it meant the device in his hair clip had either been discovered and smashed to pieces or something else had gone wrong. Irshad was betting on the latter. Pius was already in danger when he had accidentally called the killer 'Clip', compromising the entire undercover operation. *Should never have asked a newbie to go undercover*, Irshad thought. But he knew he was to blame for forcing Pius into this precarious situation. It had seemed like a brilliant idea then. But now, if the boy got himself killed, he would never be able to forgive himself.

Irshad pinched the bridge of his nose. 'How far away is the crane?' he asked the inspector.

'Around five minutes away.'

'Shit,' Irshad said again.

'A crane?' asked Simone.

Irshad exhaled through his mouth, annoyed. 'The operation was compromised as soon as our undercover guy went inside the house with the Clipper. He gave away his identity accidentally. Though he tried to cover up, the Clipper was smart enough to pounce on his mistake. I sent a team to break into the house immediately and save our guy. Unfortunately, the house is built like a bunker. Heavy metal shutters are covering each entryway. We need a wrecking ball to enter the house.'

'What about Karan?' asked Simone.

'What about him?' asked Irshad.

'Is he in the house?'

'I don't know. I didn't hear a third person on the microphone the entire time they were inside. Just Pius and the Clipper . . . umm, Pius is the undercover guy,' Irshad explained on seeing a questioning look on Simone's face.

'The crane is here!' someone shouted from a distance.

All of them turned around.

Irshad squinted at the bright yellow headlights approaching them, bumping up and down on the gravel road.

'Make way for the crane!' Irshad announced.

Zoya bolted, jumped into her vehicle and swerved it off the gravel road. So did the inspectors who were driving the two police vans that blocked the road.

'Simone, you should stay here in the van,' said Irshad.

'Please, sir. I didn't come this far to stay inside the van.'

'You shouldn't even be here, Simone. You aren't fit to be in the field. Also, I don't want you to slow down the team or hurt yourself.'

The loud, grinding sound of the crane drew nearer.

Simone inhaled. 'Okay,' she said after a moment. 'Can I at least stay right outside the house with the team manning the perimeter? I won't interfere and I won't slow them down.'

Irshad mulled over the request. 'Sorry, Simone. Stay in the van. That's an order!' Irshad shouted over the deafening roar as the crane moved past them and towards the house.

'Zoya!' Irshad shouted to Zoya as she hurried back to where he stood with Simone. 'Let's go get your son!'

They both ran after the crane, leaving Simone stranded by the gravel road.

56

Simone kicked a pebble. She clutched her stomach, trying to fight the stinging pain.

The crane worked hard to break the front door of the house, merely a few hundred metres from where she stood. She was miffed, enraged. There was no way she was going to sit inside the van while not one but two serial killers were about to be captured.

A loud noise, like heavy metal breaking, rang through the misty night air.

They have broken into the house, thought Simone. She was missing all the action, the arrest, the adrenaline.

She groaned. She'd be breaking her promise to Grandma if she went in. She didn't care about the direct order from Irshad. 'Fuck it!' she exclaimed. 'I'm going in.'

Simone trudged towards the house, as fast as the burgeoning pain in her stomach allowed.

Police personnel stood guard around the house, maintaining the perimeter. She reached closer to the house. And closer, till she reached the main gate of the house. It had been smashed by the crane. So was the front door. Large pieces of metal, wood and concrete lay scattered all around. Like bodies strewn around the victor in a battle.

There was no sign of superintendent Hussain or Zoya. They must have rushed inside to nab the killer. Hopefully, both killers.

Simone looked to her right and then to her left. All the men and women around her were her subordinates. No one would dare to stop her from going inside. She crossed the threshold and stepped into the driveway. A red Mercedes stood idle. To her right was an expansive, lush green lawn. At this time of night, the lawn looked more misty than green thanks to the single floodlight that illuminated the driveway. A cabin stood silent and dark at the edge of the lawn.

She decided to wait on the lawn. Technically, she wasn't going *inside* the house. So, technically, she wasn't disobeying a direct order.

She stepped on the grass. Some policemen stood guard behind the crane and a few more around the front door. It seemed that superintendent Hussain had used all available personnel for the operation. Then again, this was about catching the Clipper, a killer who had been haunting the superintendent for years.

Simone stood idle for a few minutes. No one came out of the house. *Why was it taking so long?* It worried her. It meant that they were still looking for the killers. It was a bad sign.

Anxious, she started pacing on the lawn.

Suddenly, a muted sound, like a child screaming, pulled her away from the anxiety gnawing at her. She looked around. It was silent again. *Am I imagining things now?*

She ignored it. Resumed her slow plod across the lawn.

Aieeee!

She stopped. There it was again. She'd definitely heard a dull scream. Possibly, from the cabin. She needed to check it out.

Simone lumbered across the lawn and stopped at the front door of the cabin. She pressed her ear against the door. Silence.

She turned the door handle. Locked.

There was a keypad next to the door. But she didn't know the code.

Aieeee!

The cry was louder this time. Definitely from inside the cabin. But what worried her most was that it sounded like a little boy screaming for help.

'Sunny . . .'

She pulled out the spare service revolver that Zoya had given her on the way over. She had to break in. *But how?*

One step at a time, Simone moved around the periphery. On the side facing the woods and Bhojtal lake, Simone found a wood-panelled window. It was open.

Simone crept next to the window; her revolver held close to her chest. She peeked inside. It was dark and gloomy. She saw the silhouette of a person standing next to an open wardrobe. The figure was draping a sari, her actions hurried, her back towards Simone.

The Doll Maker.

Suddenly, the figure turned towards the window. Simone immediately looked away, her back against the wall.

Simone decided to wait.

After a minute or so, she turned sideways, crept closer to the window and peeked inside.

Cold, hard metal jammed against her forehead.

'Hello, Simo,' said the Doll Maker, pressing the butt of the gun against Simone's forehead. 'Please drop your gun.'

It was Karan's face, without make-up, without hair extensions. Blood was encrusted around his nose, as if someone had punched him hard in the face. But his voice was the same one she'd heard before in the woods where she was shot. The voice of a little girl.

'Would you like to come inside for some tea, Simo?'

57

Simone walked into the outhouse through the back door.

'Welcome!' Karan beamed, as if he planned to do nothing else but host Simone in his home.

'I'm Nalini, by the way.'

He extended his hand to shake Simone's. The other held a gun pointed at her.

'Karan has told me so much about you!'

Simone didn't shake his extended hand.

Finally, Simone found her own voice. 'You have nowhere to run, Karan. The police have the place surrounded.'

The smile vanished from Karan's face. 'First of all, I'm Nalini. Not Karan. I can understand why you might make that mistake. But please call me Nalini. I like my name. Isn't it a lovely name? My mommy named me Nalini.' His broad smile was back.

Silence.

'Second of all, who said we wanted to run away? This is my favourite room in the whole wide world.' Karan stretched his arms, as kids do when they tell their parents how much they love them.

Suddenly, a sad, forlorn look came over Karan's face. 'It is the room where Mommy went to heaven. So, it should be the room where we all go to heaven. . . You know, I can't wait to meet Mommy again.'

Simone couldn't understand his blabbering. Not that she cared for any of it. She wanted to distract Karan long enough to save Sunny. She knew that sooner or later the police would raid the cabin. It was only a matter of time. *But where was Sunny?* She glanced around the room.

Karan grinned, 'Are you looking for my little boy?'

Simone remained silent.

'Stay right there. I'll get him.'

Karan walked backwards, one step at a time, his hand steady and the gun still pointed at Simone. He opened the bathroom door. Sunny lay sprawled on the floor. He was clutching his stomach, writhing and rolling on the floor.

'What did you do to him?' Simone pushed through the pain and stood up.

Karan chuckled. 'Don't tell me you still haven't figured out how I put my little Barbie dolls to sleep.'

Shit! Shit! Shit! He had poisoned Sunny. The same way he had poisoned the other dolls in the glass cases.

Karan closed the bathroom door, leaving Sunny to die inside.

'Oh! Where are my manners? Let me get you some water, Simo.'

He rushed to the bedside table, picked up a polythene bag and extracted two tablets. Next, he uncapped two bottles of mineral water and threw a tablet inside each.

He picked up one bottle, dashed back to Simone and offered her the bottle. 'Here you go!' he said as he removed the gun's safety. 'Go ahead! Drink some water. Please.'

Simone took the bottle from him.

'Wait! Let me get my water bottle too. We'll do *cheers* together!'

Karan rushed back to the bedside table, unexpectedly nimble in a sari. He picked up the second bottle and ran back.

He raised the bottle in the air, 'A toast to our moms, who give, give and give, seeking nothing in return except love. Cheers!'

Simone's heart started to gallop. This was it. She couldn't wait for the police any longer. The moment had arrived. It was now or never. Her options were clear: drink the poisoned water or fight. Well, Simone had never run away from a fight.

Simone raised the bottle and brought it close to her lips.

Karan grinned. He brought the bottle to his lips and took a long swig. His eyes, though, were on Simone, watching her every move.

Now!

Simone flipped the bottle hard, splashing the water on his face.

Karan closed his eyes for a long second.

That second was all Simone needed. She ducked, fighting through the agony of the torn stitches on her belly.

Boom!

Karan fired the gun the moment he recovered from the splash. But he missed. He had assumed that Simone would come at him in a straight line. He hadn't expected her to crouch. Using her haunches as a launchpad, Simone sprang up and pushed Karan's gun away with her left hand while landing a solid, forceful punch on his blood-encrusted nose with her right.

The bottle fell from his hand, spilling water over the floor. Karan stumbled back and squealed in pain, his voice shrill, like a little girl's.

Simone lunged for his gun. She grabbed it with both her hands, pulling Karan to the floor.

He struggled and screamed and cursed. But Karan was no match for Simone's brute strength. He fired the gun aimlessly. The bullet hit the Snow White clock on the wall, shattering it to pieces.

'Snowy!' Karan shrieked. Suddenly, he let go of the gun.

'No, no, no!' Tears welled up in his eyes. 'You killed . . . my . . . best . . . friend!' he said in between fitful sobs and started to bawl and kick his feet like a child.

Simone laboured to her feet. She was completely and utterly spent.

'You are under arrest, you sonofabitch!'

Karan paid her no heed. He kept weeping and kicking while sprawled on the floor.

All of a sudden, there was loud banging on the door. 'Police! Open the door!'

Finally, thought Simone. *The gunshot had helped.*

'Open the door. Now!' Simone heard a police officer say.

She huffed. Wiped the sweat off her brow. She dragged her feet to the door. Best to let them in before she got into more trouble.

She unlatched the door and swung it wide open.

There were four police officers at the door, their revolvers drawn, fingers on the trigger, ready to fire.

Their eyes widened on seeing Simone. The inspector in front said, 'Ma'am, what . . . what are you doing here?'

'Come. Arrest him. He is inside,' said Simone and turned around. This was not the time for explanations. She knew she had a lot to explain to superintendent Hussain later if she wanted to keep her job.

Simone trudged back a few steps and stopped. The police officers following her too halted mid-step.

Karan stood by the open wardrobe. He was crying profusely, holding Simone's service revolver in his hand.

All police officers raised their weapons.

'Karan, you don't want to do this. It's over,' said Simone.

'It . . .' Karan sniffled, 'it was over a long time ago. I'm just saying goodbye now.' He raised the gun. Held it beneath his chin.

'No!' shouted Simone.

Karan raised his head to the ceiling, the gun cocked and jammed to his throat. 'Can't wait to see you again, Mommy,' he whispered and then pulled the trigger.

Epilogue

Irshad walked the length of the basement in Karan's house, lost in thought that was accompanied by guilt and despair. The grey tiles in the basement reflected his mood, the mirrors on the walls showed his frailties.

Night had turned to day and then night again. Twenty-four hours.

He had seen Karan, the Doll Maker, with his blood and brain splattered across the cabin wall. Simone had briefed him and confessed to breaking a direct order. He could have been lenient with her for a job well done but chose to suspend her for two weeks—of course, off the record. At least she would be forced to rest and recover from her gunshot wound.

They had found Zoya's son lying in his own vomit in the bathroom, barely breathing, struggling to hang on to life. It was a good thing they knew about the poison the Doll Maker had used on his victims. The boy was rushed to the hospital and given the antidote. Irshad had just gotten off the phone with Zoya. She told him that her son was out of danger and would make a full recovery.

But what troubled Irshad was that they still had no clue about Pius or the Clipper. They had searched the house, the woods and the tunnel connecting the basement to the cabin. No luck. It was as if the duo had vanished in thin air.

It's my fault, thought Irshad. He had put Pius in danger. Tomorrow, he would hand in his resignation and spend the remainder of his tainted life repenting the one decision that had ended a bright, young life. He liked Pius. He would miss him.

Irshad sighed. 'Please forgive me, Pius,' he mumbled to himself.

Irshad stopped in front of the broken pieces of mirrors lying right next to the door that opened into a tunnel. They had recovered three bullets from the wall—the bullets that had smashed the mirrors. The bullets had matched Karan's gun but no one was sure why Karan had fired them. Did he have a shoot-out with the Clipper? But where was the Clipper's body?

Most importantly, who was the Clipper?

The Clipper was like a ghost. No photos, no passport, no ID proof. Judging from the clothing found in the master bedroom on the first floor, it was clear that two people lived in the house. Two men—Karan and Ranveer. Circumstantial evidence suggested that Ranveer was the Clipper but they could not establish any relationship between Karan and Ranveer. Were they friends? Brothers? Zoya had suggested lovers—considering the Doll Maker liked to dress as a woman and the Clipper liked to kill men in drag.

Two serial killers, lovers, living under the same roof. Irshad shook his head. This was too messed up, something right out of an American psycho thriller.

The fact remained: where was the Clipper? Pius was the only one who had seen the perpetrator in person. He could have helped with a sketch of the Clipper. If only they could find Pius. And, more importantly, if only he was still alive.

Irshad was convinced the Clipper had kidnapped Pius and made his getaway but was still hiding in the jungles of the national park. With the police still combing through the national park, Irshad was still hopeful. However, with each passing hour, the flame of his hope was dwindling.

Irshad exhaled, slowly, loudly.

He turned around and plodded his way to the centre of the basement. The single white tile in the middle of a sea of grey tiles had intrigued him since the first time he had entered the space. With soothing music wafting in the background, this seemed like an ideal space for meditation. He had heard of meditative techniques where people focused on one spot for hours. This could be that spot for either Karan or Ranveer.

He stopped a few metres from the white tile, enamoured by its simplicity and charm.

A thought popped in his mind. Serial killers tended to be egomaniacs. Everything was about them, about their desires or traumas. They sought the limelight, the attention, the spotlight. Perhaps this spot, with a thousand mirrors bouncing reflected light on it, is where the Clipper stood—in the spotlight, to feel like the centre of the universe.

Irshad snorted at the thought. Chuckling, he stepped on the white tile. He turned around, looking at the far reaches of the basement, trying to feel what it felt like standing in the spotlight.

'Meh . . .' he murmured. The spot felt no different from where he had been standing before.

Irshad sighed and decided to head back up. There was nothing else to do but shut the house permanently. For now.

He stepped off the white tile and started to walk away.

Suddenly, a whirring sound caught his attention.

He whipped around.

The white tile and its adjacent grey tiles, moved down and across, revealing a secret opening in the floor.

Irshad gasped. He tiptoed to the edge of the opening. A powerful and pungent smell, like the smell of a heavy-duty disinfectant, emanated from below. There were stairs that went down into nothingness. It was too dark to see how deep the opening was.

Is this how the Clipper escaped?

Irshad pulled out his revolver. Ready to fire.

He stood at the edge and pointed the gun into the opening, unsure of what he was pointing it at.

'Come out!' he shouted a fair warning.

No response.

He decided to take a chance. 'The police have you surrounded, Ranveer. It's over.'

Suddenly, light flickered on inside the opening.

Irshad ducked, thinking someone had fired at him.

'I . . . I . . .' a frail voice whispered from below.

Irshad crept closer to the opening again and peered down.

At the bottom of the stairs, curled up in a foetal position, stark naked, was Pius.

On seeing Irshad's face, Pius's cracked lips broke into a smile. 'I . . . I hope you brought some clothes.'